# John Vance
# TOUCHED BACK

Black Rose Writing | Texas

ISBN: 978-1-68433-238-0
PUBLISHED BY BLACK ROSE WRITING
www.blackrosewriting.com

Printed in the United States of America
Suggested Retail Price (SRP) $19.95

*Touched Back* is printed in Palatino Linotype

# Acknowledgements

Special thanks to Reagan Rothe, Dave King, and all the staff at Black Rose Writing, to my children, Hope and Jimmy, for their encouragement, and to my wife, Susan, for her enthusiasm and keen editorial eye.

# TOUCHED BACK

# CHAPTER 1

Running in darkness and chilled by the late December wind, Hoyt Reilly glanced at his illuminated stop watch as he passed the first hundred meters. "Slow down, you stupid prick." He chastised himself only when alone. He reserved all public censure and humiliation for those over whom he had control.

Reilly understood he was trying to speed through the planned eight hundred meters because he was anxious to continue preparations for the most important game of his coaching career. But if he took the two laps too rapidly, he would struggle reaching the end of the second one. He long ago vowed he would always finish strong, and on the days when his legs or gut told him he wouldn't be able to, he simply stopped running wherever he was on the track and walked away.

As Reilly approached the end of two hundred meters—the cold wind directly in his face—he believed he had slowed enough to regain the desired pace. Yet even the mere thought of pacing annoyed him, for he believed that those who paced themselves or who even set a pace were the losers—in football and in every other facet of life.

Such thoughts were generated by the unexpected success of his present team. With few exceptions, the experts believed the University of Northeastern Virginia—UNEV—had little business moving up from FCS status in order to play with the big boys. But Hoyt Reilly had proved them all wrong, exactly as he knew he would—all within three years of taking the job. He felt immense pride in the fact that his accomplishment easily justified the firing of his predecessor, the highly respected and beloved veteran coach Jack Ketchum. Now the college football world was talking about the University of Northeastern Virginia's sudden and shocking ascendancy to the big table.

And no less interested in the success of UNEV football were members of the present administration, situated less than fifty miles away. The White House was as much abuzz about the team as was the storied Tankard House—the favorite haunt of UNEV's students and members of the local community. The current president of the United States was a member of the initial graduating class of UNEV and a former and frequent denizen of the faux-styled English pub. The president's chief legal counsel was an alum as well, as were three other members of the White House staff, not to mention one of those attempting to stir matters up on Capitol Hill—a man in his later thirties who was seriously wounded in Iraq in 2004 and was presently the head of FVETS (Forgotten Veterans), one of the most aggressive veteran's organizations—a man who quarterbacked UNEV for Jack Ketchum sixteen years earlier.

Heading down the far straightaway of the oval track, Hoyt Reilly fought to keep his mind on the team's preparations and the further elevation of his reputation if he pulled off the major upset in the New Year's Day bowl game. As a gesture to his self-discipline, Reilly dropped his head so that his vision was limited to the ten yards of track directly in front of him. As he often argued, myopia was a condition to be actively cultivated by a football coach.

But something compelled him to lift his head momentarily. When he did, he detected an object on the track some fifty meters away. It seemed black or deep blue and around two feet or so high—too bulky to be a backpack or anything else left on the track by a careless student runner.

As he continued pounding his heavy feet onto the track, Reilly recognized the object as a person directly in his way. Someone sitting with legs drawn up, head lowered, and forearms resting on both knees. Reilly began to slow down and muttered a quick profanity at the realization he would have to alter his course to get around this idiot, who for some inexplicable reason was plopped down casually, right in his lane. Was this some gung-ho member of the student paper seeking a quotation about the big game? Reilly's breathing lost its synchronization with the pace of his running. What if this person wanted to ask something related to the head coach's controversial past and not about the bowl game at all?

With a single light pole 120 yards to his rear providing the only illumination, Reilly could just make out that the person wore a dark cap and clothing and was pointing something directly at him. A damned digital camera of some kind? Perhaps a cell phone? A candid photo taken this early in morning—here on the university's otherwise empty track?

The bullet ripped through Reilly's forehead, sending his body backwards—the legs perversely attempting to continue the mechanics of running, while his upper torso followed the head rearward.

The person in the dark blue wool cap stood and walked cautiously to Reilly's body. There was slight movement in the coach's hands and feet. The suppressor on the pistol muted the ferocity of two additional shots slamming into Reilly's chest. Dropping the gun hand, the shooter knelt to within a foot of the body and pulled out a gold pocket watch. The shooter swung it back and forth on its chain mere inches from Reilly's face and remained there until seeing the seeping blood break through Reilly's white sweat suit.

### 

"Thanks so much for agreeing to speak with me, Mr. Wells, especially at 7:45 in the morning."

"My pleasure. And how about calling me 'Daniel' while we're having this interview? You make me feel utterly venerable when you call me 'Mister.'"

Daniel Wells smiled at the writer as the server set the coffee on their table in Busboys and Poets on 14th and V Streets, one of Wells's favorite D.C. breakfast spots, patronized by many who opposed the Iraqi War.

That Wells sacrificed part of himself in Fallujah made him feel more, not less, comfortable dining there.

"Mr. Wells, please remember that this meal is being paid for by the magazine. So you can keep every penny of your money and spend it taking your girlfriend to one of Washington's most uppity upscale restaurants—of which there are so many."

"But then there are the funds required for such activity, of which there are so few."

"You know I'll treat."

"Oh, no. I give away my disability checks to those who need the money more than I do, but I do keep my speaker's fees and all of what I won this past summer in Vegas—all seventy-three dollars of it. Fortunately the slots, Black Jack, and Craps are the kinds of games one can play with just one hand." As was his custom in the cooler to colder months, Wells held up his left arm to reveal the cuff of his shirt folded up and pinned nine and a half inches below his elbow. In the later spring and summer, he usually went *au natural* and showed the world what he had lost in Iraq. "Besides, I didn't know my bank account was going to be the subject of this interview."

"All's grist for the mill, Mr. Wells. Oh, and nothing you say will be off the record."

"Then you'll be sure to tell the world that I'm one of the lucky ones who had a family who began the day I was born making investments for my future and that if my tale encourages anyone to donate, then he or she should contribute to our or any other *legitimate* veterans organization. Please remind your readers that there are some so-called veterans groups that are merely fronts for low-life bastards and others of that ilk." Wells was sickened by a recent report that four so-called veterans organizations collected thirty-five million dollars combined, of which thirty-one million were kept by the solicitors—some eighty-nine percent of the funds given by those who surely expected that ninety percent at least would be used to assist veterans in need—all points he made before the Senate Committee on Veterans Affairs at the beginning of the month.

Wells looked briefly out the window of the Busboys and Poets bistro, and turned back to the interviewer, scowled, and pointed his finger. "Let me tell you something, you low-life sports scribe. You ask me another personal question about my money and I'm going to tell you right here in front of all these people just where you can shove it."

"Is the 'it' general and rhetorical, or is the 'it' something more specific?"

Those sitting at the nearby tables spun their torsos toward the couple sitting by the window, curious as to why Daniel Wells and Andrea Chase were laughing as boisterously as they were.

"Andrea, you are both the fairest and foulest woman I've ever had the pleasure to be with."

"'Fairest and foulest'? How impressive. That's Shakespeare, isn't it?"

"*Macbeth*, actually."

"Hear much Shakespeare on your visits to Capitol Hill, Mr. Wells?"

"All the time. Especially from the Clerk of the House, who opens each day with 'Lord, what fools these mortals be.' Yet to be serious for a moment, Senator Chuck Lamont's fair-haired boy and senior aide Dylan Nieporte, one of my biggest 'fans' on the Hill, reminded me that Shakespeare used the word 'cur' to speak disparagingly of those who were no better than mongrel dogs—I being one of them. How about you, my darling? Hear much Shakespeare in your line of work?"

"Not really. But then the only reference I've heard all week has come from a very handsome and brave man, a former local football hero and dedicated advocate for those who have been neglected."

"This guy has quite a resume. Who are you talking about?"

Andrea lifted her coffee mug and rubbed the warm surface against her cheek. "All right, that's enough of the giggles. I've got an exclusive interview to conduct. Ah, but first we must order."

Wells ordered his customary two eggs scrambled with just toast, whereas Andre thought she'd try the Vegan Egg Wrap. Wells chuckled, "In the year we've been seeing each other, I've never seen you order meat with your breakfasts or steak of any kind for dinner."

"But I do eat chicken and fish."

"And tofu. Just based on eating meals with you, I would never have known you were a hell of a softball pitcher and a world-class pistoleer. And what else—a two-time Bronze-Medalist Heptathlete in the Division III Championships your junior and senior years of college."

"I was too weak to throw the shot and javelin far enough to win Gold. Oh, and don't forget that when I was twelve I caught a foul ball off the bat of Derek Jeter—*barehanded*."

Wells took her hand. "Here, let me kiss it."

"You may."

"Good thing your employer doesn't know we have a cozy relationship, or you would never have gotten this assignment."

"Oh, I would have figured a way around that, don't you doubt it."

Wells smiled at Andrea's puckish grin, so grateful for her playful demeanor and welcoming personality. "Go ahead. Ask your penetrating questions. Try and get me to trash the committee chair or his chief of staff."

"I don't give a damn about your views of the committee chair, remember? And I'd rather not talk about his chief of staff for reasons of which you are also aware. I'm just interested in your views of UNEV's football team, your excitement about the upcoming bowl game, and your impression of the job Hoyt Reilly has done since he took over the program."

"The first two I'll give you freely, with permission to print every word. But I'm afraid that I won't be as forthcoming regarding the third topic."

Andrea read her man's altered features easily enough. There wasn't a hint of levity in what he said. Her journalistic instincts began to formulate a way she could print at least some of his concerns about Reilly without firm attribution. She hadn't once heard him comment on the Cinderella story Reilly was weaving with UNEV's football team, for whom Daniel Wells once played quarterback.

Wells stared into his coffee mug, as Andrea took her spoon and stirred in additional cream, gently touching Wells's fingers, which were tightly pressed against the table.

###

"I've been instructed to tell you to go ahead and release the news of Coach Reilly's murder. The president will have a statement at noon."

"All right, Mr. Hernandez. Please tell the president we're very sorry for the first lady, okay?"

"Ms. Cameron, I know the president will appreciate your recognition of the fact that he and several in the administration are alums of UNEV and also that you've been understanding and cooperative about all of this."

"Of course. After all, Coach Reilly is—excuse me, *was*—the president's brother-in-law, and we realize the first lady needed to be told before anyone else."

Hernandez again reminded the woman that Hoyt Reilly was in fact the first lady's step-brother, whom she had not spoken to, according to Hernandez's belief at any rate, for many years.

"Let me add, Mr. Hernandez, that although we're not the Metro police, here in northeast Virginia we're still sensitive to the political ramifications of embarrassing and tragic events occurring in our jurisdiction on this side of the Potomac.

Álvaro Hernandez, President Stephen Erskine's press secretary, rubbed his temples in the way he always did when he was forced to suffer fools, particularly loquacious ones. Usually it was the occasional member of the press who didn't seem to recall that the same question was asked and answered five minutes earlier, but now it was the representative from the local police in Virginia, who had come upon Reilly's body on the university track at the same moment the paramedics and two dozen students arrived at the murder scene.

Hernandez had learned the facts an hour earlier, a little after 7:00 a.m., when apparently someone from the university shared the news with Kyle Guidry, the president's chief legal counsel. Guidry got on the phone with the president, and following a brief discussion contacted the chiefs of the local and of the university police, insisting that they keep the media from breaking the story until hearing from the White House. Guidry's next call was to the press secretary.

"Álvaro, contact the local and university police at 8:00 a.m. and instruct them to make the announcement. This is important. Answer no questions as to why we made the request to hold it back."

"Kyle, can you give me some plausible reason? When the Washington and national media start asking later this morning, I've got to tell them something."

"God damn it, just do what I ask, okay?" Guidry knew by the silence on the other end that the press secretary was indignant. It was evident to several in the White House that Hernandez had become fed up with his job. "Excuse the outburst, Álvaro." Guidry understood that for now it was important to keep the press secretary serene. It was only a little more than ten months until the next election, and securing Erskine's second term was all that mattered.

# CHAPTER 2

"How's your Vegan Egg Wrap?"

"Delicious. How are your eggs?"

"Perfect."

"So, now that that's settled, you've never told me why you're not a fan of Hoyt Reilly—even though he's led your alma mater to unprecedented heights."

Wells sighed, but maintained a slight smile. "Andrea, from where did you get that cliché—'unprecedented heights'?"

"We have a starter kit they give us when we first come to work for *Sports Word*. Contains that cliché and three dozen more."

"I thought you wanted to be serious."

"I do. I'm just trying to disarm you with my humor, so you'll give me something good on Reilly I can print."

"All right. I'll tell you whatever you want to know about Reilly—or how I view him—but promise me you'll publish not a word of it without my approval, okay?"

"My darling, I promise."

Wells looked into her golden brown eyes and saw a comfort and sincerity he had never found in any other woman, although years earlier he had desperately sought both qualities in someone else.

"When I was playing quarterback for UNEV under Jack Ketchum, Reilly coached the offensive line at a Division II school in North Carolina. One of my high-school teammates went to school down there and played guard for Reilly. He told me then—and he's repeated his estimation a dozen or so times over the years—that Reilly was quite skilled at castigating young men he felt needed motivation, as well as those he just didn't like. When he went on to the head coaching job two years later at the same school, Reilly had seventy additional young men to vent his pettiness and frustrations on."

"Lots of profanity, I assume?"

"Right—but not just the gratuitous use of standard 'coach-curse.' According to my friend, Reilly went in for personal humiliation—not about mistakes made on the field or in practice, but about each boy's personal life. I don't know how Reilly found out about these matters, but he did—and he used them, whether they had to do with a player's love life, financial situation at home, or problems the boy's parents were having. My friend quit the team in his senior year when Reilly started talking about my friend's divorced mother and her sexual habits. Yet, according to the administration down there, everything was fine, because Reilly motivated them enough—through the boys' fear and contempt of him, that is—to win consistently for the next couple of years."

Andrea saw that Wells took personally Reilly's abuse of his players. She was intrigued. Had the two men ever met? "Go on, Daniel, please."

"Reilly's success was duly noted, and he moved on to a much bigger Division 1-A program, switching to the defensive line and being named the conference's outstanding assistant coach at the age of thirty-four. Then after four additional years there, Reilly left the security of this perennial power to assume the head-coaching duty at an embarrassingly weak 1-AA—excuse me, FCS— program in Louisiana. Everyone of course thought he was out of his mind for taking the job at another relatively unknown school. But within three years, everyone knew about the program when the team led one of that season's eventual Sugar Bowl participants midway through the fourth quarter, before finally losing 21-16."

"I think I heard about that—when I was in college."

"Right. I keep forgetting that your interest in all sports began early. The one girl in your high school who knew the difference between a touchback and a safety, am I right?" At thirty-seven, Wells was both delighted and a bit self-conscious that the woman he loved was still nine months shy of being out of her twenties.

"Keep talking, Daniel. Look." She lifted up both arms. "I have no recorder, pen, iPad, or laptop to take any of this down with."

"With your impressive memory, I'm not at all comforted by that fact."

"You also have my promise, remember?"

"I know. All right. Fans began to call the small Louisiana school 'David U' for barely losing to the perennial Goliath, and the campus erupted in celebration the following year when it actually beat another, albeit weak, 1-A school 13-7. That win led Reilly to his dream job. Head coach at his Midwest alma mater."

"This is where I came in. I had just started working for *Sports Word* when I began looking up information about him. After being introduced to the media and his new players, Reilly waxed eloquently about getting the storied program back to its winning ways. But something happened."

Wells continued the narrative. "Right. Something happened. At the conclusion of spring practice in April, he faced the media again and announced that owing to 'significant family matters,' he was resigning from his dream job before he had even coached a game. He asked that all concerned respect his privacy and vowed that he would be coaching again after a year's absence."

"I don't think we ever pinned that down, as I remember. Much speculation about a number of possible causes, but..."

"Right."

She sensed her man wanted to move on to something else, but she refused to let the matter drop. "Daniel, I think the assumption was that something happened unrelated to his football program, but no one was saying. Didn't they ask Cecilia Erskine if she knew anything and were told that she never answered questions relating to her step-brother?" Andrea saw that Wells's mind was elsewhere. "Daniel? Are you with me, Daniel?"

"Sorry. I'm not at all surprised that no one said anything. After all, no one was better than Reilly at keeping his players' mouths locked shut about in-house matters."

"Well, hate to contradict, lover—and you must swear not to tell anyone—but his current quarterback, you know, the Daniel Wells of this generation...

"Thanks."

"...has agreed to talk to me exclusively following the bowl game about what has made him and his teammates unhappy playing for Reilly."

"You're kidding."

"No, I'm not."

"Jesus. Hard to believe Carter Thompson's willing to talk even though he has a year of eligibility left." Wells stared out at the street as he took another sip of coffee, prompting Andrea to change the subject to something cheerier.

"Look, how about taking me on a long drive to Baltimore. I have to see someone at the Ravens' complex next week, but then we can go to the Inner Harbor for your favorite Chicken Fried Lobster at The Oceanaire. Besides I want to take a nice drive in your brand new red Toyota."

"It's not red; it's 'Ruby Flare Pearl.'"

"Wow. Do I have to dress up to ride in it?"

"Just wear—"

Wells's attention was diverted by a young woman standing on the other side of the window signaling him.

"Who's she, Daniel? And why is she so pretty?"

"One of our tireless workers—Gina Lorenzetti. Her older brother came back from Afghanistan without his legs." He signaled for her to come in. "Anyway, Reilly was hardly out of coaching for two years before his phone rang. UNEV made an offer, after deciding to overlook both the mystery surrounding his resignation from coaching and his well-known Gestapo tactics on the football field."

Daniel, would you mind giving me the name of your friend who played for Reilly in North Carolina? I'd like to talk to him. Is he living down there still?"

"No. He's in Ottawa now. His name is Chas Overby. Did I say we went to the same high school."

"Yes. So he lives in Ottawa? An émigré?"

"No, he's an aide to the U.S. Ambassador to Canada, but he called to say he'll soon be coming down here for a few days. I have his cell number on my phone. Remind me to give it to you when we leave. Ah, here she is. What's up, Gina? Senator Lamont calling his committee back in session to rip me a new one?"

Gina Lorenzetti's normally animated face was frozen in concern. The attractive young woman seemed unsure of how to deliver the news she possessed. She bit down on her lip before responding. "Daniel, I was sent here to tell you that Coach Hoyt Reilly of UNEV was shot and killed this morning out on the university's track."

### 

Jack Ketchum held the phone in his hand for almost thirty seconds after the caller hung up. Someone from the local Leesburg, Virginia press had called him as soon as the news broke about Hoyt Reilly's murder. Ketchum's initial reaction was to show frustration at having his routine interrupted. The morning paper was on the kitchen table ready for him to read—placed there by the news carrier as part of an agreement with Ketchum, who in a quaint nod to his past, left a key to the kitchen door under a three-foot statue of St. Francis near his back patio. As Ketchum began to scan the front page, the oven was preheating for the insertion of the daily frozen breakfast meal, the kind he started eating following the death of his wife four years earlier.

When he coached football, he drilled his teams in the same way at every practice and scrimmage. He insisted on following the same regimen for each game. "I don't want you to *think* too much," he always told his players. "I just want you to *do*." Ketchum prided himself on treating every player the same—whether starter or third string. His players genuinely respected him—there were very few who didn't during the thirty-five years he coached, the last twenty-seven years spent at UNEV. He was proud of all his boys who did the right thing and was deeply disappointed by those who didn't. But no one pleased him more than Daniel Wells—his starting quarterback for two years in the early 2000s—now a decorated war hero and vigorous advocate for so many scarred and needy veterans.

As for the current president of the United States, Stephen Erskine—the school's first senior class president—Ketchum sat him down back then in his make-shift head-coach's office and told handsome Steve Erskine that he wasn't good enough to start as quarterback on the inaugural UNEV football team Ketchum cobbled together in the late 1980s. Over the years, Ketchum had kept that little fact quiet and refused all requests to talk about Erskine's abilities behind center. Ketchum smiled on inauguration day remembering how Erskine thought he was a hell of a lot better than he was, but in truth he had a weak arm and couldn't throw a deep sideline route to save his life. In addition, Erskine was both hesitant and immobile in the pocket, and Ketchum explained to him that he'd not only hurt the team but also get himself killed if he was given the starter's job. That Erskine quit the team learning he'd not be the QB didn't surprise Ketchum, but as in all such cases, it disappointed him.

Ketchum poured a cup of black coffee and sat at the kitchen table in a futile attempt to read the paper and forget about how he lost his job to Hoyt Reilly three years earlier. But it was useless. The manner in which he was treated by the UNEV athletic director and university president still rankled deeply and Ketchum imagined it would for the rest of his life.

The athletic director came to his office one mid-winter morning for a "chat about the future of the program." Having just turned sixty-one, Ketchum planned to coach at least until he was sixty-five—especially since his wife had recently died and he needed his team more than ever. Initially, there was no discussion of retirement. The AD insisted that Coach Ketchum see the wisdom of moving up to 1-A status—or FBS as it was presently called—and playing in the American Athletic Conference, with out-of-conference games against ACC and Conference USA schools. Ketchum reluctantly agreed in the previous two seasons to getting two games with ACC programs, but although the payout was welcome, UNEV ended up being homecoming fodder for the more senior and talented programs.

UNEV's AD and university president were fairly new on the job, just completing their second year, and Ketchum attempted to convince them that such a move to 1-A/FBS would ill serve both the players and the university. Although he had gotten his team as far as the 1-AA/FCS semi-finals and championship game in two of the previous five seasons, less than a week after his meeting with the AD, the university cut Ketchum loose because he didn't have "the kind of daring vision we want for the UNEV's football program."

Rumor had it that a series of calls from someone in Stephen Erskine's office convinced UNEV to contact Hoyt Reilly, then serving his apparently self-imposed athletic exile. Erskine was at the time chalking up a series of primary victories and becoming the prohibitive favorite to take both the nomination and the election in November.

Crushed by the termination of his contract, Ketchum was stunned by the choice of Reilly to succeed him. He was well aware of Reilly's objectionable coaching manner and the common belief that Reilly had played the system to his advantage wherever he coached. And he heard further unsubstantiated rumors about Reilly's sordid personal life, all of which Ketchum wanted desperately to believe. To cauterize the wound caused by his humiliation, Ketchum began investigating these assumptions and rumors, finding evidence that at least two-thirds of them were true. He wasn't proud of himself for doing such espionage, but he kept a file in his desk of what he had found, along with dates, names, and contact information.

Ketchum wanted to give what he had to the *New York Times*, *Washington Post*, or *Sports Word* magazine, but a long discussion with the man he loved like a son, former player Daniel Wells, convinced him to hold off—for the sake of the university they both cared for and for Ketchum's own legacy. Wells reminded Ketchum of what he told his players about "not getting in the swamp" with the "many snakes" in the sport. "Stand up. Hold up your chin," he insisted. "Never bend, squat, or crawl as many will tempt you to do." Reluctantly, Ketchum agreed to remain silent, supported by his affection for Wells and the realization that he had indeed touched the younger man's life in the best way possible.

The file was in a locked desk drawer in Ketchum's study on the other side of the kitchen wall. Owing to the increasing incidents of forgetfulness and the memory of his own mother's Alzheimer's, Ketchum feared he would succumb to the disease and wanted to cover his bases before he felt the symptoms. A printed copy of the updated file had been mailed to his daughter in North Carolina with the instructions to send it to Daniel Wells when her father passed on.

Ketchum entered the study and sat behind the desk. He tugged at the drawer to check that it was locked. It opened easily. Ketchum stepped back as if his hand had been scorched. Had someone broken open the lock, or had he simply forgotten to secure it the last time he looked at the file? Ketchum strained to remember when he last perused the information on Reilly. He believed he put something new in the file three or four days previously. But why would he forget to lock the drawer? He moved to his book case and lifted one of the thicker volumes off the shelf. The key was inside the book, where he always kept it. Ketchum returned to the desk and checked the drawer for evidence of forced entry. There was none. He finally pulled out the file and checked every page. All the pages were present—and in the same order he was sure he left them several days earlier.

Ketchum sat at his desk and placed the file under both his open hands. Reilly was now dead. So why not reveal everything he had on him? The press would be hungry for any information on the murdered coach. They would follow up on what was in the file. Now would be the time to expose Reilly for the kind of man he was and had always been. To hell with the ancient adage, "Of the dead say only good." Ketchum heard the beep. The oven had now pre-heated to the required temperature. He got up and took the file with him.

Turning the corner into the kitchen, Ketchum saw the frozen breakfast meal on the counter. He looked further down the counter to the kitchen phone. He decided that he owed Daniel Wells a call to explain why now would be the ideal time to give his information to the press. Ketchum reached for the phone. Yes, he had to have Wells's approval before he'd turn over the information on Reilly. And Ketchum decided that his former quarterback's lovely girlfriend, Andrea Chase, would be the media person he'd trust with the document.

Ketchum was about to grab the phone, but thought that he might as well slide the frozen meal in the oven while he punched in Wells's number. Ketchum placed the file folder on the counter and reached for the oven door handle. He jerked it open.

The explosion obliterated almost everything in the kitchen, setting parts of the adjoining room on fire.

# Chapter 3

"Un-fucking-believable."

"That son-of-a-bitch."

Mike Cipriano slammed the back of his fist against one of the outdated metal locker doors. "Hey—Thompson, Roebuck—we don't want that kind of foul-mouthed talk around here *anymore*. You're supposed be the leaders of this team. Clean it up. Got that?"

"Sorry, coach." Darryl Roebuck, UNEV's starting middle linebacker, understood that his defensive coordinator—less than an hour ago named interim head coach—was certainly capable of getting them through final bowl game preparations, but he also believed that the murder of Coach Hoyt Reilly would make almost impossible the team's ability to concentrate full-out before the biggest game in the school's history. The media would be probing up and down their backsides from now until kickoff less than a week away. Just one more thing to resent that bastard Reilly for.

But starting quarterback Carter Thompson heard something else in Coach Cipriano's reaction to the profanity. That emphasized word *"anymore"* told Thompson that Cipriano, who certainly expectorated his share of salty speech—though never the "GD" or "F" words—had come to despise his former boss and the manner in which he treated his players. In addition, Thompson recently confided in Cipriano that he twas thinking of leaving the university and using his final year of eligibility to play for another school.

Cipriano had listened for a good fifteen minutes to Thompson's complaints—just asking once if the quarterback thought of going to the offensive coordinator instead of him, since the OC also doubled as Thompson's quarterback coach. But Thompson made it clear he trusted only Cipriano; therefore, the coach let him vent, although Cipriano offered no balm for Thompson's grievances, except to tell him that he should stay at UNEV for his senior season, even though the quarterback would have graduated three months prior. Thompson had one year left of eligibility, since he was red-shirted as a freshman, and his grades were good enough to be accepted into the school's Master's program. It was following their talk that Thompson contacted Andrea Chase of *Sports Word* magazine and promised to give her a "major story" on the heels of the bowl game in January.

Carter Thompson was the athletically gifted son of a Caucasian mother and African-American father, the latter having played seven years in the NFL as a defensive back before suffering a career-ending shoulder injury. Miles Thompson taught his son never to accept any abuse beyond the harmless hazing that accompanied a young man's rite of passage in the game of football. As a young boy, Carter witnessed his father punch out an NFL teammate—a fellow African-American outweighing the senior Thompson by eighty pounds—for making fun of young Carter's "white traits." The boy moreover watched his father get in the face of his position coach, an overt racist, for asking Thompson to leave his white wife and mixed-race son at home during a team social function.

In the middle of UNEV's Cinderella season, Carter saw more evidence of his father's agitation and mood swings than he ever remembered. He wondered what the senior Thompson would say or do if his son took an additional year of abuse from Hoyt Reilly—which included the patronizing allusions to Thompson's mixed racial heritage and the hardly-subtle references to the loose morals that resulted in unwanted pregnancies, forced unions of men and women "not really meant for each other," and the "unfortunate burdens" children of such parents were forced to endure.

Reilly never pointed to Thompson when others were around, but the coach managed on one occasion to corner his quarterback while

Thompson was alone in the whirlpool. Pulling up a chair, Reilly asked Carter what it was like growing up "with a white mother." Reilly was keen to know all about Jana Thompson—her family, her popularity in high school and college, and what her other friends were like. Thompson vowed at that moment he would be paying the bastard back in some way for asking these inappropriate questions, most notably the one that terminated their little one-on-one meeting: "I'm curious, Thompson. Has she kept her looks—you know, her 'style'—since she married your father? Does she still look... you know?" Thompson detected in Reilly's disgusting grin that he didn't want to know if Jana Thompson still looked attractive. What he meant was "Does she still look... white?"

Carter Thompson hadn't mentioned a word to his father about this and other similar incidents involving his psychologically-abusive head coach. He knew that even with his damaged shoulder, Miles Thompson would punch the crap out of Hoyt Reilly if he learned any of what the coach had said or had asked about his wife. Besides, his father long ago taught him to solve his own problems. Throughout this season, Carter chided himself for not living up to his father's example—simply because he wanted to play quarterback and look forward to a possible career in the NFL. Now twenty-one, he hated himself for not already standing up for himself and for the honor of his family. Fortunately, Thompson had his best friend on the team—Darryl Roebuck—to share some of his frustrations with.

The rest of the team, along with Coach Cipriano, noticed Carter growing anger as the regular season came to a close. He just yesterday hurled a full plastic water bottle past the ear of a lineman into the locker room wall and violently brushed from his shoulder the hand of a concerned teammate. Darryl Roebuck knew why his friend wasn't at present relieved or joyful over news of Reilly's death. Roebuck was sure young Thompson was bitterly disappointed that he didn't shoot the son-of-a-bitch himself. Roebuck was moreover certain his friend would expect to release a good deal of his pent-up frustration and anger by letting it all go in his interview with that female writer for *Sports Word*—whose attempt to play down her looks by wearing turned-around baseball caps and glasses hadn't made her any less desirable to Roebuck, who furtively downloaded many photographs of her from the internet.

###

Back at his apartment, Wells dialed the number again. Given his life of unalterable routine, Jack Ketchum should still be home. Nothing less than an emergency would get him out of the house before noon when the weather was this cold. Nonetheless, his old coach might be taking his daily walk several hours early. Or had his phone been somehow disconnected?

Hearing several knocks as he poured another cup of coffee, Wells dropped in two pellets of artificial sweetener and approached his door. When he opened it, he beheld a fellow alum from UNEV.

Hey, Daniel. Have a minute?"

"Sure, Grant. Come in. Like some coffee? What drags you out of the White House and over this way?"

Grant Paulson, President Erskine's Director of Public Liaison, had plenty to do in any given day, but without complaint he also served as UNEV's de facto booster club president—at the request of the president. One of his tasks included coordinating visits to the university by its distinguished alums serving in the Erskine Administration, Congress, and throughout all government agencies and bureaus in the city. The president himself had made one visit to Costello Field in each of his first three years in office. Named for Mitchell Costello, the president of the school who was instrumental in changing it from a two- to a four-year institution, Costello Field would in either thirteen months or more likely five years—at the end of Erskine's second term—change its name in honor of the current President of the United States, with the remaining Costello family's blessing, particularly since the deceased Mitchell Costello was never a fan of collegiate football, viewing it merely as a necessary evil. The deal to change the name of the stadium had been finalized, although so far it had not leaked to the press.

"Daniel, the president would like you to make a public statement about the tragic loss of Hoyt Reilly. Wait, I'm sorry. I'm assuming you've heard, right?"

"Yes, I've heard."

"Do you know Mike Cipriano has been named interim head coach?"

"No. But a good choice, I think most would agree."

"Damn. Reilly murdered while he was running on the god-damned university track.'

"Right."

"Anyway, the president feels the UNEV nation will be shaken up pretty hard by this, and that it's up to all of us to console the university community and the alums. He's already decided to attend the bowl game in January and wants you there with him."

Wells was taken aback. "He's never asked me to be at any of the small alumni functions he's sponsored at the White House. We're not by any stretch friends or even acquaintances. So why now all of a sudden?"

Paulson took a sip of the black coffee Wells just poured him. "You know god-damned well why, Dan. You've always been Jack Ketchum's fair-haired boy. The president never could stand Ketchum. Unfortunate that you had to bear the brunt of Erskine's grudge through his neglect of you, but... hell..."

"Okay, but why does he want me to be with him now?"

"Honestly, I can only guess that Reilly's murder might have shaken him loose from old resentments."

"Doubt that."

"Then maybe it's because Erskine is primarily thinking of the university and what it needs at this time."

"Doubt that too."

"Jesus Christ, Dan. Perhaps *you're* the one who can't shake free of his resentments."

Wells turned and walked to the shelves where he kept his old UNEV game programs and media articles about his athletic exploits. He placed his hand on the thin university yearbook for his senior year.

Paulson saw him open to one of the pages and gaze at the photos—it seemed at one in particular.

"Sorry, my friend."

"No, no, Grant. You're probably right. But let's be honest. It's for other reasons that I shouldn't accompany the president to the bowl game."

"What the hell's that supposed to mean?"

"Just respect my feelings on this, all right?"

"Look, I know you weren't a big supporter of Reilly's style."

"His 'style' was only part of it." Wells thought of Jack Ketchum and his extensive research on Reilly. Now, he wanted to see that evidence—to examine it carefully—to determine whether it might be made public. He decided that when he reached Ketchum by phone, he would ask to come over and take a look at the file his old coach had locked in his desk.

"Grant, I don't think I should accompany the president to Arizona next week. Before you arrived, I contacted the AD and asked if I might talk to the team tomorrow morning before practice. I'll be driving to the university later today and spend the night. So, I'll be making my contribution. You can tell the president that." Wells closed the yearbook and began to place it back on the shelf.

Paulson was ready with his trump card. "I should add that the first lady specifically asked me to convince you to be with the president at the bowl game."

Wells slowly slid the yearbook back in its place and without turning around asked, "She's not going?"

"No. As an alumna, she feels badly that she can't go to Glendale. But six weeks ago she had scheduled a Breast Cancer Awareness symposium and reception at the White House at the same time as the kickoff. Like the rest of us, she had no idea in October that Reilly would get UNEV into a major bowl game."

Wells took his time shaping his reply. "Right, no idea."

###

"Oh no, please don't tell me that." Andrea Chase shut her eyes and listened intently to the sketchy information so far accumulated about an explosion at Jack Ketchum's place in Leesburg. Most of the house was demolished beyond salvage by the blast which emanated from the kitchen and the accompanying fire. Just the garage and part of Ketchum's bedroom were "saved" by the efforts of the fire department. The official identification of the victim had not been released, but based on what was seen of the body's remains, there was little doubt Jack Ketchum was standing in the kitchen when the blast occurred.

Andrea thought of little other than what Daniel Wells's reaction would be to the horrific news. She struggled to find a question to ask. "Was... was it the gas stove that blew everything up?" The caller, a friend working at one of the northeastern Virginia television stations, said they all believed Coach Ketchum had electric appliances.

"Then you think it was a bomb of some kind?" The caller replied that nothing was official—but, yes, that's what it looked like.

"But who would want to kill him?" The caller had no answer, for she, like everyone in the area, considered Ketchum a local treasure and a reluctant celebrity whom no one would criticize—not even those who came to the conclusion that it was ultimately wise of UNEV to let him go in favor of Hoyt Reilly.

Andrea waited a full five minutes before she gathered the courage to call Wells. When she finished telling him the horrible news, she was a bit stunned to hear his initial reaction. "Andrea, did they say if the desk in his living room survived the blast?"

### 

"What the hell are you talking about, Álvaro?" Kyle Guidry was in the middle of a fifty-four page "working draft" of the administration's response to the Ninth Circuit's 2-1 decision in a First-Amendment case the solid majority of Californians did not support. The decision was particularly galling to Erskine since he had two years earlier appointed the swing judge who wrote the majority opinion. Guidry was determined to do everything possible to encourage a writ of *certiorari* and ultimately a Supreme Court reversal of the lower court's decision.

Erskine and Guidry knew damn well this was an opportunity to grab California, which Erskine had narrowly won three years earlier. Enough Californians would appreciate the president's efforts in this matter to cast more of their votes for him next November, assuring him of the grand prize of fifty-five electoral votes and easy re-election. But Álvaro Hernandez had interrupted Guidry with news of an explosion across the Potomac.

"An explosion, Kyle. Didn't you hear what I said?"

Guidry slammed his open palm on the scattered pages of the draft. "No, Álvaro, I didn't. Fuck, all right. What blew up again?"

"The home of Jack Ketchum. You know, the former head coach at UNEV."

"Jesus Christ. Was he harmed?"

"Apparently he was standing in the kitchen when the oven blew up. Or rather, when the explosive device placed inside his oven detonated. They haven't made it official, but there seems to be little doubt the bits and pieces of the body are Ketchum's."

Guidry appeared annoyed by the details. "God damn it, are you sure it was a bomb that was planted in the oven?"

"They tell me it couldn't have been anything else. They've extricated enough tell-tale signs of an explosive device—so they're sure." Hernandez was surprised to see the look on Guidry's face. He had never witnessed anything like it before.

"Oh, Christ. Jesus Christ. All right. All right, does the president know?"

"Cabinet meeting isn't over. I'll inform him as soon as he comes out."

"No, no. I'll tell him. You just get busy on a statement we can get out in the next fifteen minutes. Keep it brief—to the point. Something about how the loss of both Reilly and Ketchum has deeply saddened—"

"God damn it, I know my job, Kyle." Hernandez looked as though he was begging Guidry to patronize him again. Guidry momentarily halted before turning his back.

"Fine. Then just do it."

Guidry waited until Hernandez left his office before he lowered his head into his two open hands. "What the hell? What the fucking hell?"

# Chapter 4

"Gina, remind Rod that I'll be gone from my office for the rest of the day. I'll be heading to the university, where I'll be spending the night. I hope to be back by eleven tomorrow morning. But I might be delayed, so ask him to switch tomorrow's scheduled 11:45 meeting with Warren Brown of Veterans National to later in the afternoon. Do you have all that?"

The young woman winced. She was certain Wells's right-hand-man Rod Pritchett didn't like her and would somehow blame her for the change of plans. "Okay. Now Mr. Brown may be willing to open his books to the media, right?"

"Yes—if I can stroke him the right way. Warren's a royal pain in the ass and he has a natural antipathy for people who pry into anything he's involved in. Still, he's as sick as I am about the statistics I showed him—so I think he'll come around."

Gina Lorenzetti doubted seriously if anyone was as sickened by the numbers as Daniel Wells. He frequently complained that a good number of so-called veterans organizations weren't exactly divvying up the pie the way they should have. As he told her, some of these organizations gave only "slivers of crust" to those who need "much more of the pie." Wells shocked her when he mentioned the percentage of true aid as opposed to money raised by the solicitors and spent on "administrative costs," marketing expenses, and lavish salaries. Whereas one major organization passed along but forty-eight percent of funds to those who needed assistance, still others were even more shameless in their handling of donations made by generous and concerned citizens and organizations. One group raised 2.6 million and send on a scant three hundred thousand to vets. Another kept 7.2 million of the 9.3 million raised, while a third raised 12.6 million and kept 10.2 million of that amount. Finally, Wells informed Gina that a larger organization pulled in 70.2 million and sent along just a measly 7.8 percent of it. Gina was proud to work for a man as impassioned as Daniel Wells, who constantly spoke out and warned against a series of scams trading on the good will, gratitude, and patriotism of so many generous Americans.

"Anyway, make sure that Rod understands the rescheduling, okay?"

Gina groaned. "Hope he doesn't yell at me. Wait. Why are you smiling?"

Wells knew the problem was that Pritchett's aloofness was a protective mechanism because he was actually quite attracted to her.

"It's nothing, Gina. I was trying to imagine Rod yelling at you."

"Hang around a little longer and you won't have to imagine it."

Wells appreciated Gina's wit at this moment. He was having difficulty dealing with Andrea's phone call about the death of his mentor Jack Ketchum.

"Can I ask you something?" She was fidgety and seemed troubled.

"Sure, what is it?"

"What's the deal with Senator Lamont's chief of staff? What's his name again?"

"Dylan Nieporte. Why? Did he do something to you?" Wells assumed Lamont's chief of staff had overstepped his bounds with the comely young woman.

"Not exactly. I hand delivered the letter you wrote the senator, and Mr. Nieporte came out of his office and took it from me. When he saw it was from you, he shook his head and asked me if this was the best I could do. I wasn't totally sure what he meant, but it seemed to me he thought my working for you wasn't a good job."

Wells laughed. "Oh, you can be sure that's exactly what he meant.

Don't tell me. He asked if you'd be interested in working for Senator Lamont."

Gina's mouth fell open. "How did you know?"

"Did he mention a salary?"

"He did. Between thirty-three and thirty-five thousand."

"Hmm. That's a bit more than you're making here. Are you going to take it?"

"No, I'm not. He didn't mention what my duties would be, and I didn't like the fact that he said I'd add a 'little pulchritude' to the staff. I mean, who talks like that? Pulchritude?" Wells laughed again, prompting Gina to do likewise. "Does he have reputation for coming on to the female staff?"

"And not just the female staff—females of all occupations. But recently he's cleaning up his act since the culture on Capitol Hill has changed—at least rhetorically. Look, I need to go, so I'll give you the Cliff's Notes version. Dylan Nieporte hates my guts—for several reasons. One, he doesn't think I respect his boss enough because we've butted heads a few times regarding Veterans affairs—particularly at the hearing early this month—and I've written several articles criticizing the committee for slow-walking many needed changes. Second, I don't take Nieporte's calls. I insist on speaking just with the senator. Third, he hates me because I have the relationship with Andrea Chase he wanted to have."

"Whoa."

"You got that right. Later I'll share with you the specifics of that little matter, but it's time for me to get out of Washington and drive to Leesburg. I have to find out all I can about Coach Jack's death."

Gina frowned, fearful that Wells too might be in danger. "Please be careful, Daniel."

###

Glancing to his right as he crossed the Potomac on the Theodore Roosevelt Memorial Bridge, Wells took in as much of Theodore Roosevelt Island as safety would permit. It was a place he often enjoyed visiting, because it gave him a sense of remoteness and escape from the congested capital city—its access limited to a footbridge near the George Washington Memorial Parkway. Wells made it a point to come to the island at least once a month to think about his satisfactions and regrets and to make or renew promises to himself. He was due for another visit--although Andrea insisted she accompany him the next time he went.

His visits often encouraged Wells to recall the major event of his life, the one that changed everything for him—in so many ways. Following his graduation from UNEV, he was committed to seeking a job in the NFL through free agency. He believed he'd at best be a late round draft choice in the April draft—in the sixth or seventh round—but when the Oakland Raiders didn't take him for the 262nd and last pick in the seventh round, Wells made a call to Jack Ketchum, who also made a call, and Wells was offered a free agent contract with the Denver Broncos. But Wells knew his chances were slim. He was a quarterback, and very few free agents QBs ever escaped training camp without being cut. At least he made it until the second pre-season game, where he went in for two plays in the fourth quarter—both simple handoffs. He was cut two days later. It was small comfort to him that from that year's draft class there was but one quarterback from the thirteen drafted who made it as a successful starter in the NFL—Carson Palmer, the number one player taken that year.

Jack Ketchum then pulled some other strings and secured Wells a position in the UNEV athletic department, with the thought that Daniel would either work out during the year and try the NFL again or take a coaching position on Ketchum's staff when a position opened up for the following season. But those plans were sideswiped by the event of March 31—the ambush of four American security contractors in Fallujah—to the west of Baghdad. As reported, the men were escorting a Eurest Support Services Catering convoy when they were attacked and killed. After their bodies were bludgeoned and burned, their charred corpses suffered the indignity of being dragged through the city and then hung over one of the bridges crossing the Euphrates. The event deeply affected Wells because his family knew the family of one of the slain men, who played catch with Wells when Daniel was a boy. Photos were widely disseminated showing several elated Iraqis posing with the burned corpses.

Wells wasn't one to wear his patriotism on his sleeve, but the fall of the Twin Towers enraged him when he was in college and he was briefly tempted to delay his schooling and enlist in the Army. But his football and other social activities convinced him that then wasn't the time, but now there seemed no excuse to stay out of the military. On the advice of his family and Jack Ketchum, he took three weeks to think before he acted on his initial impulse. He came down to Theodore Roosevelt Island for the first time and returned twice again during those three weeks. Yet he never wavered from his initial inclination, and in the spring of 2004 he joined the Marines, the branch of service chosen by two of his uncles, both having served in Vietnam from 1968 to 1969.

Five months later, and as the gods of coincidence would have it, Wells was part of the second battle of Fallujah in November as part of the "Darkhorse" 3rd Infantry Battalion, 5th Marines. Their mission was to work with other Marine, Navy, Army, and Iraqi units and capture the city from the insurgents. Because the enemy had prepared for such an attack by digging trenches, tunnels, and spider holes, as well as setting booby traps and IEDs, the battle resulted in the heaviest urban combat since Huế in 1968. Moving into the city under the cover of darkness, Wells and his fellow Marines waited for the other units to coordinate before launching the initial attack on the morning of November 8. Air cover allowed his unit to move to other sections of the city. It was during this move that he and his fellow Marines were hit by small-arms fire. Not long after, Wells's consciousness of the battle was interrupted. When he regained his faculties in a hospital bed, he found himself conversing with a Navy doctor and chaplain—both men smiling and assuring him that he'd soon be going back to the States. Wells was confused at first until he remembered the searing pain in his arm that caused him to black out on one of Fallujah's bullet-ridden streets. The pain medication having lessened, his memory pieced together what had occurred when he was under fire. While taking cover during a volley from the top of a building, he heard screams from one of the men who'd been hit. The solider kept repeating "My leg! My leg!" Wells saw that it was one of the men in his unit he had never even spoken to. The man lay in the open some ten meters away. Bullets splayed the sand and broken rocks around his body, but no other rounds struck the wounded Marine. Wells knew it was only a matter of time before the man would be mortally wounded if not blown apart. Shouting a profanity, Wells dropped his rifle and made it clear to the others that he was going out for his wounded comrade. He waited until his unit returned fire before he headed out, running as low as he was able. But he tripped over several rocks, which messed up his stride and timing. By the time he reached the wounded man, renewed insurgent fire peppered the area, causing him to drop face down to the right of his fellow Marine. Wells felt a burning sensation between his right calf and ankle and knew he'd been hit at least by a bullet fragment. Other men in his unit saw his predicament and stepped up their return fire, giving Wells a chance to drag the Marine back to relative safety.

Wells told the wounded man to turn over so that he might at least crawl back if Wells couldn't lift or drag him, but he was unable to move his body. Still on his stomach, Wells lifted his left arm to pull at the man's shoulder in an attempt to turn him over. But the moment his arm reached out, an RPG exploded on the other side of the wounded Marine, riddling him with shrapnel and killing him instantly. The explosion also took Wells's left hand and part of his wrist. That was all Wells recalled until he was in a medevac helicopter where he was told that the man he tried to rescue hadn't made it. No one said anything about his left arm, only that the wound in his lower leg was minor.

"You should get a nice commendation for what you tried to do, Marine."

Ignoring the compliment, Wells looked at the Navy doctor and took a deep breath—his throat constricted by his anxiety. "My arm?"

The chaplain reached for Wells's right hand as the doctor informed Wells what his effort at gallantry had cost him.

"You know, sir, I was afraid you'd have to take off the whole damn thing—so I guess I didn't come out too badly." Wells managed a smile, but his face suggested to the two men that this young man was going to make the most of all that wasn't affected by the RPG.

Following his medical discharge—he had received a Silver Star Medal for his valor and sacrifice—Wells returned to his job in the UNEV athletic office and within a month he was doing volunteer work for veterans and then--seeing the number of dead, maimed, and wounded proliferate because of the wars in Afghanistan and Iraq--he devoted his time to the returning wounded and learned that physical deficiencies were rivaled if not surpassed by the psychological ones. In 2007, at age twenty-seven, Wells began his own organization and began establishing a national profile. Although he declined Jack Ketchum's offer to join his coaching staff, Wells often came by and worked with the quarterbacks and addressed the team. To a man, the players respected Daniel Wells for what he endured, for what he attempted, and for what he had done with his life.

### 

As he drove on, Wells brought his thoughts back to the present and understood that he had to make some decision regarding his future with Andrea Chase. Yet he couldn't do so until he shared with her one aspect of his past. Perhaps the death of Jack Ketchum might make it easier for him to confide fully in Andrea, although he wasn't quite sure why. Would the death serve as a catalyst for revelation? Perhaps he would need her more now that his mentor was dead. Still, how would she react if she knew everything?

Wells made the turn right on the George Washington Memorial Parkway and headed west toward Leesburg. It was a drive he had taken a number of times to have lunch with Coach Ketchum, who made it a point never to come to Washington. The last time Wells visited his mentor, he brought Andrea Chase, who received Ketchum's seal of approval within half an hour of their visit. Today, Wells was determined to see Ketchum's house and find out what he could about the explosion. He would grab some fast food for lunch, stop at Ketchum's, and then head southwest to UNEV to spend the night.

### 

Twenty miles outside Leesburg, Wells noticed a new GMC truck in his rear view mirror. He identified it as a Canyon—the very model he had been encouraged to buy from one of his friends, who owned an auto and truck dealership. Wells had the money, but he saw himself as an unpretentious, sedan kind of guy and bought a new Camry instead. Then something caught his attention other than the attractive look of the black truck. The driver's right hand was off the steering wheel and lifted above the dashboard. Something was swinging in that hand. Wells couldn't see the face of the driver, owing to the sunglasses and pulled down ear flaps of his camouflage hunter's cap. The item seemed to be something dangling from a chain. Wells guessed that it was gold pocket watch rocking back and forth. Perhaps the driver was engaged in self-hypnosis. Amused, Wells returned his eyes to the road and continued his drive to Leesburg.

# CHAPTER 5

"Mr. President, excuse me, but the first lady is considering making her own statement to the press about the death of Jack Ketchum."

Stephen Erskine reacted as if he felt the onset of one of his frequent sciatica attacks. "Christ. Look, Álvaro, do what you can to dissuade her. If she says anything formally about Ketchum, everyone will want to know why she's decided to say nothing about her step-brother."

"I understand, sir."

"And ask Kyle to meet me in the Oval at 11:30."

"I will, Mr. President."

"I'll have lunch after I see him. All right. How much time do we have before I make my statement?"

"Ten minutes, sir."

"And you have everything ready for release?"

"Of course, Mr. President."

"Good, good. You're doing an excellent job, Álvaro."

"Thank you, sir."

Hernandez was struck by Erskine's verbal fidgetiness. He was rarely one for issuing compliments, and he made Hernandez feel he was one step ahead of the press secretary on all matters. But not this morning.

"Here's the first lady. Thank you again, Álvaro—and have Kyle meet me in the Oval at..."

"...at 11:30. Got it."

Hernandez smiled at Cecilia Erskine as she came up to her

husband. The president realized he'd have to be the one to convince her not to avoid a public statement about Ketchum's death.

Erskine's heart both warmed and ached at the sight of his beautiful wife—as it always did. Against the advice of his political advisers and members of his family, he married Cecilia Finch, twelve years his junior, when he was thirty-eight. Coincidentally, earlier this year they celebrated their twelfth wedding anniversary and she had turned thirty-six. Erskine found the chronological connections both intriguing and depressing.

His marriage to Cecilia was Erskine's second and her first. He had met her at a UNEV alumni re-union while serving in Congress in the early 2000s. She had come up from Charlotte, North Carolina, where she worked for the then mayor of the city, and following six months of long-distance courtship, Erskine convinced Cecilia to come to Washington and become part of his congressional staff. Soon after, they wed.

The president's divorce—four years before he met Cecilia—was prompted by his wife's adultery. Accordingly, no one held the second marriage against him politically, although the age difference between the congressman and his second wife did provide initial discussion—until his constituents were won over by her beauty and charm, allowing Erskine to seek and win the state house and re-election—the second term as governor being cut short by his run for the presidency.

During the campaign, the press again paid what Erskine believed was inordinate attention to the age difference of twelve years, which the couple addressed in a joint interview on one of the major television networks. Cecilia charmed a national audience by informing them that John Tyler's second wife Julia was a full thirty years younger than he and that Grover Cleveland was twenty-seven years older than his wife Frances. The couple also wished to note that John and Jacqueline Kennedy were separated in birthdates by over twelve years. Indeed, given the personal attractiveness of the Erskines, many comparisons were made between them and the Kennedys half a century earlier. After all, Stephen Erskine was forty-seven when he was inaugurated; JFK forty-three.

But what the public didn't know was that the present first lady suffered from periodic bouts of depression and an occasional predilection to act impetuously, as was evident in her desire to speak publicly about Jack Ketchum. The public was moreover unaware of her true feelings for her step-brother, although the media would certainly want to know what she felt now that he had been murdered. Erskine had already armed his press secretary with the response he was to give to all requests to speak with his wife. "The first lady wishes to deal with tragedy of Coach Reilly's death privately. She will offer no public statement." Again, Erskine couldn't allow her to speak about Ketchum, for then she would be forced to field the inevitable questions about her step-brother. As he walked forward to embrace his lovely wife, the president had but one thought: thank God that goddamned bastard Reilly was dead. Perhaps in some way, that fact might draw her closer to her husband, who over the past several years anguished over the growing distance between them.

### 

Taking the last bite of his fast-food chicken biscuit, Wells parked his car as close as was permitted to the smoldering remains of Jack Ketchum's modest home just outside Leesburg. What kind of explosive charge wreaked such destruction? All Wells learned from a quick call to his friend Henrik Nordenson—Metro's resident weapons and explosive expert, who had come over from Washington to help out the Leesburg and Loudoun County authorities—was that the device was detonated in the kitchen. But who would have wanted Ketchum dead, and why go to such elaborate means? Wells was unable to get his thoughts past the file his mentor mentioned he had locked in his desk, which was situated on the other side of the kitchen wall. Had Hoyt Reilly not been murdered earlier in the morning, Wells would have thought of him as the one responsible for Ketchum's death. Yet, was Reilly aware of what exactly Ketchum supposedly had on him? If so, could the man have in the middle of the night driven the short distance from his home near the UNEV campus, broken into his predecessor's home, set the charge in Ketchum's kitchen, and then returned to campus—only to be shot dead on the university track?

"So you came after all."

"Told you that I might, Henrik."

"I'm awfully sorry, Daniel. This is just horrible. So damned horrible."

Henrik Nordenson had picked up the nuances of English fairly easily, moving to Virginia when he was six. Although he and his father already spoke a qualified form of English, his skill in the language was enhanced by his then new mother—the young American assistant professor of European history from UVA, who encouraged his widowed father to leave Kristiansand on the southern coast of Norway and continue their relationship in the States—resulting in their marriage less than a year after he brought his son to Virginia.

But the marriage ended after five years, prompting Henrik and his father's return to Norway, where the boy finished secondary school and took a degree at the University of Oslo. He intended to become a lawyer, but soon found his nature demanded considerable physical activity with a hint of danger—and therefore joined the Norwegian Police Service until deciding to return to the States eleven months earlier. He and Wells met when a false bomb threat at the building next to Wells's office was called in the previous February.

"Henrik, what the hell happened here?"

"From what we can gather so far, it seems to be a VOIED."

"Sorry?"

"Victim Operated Improvised Explosive Device. Just one of the many varieties of IEDs. A kind of booby trap, if you will. VOIED triggering devices are normally disguised as something seen every-day—something completely innocuous."

"Like a trip-wire in Jack's kitchen?"

"Maybe—but it can be anything that's set off by movement. Brushing against, tripping over, stepping on, pushing, or pulling. Long history of these mechanisms, starting in World War II—then Vietnam, North Ireland, Afghanistan, Lebanon, and of course Iraq." Nordenson paused before adding, "As you well know."

"What do you think set it off?"

"Something likely on the stove. It was an electric oven, so it was probably rigged to go off when one of the knobs was turned, when bake or broil was pressed, or when the door was opened."

"Jack told me that he had stopped scrambling eggs for breakfast and started heating up those frozen breakfast meals in his oven."

"Then that may have been it."

"Jesus, if someone wanted him dead, why do it this way?"

"Several possible reasons—and you can be sure that they'll all be considered."

"Are you saying you have an idea of who might have wanted Jack dead?"

"No, I'm not. I'm just saying that all possible motives will be considered. Standard procedure, really."

"But when was the charge set? Jack didn't go out much. He probably used the oven for dinner last night."

"If so, the explosive was set in the middle of the night while Ketchum was asleep. Hate to say it, my friend, but creativity is not simply limited to those in the arts."

"Wait. Wait a minute. I can't believe I..." Wells shook his head at the embarrassing revelation.

"What is it, my friend?"

"Motive. How goddamned obvious. Hoyt Reilly was killed this morning. Jack Ketchum as well."

"They already have two officers assigned to UNEV's interim coach, if that's what you're getting at."

"Right."

Nordenson perceived that Wells was thinking of something else. He smiled and put his hand on his friend's shoulder. "We'll find out who did this to your old coach. I promise."

Wells expected such a response, but it soothed him nonetheless. "Thanks, Henrik. Look, is it possible that the murders of Reilly and Ketchum were unrelated?" Wells hoped Nordenson could convince him they were. "I mean, one was shot to death, right? The other..."

"We're going first on the assumption that they *were* related. If it's difficult for the killer to confront one of the victims, it does happen that two widely different manners of killing are used on multiple victims. Poison, explosives, firearms, and more assorted booby traps than you can possibly imagine."

Nordenson looked around to be sure that no one could hear them. "Okay, for your ears alone, Daniel. Right before I left Washington, I saw via computer one of the bullets extracted from Reilly's body. They asked my opinion and I told them it looked to me like a 9 x 18mm. cartridge fired from a Makarov."

"Makarov? Sounds Russian."

"Well done, my friend. For forty years a pistol of choice for the Soviet police and military—not to mention the Spetsnaz."

"You mean the Soviet version of the Green Berets?"

"Something like that. Russian Special Forces, if you will."

"You're not trying to suggest some kind of Russian operation here, are you?" What possible connection was there to Ketchum and Reilly to prompt double murder by the Russians?" Wells felt pressure in his gut.

"No, not saying that. First of all, the autopsy will pull the two other rounds out and we'll check to be sure. The round I saw on screen was easily extractable—the two others, not so much. And the Russians stopped relying on the Makarov twenty years ago. They've used the MR-443 Grach—the Yarygin Pya—in recent years." Nordenson smiled at the confusion on his friend's face. "Sorry for the jargon, Daniel. My point is that it might be someone who collects guns and got the 'bright' idea of using the Makarov—for a dozen possible reasons. But no, I wouldn't go so far as to say that the Russians are attempting to bring down this country by taking out a few college football coaches." Nordenson saw Wells's eyes close and realized his *faux pas*. "Sorry, my friend. I didn't mean to sound so flippant."

"It's all right, Henrik. It's just all damn confusing." Wells was tempted to tell Nordenson about Ketchum's supposed evidence against Reilly, but thought now wasn't the time—not until he was convinced there was indeed something there. He made up his mind to call Ketchum's daughter in Chapel Hill to express his condolences as soon as he had the chance. He assumed she'd been contacted by now. If not, it would perhaps be appropriate that he was the one who informed her.

When Wells moved toward the house, Nordenson stopped him. "Sorry, we can't let you get any closer. But there's nothing much to see. What was left of him they took... They've already removed him."

Wells took a deep breath. "Henrik, what about Ketchum's possessions—his papers and such?"

"What hasn't been destroyed in the explosion and fire will of course be examined for any possible clues as to who might have done this. It seems from what I've been told that whatever was in his den on the other side of the kitchen wall has been incinerated. But I haven't been here that long—so I know only what the police and fire department have shared with me." Nordenson smiled mischievously. "Why do you ask? You think there may be something relating to a possible attempt on his life that Ketchum kept in the house?"

"I don't know. I was just trying to think like a cop."

Nordenson nodded his head. "Ah, you're trying to tell me you missed your calling. Is that right?"

Wells couldn't help grinning at his friend's remark. "Something like that." Wells's father and one of his uncles were cops.

"Come on, Daniel. I'll walk you to your car."

"You going to hang around?"

"Yes, and I promise to let you know when we find anything or I learn anything else about the explosion or who might have rigged it. I'll be here for another hour or so. Then I'll go back to the city and see what else I can learn about Reilly's murder—which I'll share with you if I can."

"And I'm off to UNEV."

"Daniel." Nordenson once more placed his hands on his friend's shoulders. "Watch yourself, all right?"

Nordenson walked back toward the smoldering house, and for the first time, Wells felt that he too might be in danger.

# CHAPTER 6

"This is Andrea Chase. Hello?" The delay on the other end of the line prompted her to repeat her "Hello?"

"Ms. Chase, this is Darryl Roebuck."

"Yes?"

"You know, Darryl Roebuck. I play middle linebacker for UNEV."

"Of course. What can I do for you, Mr. Roebuck?" Andrea recalled her conversation with Daniel Wells about Roebuck's notorious "nasty streak" on the field. She and Wells were aware Roebuck had been kicked out of the second game of the season after incurring a second unsportsmanlike conduct call, when he slammed his fist against the side of an offensive lineman's helmet, after shoving him to the ground earlier in the game. Even though Roebuck was required to sit out the rest of that game and the first half of the next one, Hoyt Reilly praised his middle linebacker for his "spirit"—informing the press that Roebuck played the position "as it damn well was meant to be played."

Andrea and Wells also discussed the close friendship of Roebuck and Carter Thompson and the rumor that Roebuck deviated from the more admirable example of his best friend by roughing up two young women over the previous summer. Jack Ketchum informed Wells that Reilly had intervened with both the local police and the two women to prevent the matter from putting in jeopardy Roebuck's eligibility for the coming season. Andrea included the two incidents in a piece she wrote about off-field violence against women. And now Roebuck was calling her—for what she wasn't quite sure. Delayed or simmering anger over her piece?

"Ms. Chase, I know that you're soon going to be talking to Carter about Coach Reilly, but I thought I'd let you know that I might have some information about that fucking dead bastard you might find of interest."

Andrea didn't expect the brash profanity, even though she knew most of the team felt similarly. She simply felt uncomfortable talking with Roebuck—there was something about his manner that unnerved her—and coupled with what she knew of his temperament, she was reluctant to agree to speak with or interview him. But as a journalist, she knew she couldn't defend a decision not to.

"I see. All right. If I can call you back in about an hour, I'll have my—"

"No, I can't be available then. Coach Cipriano is calling a team meeting in an hour."

"Tomorrow, then?"

"Not sure what we have for tomorrow. We have to get ready to fly out to Arizona and all that. Wait, I know that Mr. Wells is going to address us in the morning, but I don't know what else is scheduled. Look, I'm driving down to Alexandria to see my parents tonight. I could meet you after I have dinner with them. I can come into the city. It would be no problem. None at all."

Andrea was even more discomforted by the sudden lilt in his voice. "Okay, Mr. Roebuck. Let me check what I have going on. Can you call me back at this number before 5:00?"

"I think I can get free to do that."

"All right. I'll talk to you then and let you know where we can meet."

"That's great. I'll call you back, Andrea. Bye."

She held the cell phone in her hand for a good fifteen seconds before placing it back in her jacket pocket. She wasn't at all pleased that he took the liberty of using her first name.

### ###

"Then, my darling, you understand why it wouldn't be wise to issue a public statement about your affection for Coach Ketchum."

"He was a very special man to me, Stephen. Besides, I feel I should say something about what he meant to the school."

"I know that, Cecilia. But I'm afraid you'll be asked about Hoyt, and then..." The president stopped when he saw his lovely wife lift her head, as if to say she was finally free of the psychological burden her step-brother had long ago imposed upon her. She admitted her step-brother "tormented, ridiculed, and embarrassed" her, but she never revealed any specifics, preferring "not to live any of that again." Erskine assumed Reilly made her transition into puberty most difficult, likely poking cruel fun at her budding breasts and her menstrual periods and probably shocking her and her friends and boyfriends with private tales of everything from Cecilia's bathroom habits to her supposed solo bedtime activities. The man was a "disgusting lout" as the president told select members of his staff.

"I see your point, Stephen."

Relieved, Erskine smiled and watched his wife touch her neck and take a deep breath. She turned slightly toward him and commanded his attention. He understood she had something else to say.

"I want to think further about exactly what I want to say about my step-brother and Coach Ketchum. Then I will say it. Excuse me."

Checkmated, Erskine watched her walk out of the Oval Office—her stylish gait and her highly attractive shape had elicited almost daily remarks of appreciation in both liberal and conservative blogs, not to mention the flirtatious offerings of cabinet officers and particularly the older male members of the House and Senate. Erskine understood the futility of indulging his jealousy, but he felt it—and lived with it every day. He wondered if this was the unalterable fate of any man who marries an attractive woman too many years his junior. But he reminded himself that she was twelve, not twenty or thirty years younger. The names were familiar, because he researched the matter and memorized eleven of them: Larry King, Hugh Hefner, Humphrey

Bogart, Clint Eastwood, Michael Douglas, Harrison Ford, Woody Allen, Jerry Seinfeld, Frank Sinatra, Paul McCartney—even Nelson Mandela, for God's sake—all married women more than twelve years younger, and a good number of these unions remained unbroken. Still, the current state of his marriage left him generally insecure about his wife, and he occasionally allowed a few revenge fantasies to enter his mind. Not simply other men who ogled Cecilia but oddly enough, Hoyt Reilly. Erskine constructed a theory that the vulgar man's torment and humiliation of his step-sister formed a need for her to be flattered and even wanted by other men. Even Reilly's sudden death could not alter this desire of hers. It was too late for that.

### 

Wells took a full breath after expressing his deepest condolences to Jack Ketchum's widowed daughter and only child, Carla Aronson. Ten months earlier, her forty year-old husband—a professor of Economics at UNC—died from a gunshot wound by a disturbed student, a young woman to whom he had just given a B. And now Carla had lost her father. At least she wouldn't be alone for long, since her deceased husband's sisters were tomorrow morning driving east from Oregon to accompany her to Virginia for the funeral services, once they had been formalized.

"You will speak at the service, won't you?"

"Of course I will, Carla. I am honored you want me to."

"Oh Daniel, daddy loved you and thought of you as a son."

Both Wells and Carla recalled as well how keen Jack Ketchum had been to get the two of them together when they were students at UNEV, although both had other love interests at the time.

"You know how much I admired and respected him, Carla."

"I know. That helps more than you can imagine."

Wells recognized his timing was dreadful, but he couldn't help shifting the subject. "Carla, forgive me for mentioning this, but it seems as though all your father's papers were destroyed in the fire, and—"

"Papers. Oh, wait. I have to tell you something. Something very important."

Wells conceded he would have to call her again about the file on Reilly or wait until she came up for the funeral. "Of course. What is it?"

"My father made me promise to give you a printed copy of a file he was keeping on Hoyt Reilly. Made me promise to give it to you if... when... Oh, Daniel, he told me to give it to you when he died—and added that I was to give it to you 'however he died.' I never understood why he had said that. But I now believe he knew he might be killed because of it."

"We can't conclude that for sure, Carla, because..." Wells couldn't complete the thought. He believed in the possibility as much as she did.

"Should I bring the file up to you when we have daddy's services?"

Uneasy, Wells felt he couldn't wait that long. Again he risked offending her sensibilities.

"Carla, I have promised a friend I served with in Iraq that I'd come down to Greensboro sometime before the New Year and chat with him about his campaign for a congressional seat from the 13th District. I can swing over and see you, and you can show me the file." Wells was disappointed with himself for making so clear the true reason he was coming down to North Carolina.

She didn't hesitate. "Should I pick you up at the airport?"

"No, I'll drive down tomorrow morning after I address the team here at UNEV." Wells would again have to call Gina Lorenzetti or Rod Pritchett and make still another adjustment to tomorrow afternoon's schedule. "It's about four hours to Chapel Hill by car—so expect me sometime in the early afternoon."

"Let me give you my address and directions."

"Thank you."

"Daniel?"

"Yes?"

"I'm frightened."

"I know, Carla. I know."

###

After noting the time—5:05 p.m.—the man began walking the two blocks to the administrative, training, and locker-room areas that served UNEV's football team during the fall. No one would know him here. Besides, he had donned a UNEV sweatshirt complete with hood—reflective of the recent student body sartorial trend that reflected school pride for the team's initial foray into the college football stratosphere—the big bowl game in Glendale, Arizona.

As he came toward the main entrance of the complex, the front door opened, and a group of five UNEV football players emerged and headed down the entrance walk toward the sidewalk. They turned to their right and continued their animated discussion. The man was less than ten feet behind them, accidentally banging shoulders with a tall middle-age jogger. "Excuse me, ma'am," he cheerfully said, after she flashed him a cheerless look. Given the volume of the young men's voices, the man had no difficulty hearing everything they were discussing. The athletes expressed their contempt for the now deceased head coach Hoyt Reilly, their concerns over a change of the bowl game plan now that a new coach was in charge, and their anticipation of a visit in the morning by one of their distinguished alums and former letterman, Daniel Wells. Twice, one of the players looked back at the man in the hood, but none of the five lowered their voices for fear of being overheard. The man knew that subtlety and discretion were not qualities these young men were ever expected to cultivate.

"So, you're going home tonight, Darryl?"

"Got to. My old man's birthday."

"Carter going with you?"

"Fuck you. We're best friends, but he's not my goddamned wife."

"You ought to change positions for your senior year, Darryl. Switch to center so that Thompson can tickle your sack on the field as well as off."

"As I said, 'fuck you.'" Roebuck was only mildly annoyed by the teasing. He had heard it all before—and daily.

"Seriously, be sure you're back for Wells's big pep talk tomorrow morning."

"Cipriano knows where I'm going tonight." Roebuck paused. "But he doesn't know all the places I'm going."

Another teammate playfully shoved the burly linebacker off the sidewalk. "What the hell are you talking about?"

Normally, Roebuck would make it a point to shove back hard enough to knock his teammate off his feet, but he suppressed the urge. The others saw that the linebacker was uncharacteristically relaxed and delighted about something.

"You seeing some fine female flesh tonight in Alexandria, Darryl? Father's birthday just an excuse, that it?"

"No, I'm having dinner and cake with the folks, but yes, I am seeing some 'fine female flesh' tonight in the capital city."

"Anyone we know?"

"Oh, yeah. Someone you know."

"Well, shit, man. You gonna tell us?"

"Why not? It's Andrea Chase of *Sports Word*."

"That is indeed fine female flesh. But what the hell does she want to see you about?"

"Officially, she wants to interview me about the bowl game and that mother-fucker Reilly."

"Hey, Darryl, seriously—you'd better be careful what you say. Cipriano's likely to bench your ass if he doesn't throw you off the team first."

Roebuck sensed his four teammates were genuinely concerned that his admissions to Andrea Chase would become too much of a distraction between now and game day. Media interest was bad enough with Reilly's and now old Coach Ketchum's deaths.

"No, no. I'll only agree to talk to her on the condition that nothing I say about Reilly comes out until after the game."

"You trust her?"

"Oh, yeah. I trust her."

The smugness of Roebuck's response prompted one of the players to seek further explanation. "You just said that the 'official' reason was the interview. What do you mean by that?"

"You never know what might happen when a beautiful woman reporter spends a little time alone with a virile and younger male—you know, the best at his position in college football."

"Oh, so Carter's going to meet the two of you there?"

The others roared with delight, but this time Roebuck's reaction was more characteristically sour. "As I said, 'fuck you.'"

"Hey, hey, man. Lighten up. Okay, so you and Ms. Chase are going to a fancy hotel for cocktails, and interview, and perhaps some cock in uh... the tail?"

Roebuck managed half a smile at the bawdy adolescent pun. "No hotel. We're meeting tonight at 10:30 at the Tryst Coffeehouse on 18th. After that... well... you never know if a hotel might not be in fact be in the plans."

"A coffee house? You're idea, Darryl?"

"No. Hers." The others noted the disappointment in his voice.

"Thanks for telling us where you'll be, Darryl."

The men had reached the end of the block where they would turn and cross the main street. Roebuck was visibly aggravated at himself for giving his crew the exact location.

"If any of you assholes think you're going to drive into Washington and interrupt my meeting with her, I swear I'll fuck you up big time."

The men protested their innocence, until Roebuck felt assured that they wouldn't dare show their faces in the coffeehouse.

"I'm telling you, next to the current first lady, Andrea Chase would rank second in the D.C, celebrities I'd like to shove my cock into. Fucking them both at once wouldn't be too bad either." The others mocked the anatomical impossibility. "Fuck you guys. I meant fucking Andrea Chase right after making Cecilia Erskine howl like a bitch in heat." Now the others laughed at his ludicrous fantasy as well as his comical vanity.

The man stopped behind the five players as they waited to cross the street and was but two to three feet to their rear as Roebuck finished discussing his lurid plans for the evening. When the players crossed, the man turned and retraced his steps, walking casually until he reached his vehicle parked over two blocks away. He felt satisfied that he could leave the university area now. And he knew he wouldn't have to come back. The trip wasn't wasted as he feared it would be. What he heard from another source was flat-out accurate.

# CHAPTER 7

"You're already in Washington, Chas?"

"Let's just call it part of a long Christmas holiday. Where are you, Daniel? Can we have dinner?"

"Actually I can't. I've just arrived at a hotel up in Leesburg. I'm talking to the UNEV team early tomorrow morning."

"Yes, I just learned about the shooting. I'm sorry for the university, not for Reilly, obviously. And I feel awful about Coach Ketchum's death. I know how close you both were. So tell me. How did it go before the committee earlier this month?" That was Chas Overby—a man known for his quick and occasionally tactless transitions. Wells informed his friend he'd tell him all about it when they got together, but Overby was insistent. "Were you intimidated by the surroundings, not to mention by the senators scowling down at you from Mount Olympus?"

"Actually, no. And how could I be when at the beginning they treated me like royalty and used me to announce to their constituents that I'm what America is all about."

"Sounds like you enjoyed it, then."

"Not quite. Besides, I wasn't long into my testimony before they thought of me as anything but a paragon of American virtue."

"Can't wait to hear the details." Overby made another one of his leaps. "Don't know why you don't run for Congress."

"Not interested."

"Oh, that's right. You always thought small. One of the reasons why you preferred little old UNEV to Penn State. You realize, don't you, that you were an idiot for not accepting their scholarship offer? You might have had a better shot at the NFL if you had. I would have crawled to State College on my hands and knees had they offered me one." Overby's tone was jocular, but Wells knew his friend was still confused as to why he hadn't chosen a bigger program than Jack Ketchum's at UNEV."

"Maybe. But I never felt comfortable with their offensive coordinator when I visited. I probably wouldn't have seen the field the entire four years."

"Hey, buddy, I know what you mean. Besides, playing for Coach Ketchum must have been special. Again, I'm so sorry to hear about his death."

"Thanks, Chas. He was a great guy. Truly a great guy."

"What I wouldn't have given to have played for him, rather than that son-of-a-bitch Reilly. Sorry, Daniel. I know it's not proper to speak ill of the recently deceased."

"In Reilly's case, such rules do not apply, so go right ahead."

Wells first met Overby when they were teammates in high school. Reilly recruited both of men hard when he was coaching at the up-and-coming Division II school in North Carolina, but Wells disliked the coach and his petty manner, whereas Overby bought into the promise that Reilly would get him ready for the pros at Overby's position—offensive line. When Overby made it to campus, Reilly acted as though he hardly heard of him. Overby finally started at right guard when he was a junior, but he was benched by the fifth game and only saw spot duty from then on. The constant harassment he took from Reilly at practice made his football experience even more regrettable.

"Daniel, I know I've told you how much 'fun' it was like playing for him, but..."

Wells was intrigued by Overby's hesitation. "Chas?"

"I can tell you more if you'd like to hear it."

"You got it. I'll check my calendar and get back to you later tonight or in the morning about when we can get together. As soon as possible,

I promise."

"Great. I'll be at the D.C. St. Regis until the thirtieth. Then I'll be going to my sister's for the big family New Year's gathering in Knoxville."

"The St. Regis—well, well. Now I understand why you took the embassy job."

"Not coming out of my salary, my friend. You forget that my father is a hotel magnate of sorts. He's taking my younger sister Ellen away on an exclusive father-daughter jaunt to Vienna, and he doesn't want me to feel neglected. I'm telling you, Daniel, you should follow my advice and marry Ellen, because she'll then be able to get you into first-rate accommodations."

Overby expected a witty comeback, but his friend was dead silent on the other end. "Daniel?" There was no answer, but he could hear Wells breathing.

"I'm sorry, Chas. I got distracted. Look, I'm getting picked up for dinner in about three minutes. I need to slap some water on my face."

"Okay, buddy. Hey, you're not picking up the check tonight, are you?"

"No, UNEV is paying. I'm eating with the president and athletic director."

"Sounds impressive."

"It isn't. They're both first-class jerks. This is the duo who saw to it that Jack Ketchum was removed from his duties and that Reilly was given the job. But considering what happened and the fact that I'm going to address the team in the morning, I feel I have to play nice."

"Hey—have four of five drinks and then tell the bastards what you really think of them."

"Wish I could, Chas. Wish I could."

###

Cecilia Erskine finished her brief chat with one of the White House chefs regarding the menu for a forthcoming state dinner. It was one of the responsibilities of her position she most enjoyed. In the first months after she and Erskine moved into the White House, she fretted over not advancing an issue with which to be identified. But with her husband's tactful encouragement, she concluded that she would make her mark with her style and taste—in clothing and in the arts. The White House had not seen so many classically trained performing artists since the Kennedys were in residence—from intimate poetical readings and concertos to full symphonic and operatic selections.

Now alone, the first lady sat in one of the cushioned arm chairs in her East Wing office and directed her attention to two items of memorabilia resting inside a glass-enclosed bookcase. One was a cameo of a woman blowing a swirled horn held up by a miniature gold easel. The other was a small-scale model of a Civil War cannon. After staring intently at both items, she closed her eyes and touched the spot on the back of her head that fifteen years earlier had been left bruised and bleeding. She pressed her eyes as tightly shut as she could. But within moments the tears broke through the barrier she had tried to form and cascaded down her cheeks.

###

Kyle Guidry checked the area around the World War I Memorial in West Potomac Park, a little southwest of the Word War Two Memorial on the National Mall. The domed peristyle Doric temple, where Guidry had recently seen a Marine Corps band play, was empty of visitors. He placed the cell phone to his ear.

"Helene, what would be the best way to console her at the loss of her step-brother? A sympathy card seems trite and not at all special. What?" As he listened to the woman discourage him from any overt gesture, Guidry grew impatient. "I have to do something to express my—look, why not? God damn it, I'm sorry I called you. Goodbye."

Taking rapid breaths, Guidry staggered from the Memorial. It took him thirty yards before he regained his normal stride. He would find another way to express his love for the first lady. He had already performed several "favors" for her of which she was completely unaware. But he was no longer satisfied with anonymous gestures of devotion.

### 

Wells was relieved that neither the university president nor the athletic director invited him for a drink after dinner. It was trying enough just getting through the meal. Neither of his hosts wished to discuss the death of Jack Ketchum—the man they had unceremoniously fired three years earlier. All their conversation was about Hoyt Reilly and how best to turn the murder into a plus for the team. The AD was delighted that "consolation funds" had already begun coming in. Seven well-heeled boosters increased their contributions to the top level and another offered to purchase brand new uniforms for the team, in order to provide a "fresh start" commencing with the bowl game in Glendale. The university's president asked Wells whether the team should go all the way with that fresh start and consider changing the team colors. Wells remembered vividly Jack Ketchum's telling him that he originally chose green and gray as a tribute to the memory of his late son, whose pee-wee football team wore the colors—his son having died of leukemia when he was eight. Wells maintained a polite demeanor but put an extra stress on his reply, "I would strongly suggest that you leave the colors *as they are.*"

Now alone in his hotel room, Wells formulated what he would say to the team in the morning, what he would say to Ketchum's daughter Carla Aronson when he drove down to Chapel Hill, and what he would say at Ketchum's funeral service several days hence. In spite of the day's events, he couldn't help chuckling at the irony. He had recently paused on the footbridge going into Roosevelt Island Park and watched the waters of the Potomac while he thought how settled his life had been since he established his relationship with Andrea Chase. He believed he had forged a satisfactory link between his past and present—first the good memories of UNEV, embodied by his old coach Jack Ketchum, and now his new love interest being a sports writer for a national magazine. Yet, it wasn't all that it could be, but that was to be expected. Wells knew he had some more work to do in setting his past in its proper place.

But Ketchum was dead—murdered, surely. And the man Wells despised, for so many reasons, had also been slain. He couldn't help thinking that these two killings wouldn't be the last to touch those connected with UNEV. Wells pulled back the drapes of his hotel window and looked out on the university quad. Because it was brightly lit, he could see everything and everyone quite clearly. That wasn't the case back then.

### 

"No, I'm not kidding, Andrea. Sorry. Can I call you Andrea or would you prefer Andie, as you're sometimes called on TV?"

She replied with a half-hearted "Andrea." She sipped her latte and took down a few notes. "So Coach Reilly actually asked you if you could 'hook him up' with some undergraduate women?"

"I swear to God he did. Reilly laughed when he said it, which told me that the fucker was protecting himself. Sorry."

She ignored the apology for his profanity. "What do you mean?"

Darryl Roebuck took his first swallow from his third draft beer and lowered himself even further into his comfortable chair at Tryst. He had pushed up the sleeves of his pull-over shirt, exposing his muscular forearms. "If I let it be known that he asked me to set him up, he'd simply say he was joking, you see? He did that kind of thing all the time. 'Hey man, I was kidding.'"

"Any evidence that he was really serious this time?"

"I think there was. He'd get point specific with me and Carter about what kind of girls he wanted. Wanted the "slutty types" and said he had no problem if they—excuse my being so direct—if they brought their mothers along."

"Mr. Roebuck, let me ask it this way. Any evidence that he actually had sexual relations with any undergraduates—or their mothers?" Andrea knew she'd take it no further, unless Roebuck had hard and fast proof. The topic of the conversation was upsetting her, and she regretted agreeing to meet UNEV's middle linebacker for a latte, three drafts, and unsubstantiated and sordid gossip.

"How can I put this without... Okay, there's evidence that he had something sexual with at least one co-ed—and it wasn't exactly consensual."

Andrea leaned forward and pulled the beer away from his hand. "Are you saying rape, Mr. Roebuck?"

"Come on. Call me Darryl."

"And you have proof?"

"Best you can have. The victim herself."

Andrea turned the page in her small notebook and wrote "Reilly—rape?" on a clean sheet. "All right, will you tell me who she is—or how I can get in touch with her?"

"I'm going to have to think about that, Andrea. I'd like to spend more time with you so that I can feel more comfortable you won't abuse the information and make things difficult for the victim."

"You won't tell me, then?"

"I didn't say that. I just said that I want to get to know you more... a little better, I mean. Why don't we pay up and we can take a walk. It's a little loud in here for one thing. And for another, I don't want anyone overhearing anything else I might say. Come on."

A few minutes later, Roebuck crossed 18th Street NW and started walking south to where he had parked his car—in a darkened area near Belmont. "Fucking bitch," he muttered to himself. Andrea Chase said nothing to him about his invitation to get to know her better by taking a walk, refused his offer to drive her back to her place, and called a cab from inside Tryst. When he got to his car, he saw that the left rear tire was flat. "God damn it." Roebuck slammed the back of his fist into the rear side of his car, denting it slightly.

He couldn't believe the last ten minutes of his life. His attempt to make a move on Andrea Chase had utterly failed, even with the inducements he offered. She was having none of his revelations about Reilly or about the young woman Reilly had assaulted or raped—Roebuck hadn't made up his mind which of the two stories he would go with. The sports writer even refused to thank him when he promised he'd send her the name of Reilly's supposed victim. She further insulted him by insisting on paying for her little piss-ass latte, and then she called a goddamned cab. And now a fucking flat tire.

Roebuck reached for his car key and lined it up with the lock on the trunk hood. He jammed the key into the lock. He barely had enough time to realize the trunk was already cracked open when it jerked upward and a twenty-two inch blade entered his throat and slid unimpeded through the back of his neck.

### 

The man checked for the pocket watch. He was momentarily concerned it might have slipped out of his pants when he was lying inside the trunk of Darryl Roebuck's 1984 Pontiac Bonneville. He simply couldn't afford to lose the watch. It was there, however, and the man noted the time. He moreover saw the blood on the sleeves of his dark sweat shirt, the one he wore when he shot Hoyt Reilly fifteen and a half hours earlier and set the explosive charge at Jack Ketchum's four hours earlier than that. Three deaths in a mere three-fourths of a single day. Would he keep to such a schedule in the days ahead? The man knew it might be impossible, but he wanted it all over by the end of the weekend, six days from now. Sunday was his birthday, and he wanted—dearly hoped for—a new start free of all the responsibilities the past had burdened him with.

The man stood under the running water, turning it up as hot as he could stand. He closed his eyes and quickly visualized the faces of his first three victims, two of whom he had seen on several occasions, the third he had seen for the first time in the late afternoon on the campus of UNEV. He also briefly visualized the faces of others he would or might have to kill, but spent most of his time in the shower contemplating the visages of two faces in particular. One of them belonged to the former UNEV quarterback Daniel Wells.

# Chapter 8

At 7:30 a.m. Wells sat in the dining hall of the UNLV Athletics complex, speaking with Coach Mike Cipriano and other members of the coaching staff. Two officers from the local police stood a few feet away scanning the entire area.

"Jesus, Daniel, my protection detail has spooked the entire team. As I told them several times, I'll be fine."

Wells nodded, but was concerned that Cipriano would end up the next victim of the person who murdered Reilly and Ketchum—someone who apparently had a grudge against the coaching staff or the university as a whole. Wells pondered the matter for an hour before falling asleep the previous night and in the hour after awakening this morning. From what he could gather from the university's president and the AD at last night's dinner, there was no one on file with any active grievance against the university or athletic department. No threats had been noted by anyone involving the football team. Wells thought the first place to look was at former players who either didn't make the team or who never started—or who quit outright owing to a benching or disagreement with the head coach. Wells couldn't help thinking someone like Stephen Erskine—the president of the United States? Might it have been a former player Reilly abused in some way? Someone who felt about the coach as did his friend Chas Overby? Wells quickly dismissed that possibility, disappointed with himself for having come up with such a thought.

The candidates with a grudge against Reilly were surely many—but who would have wanted Jack Ketchum dead as well? Wells looked around the room and noticed an empty place next to where Carter Thompson sat eating his breakfast. Then it hit him. Why consider just former players? Perhaps it was a current player who was responsible for the murders.

"Coach Mike?"

"Yes, Daniel?"

Wells pointed to the empty place next to Thompson. "Someone missing this morning?"

Cipriano lowered his head and muttered a broken profanity. "Yes. Darryl Roebuck—our starting middle linebacker. He went home to Alexandria for his father's birthday last night. He didn't come back. And now I'm going to have to sit him for at least the first two series of the bowl game. And if I don't hear anything from him before the morning's out, he might not play at all, damn it."

Roebuck? Wells recalled what he knew about the rumors and evidence of the linebacker's off-the-field aggressive behavior—some of which Wells discussed recently with Andrea Chase. Wells glanced at Cipriano to see if the interim head coach was thinking along the same lines. Did Cipriano at least consider the possibility that Darryl Roebuck might have murdered Reilly and Ketchum?

"You know, I was just thinking."

"Yes, Coach?"

"Let's move the team out to the practice field for your talk. It's a bit too stuffy in here, and the acoustics aren't worth a damn."

###

"I appreciate you guys taking time to listen to an alum and former player from back in the day." The crisp weather invigorated Wells. Just forty-one degrees but sunny and relatively windless. Though much warmer, it was such a day as this that Wells first set foot on campus during his recruiting visit and fell victim to the irresistible force of Jack Ketchum's argument as to why the young man ought to sign with

UNEV.

The team applauded politely, and Wells didn't think the response was orchestrated. Mike Cipriano twirled his whistle around his finger, while keeping his eye on his quarterback Carter Thomson, who was visibly unsettled. It was obvious to all that Thomson was concerned about Roebuck's absence.

The team huddled around Wells. "I don't have any magic words, guys. I just remember what Coach Ketchum told all of us back then. He said that sometimes the mark of a good football player is no better demonstrated than in how he handles distractions—on the field, off the field—about his own life or about the lives of those we care for. Practice might be tough going for awhile, but you owe it to... "

Wells stopped in mid-sentence. With the exception of Carter Thompson the rest of the team looked like a relaxed lot. Many were smiling and nodding their heads. And why not? They were probably all relieved Hoyt Reilly was out of their lives forever. As for the loss of Jack Ketchum, only two seniors were left who were on the squad in the old coach's last year. The others who were then freshmen quit or transferred after meeting Coach Reilly the following February. Wells knew the team had no worries Cipriano would become another Reilly, and no one appeared alarmed that someone might be planning on murdering the interim head coach, let alone any member of the team.

"You owe it to yourselves to go out to Glendale and show the world what kind of a kick-ass football team and tradition we have here at UNLV." The team, again with the exception of Thompson, cheered vociferously, adding unintelligible hoots and grunts to punctuate the sentiment.

"Hey Mr. Wells." One of the team's wide receivers had raised his hand.

"Come on guys—I'm an alum. Call me Daniel."

"Okay. Hey, Mr. Daniel." Half the team laughed, while the other sent forth a volley of good-natured boos. "How about throwing a few to the wide-outs? See if you can still chuck it. We hear you once out-threw Chris Weinke when you were a rising sophomore and he was about to enter the NFL draft. Weinke had just won the Heisman Trophy at Florida State, and he and Wells worked out together before the NFL combine in the spring of 2001.

"Wait now. We both threw ten balls each—and Chris out-threw me nine out of the ten. It would have been ten out of ten but on one of his attempts the wind came up in his face."

"Yeah, but you still out-threw him, didn't you? No excuses—just throw."

Wells couldn't have been more delighted. These guys weren't going to let him just wave and walk away just because he was missing the lower part of his left arm. "Okay, you win. Go deep, young man. Go deep." Wells took the football, went through his seven-step drop, and hurled the football as far as he could. It was long enough, but a little off the mark. Wells thoroughly enjoyed the boisterous teasing he received and waited until it died down before he offered his own retort. "You ran the wrong route, number 17." Many on the team came up to him and shook his hand or patted him on the back. No one offered an "I'm sorry about what happened to you in Iraq," and that was the way Wells wanted it—here and everywhere else in his life. The last to shake his hand was the team's current quarterback. Wells wanted to share a little advice about playing confidently, but Carter Thomson turned and headed back inside the locker room.

###

When he was back in his hotel room packing his things for the trip down to Chapel Hill, Wells thought he'd call Henrik Nordenson's cell and share with him the fact that Darryl Roebuck didn't make it back to campus the previous evening. He wanted to express to Nordenson his nagging suspicion that Roebuck might have been responsible for Reilly's death—if not Reilly's and Ketchum's.

"Daniel, have you talked to Andrea late last night or anytime this morning?"

"No. Oh, Christ. Is she all right?"

"Yes, yes. I'm sorry. I should have prefaced that with... no, no, she's fine. But she met Roebuck last night in the city for an interview."

"What? She didn't tell me she was going to do that."

"I talked to her less than an hour ago. She said she was afraid you'd be upset with her, since the two of you had talked about some of Roebuck's distasteful antics."

Wells knew he would never have allowed her to meet Roebuck alone. He would have driven back to D.C. and accompanied her. "So, she met him. Did she sense anything about his behavior?"

"She'll talk to you about that."

"But you're certain she's all right."

"Yes. She insisted that nothing happened to her."

"Henrik, did she see any indication that he might have killed Reilly—and Jack Ketchum?"

"She said no. But I don't think that's at all a possibility now, Daniel."

"What do you mean?"

"His body was found earlier this morning. He was inside the trunk of his car. He was almost decapitated."

### ###

"Álvaro, is this just some rumor? Please, for the love of God, tell me that's all it is."

"Kyle, it's no rumor. Official word is that the body of the team's starting middle linebacker was discovered by a pedestrian early this morning. The woman said she saw blood splatters on the road near the kid's car and saw a pool of blood underneath the trunk area. She lifted the opened hood and saw him jammed into the trunk. Police report that half his neck was sliced all the way through. Some kind of long bladed weapon, they think."

"Was the murder weapon left at the scene?"

"No. No trace of it."

"Does the president know?"

"Yes, I informed him."

"The first lady?"

"I don't think she knows."

"Fuck. Why don't you know for sure? That's your job."

"Why the hell would she need to be told, Kyle? She didn't know the kid."

"All right, all right. Let me know the minute you hear anything else."

"I will." Angered by Guidry's disrespectful response, Hernandez reached the door of Guidry's West Wing office, stopped, and said over his shoulder, "Kyle, I'm afraid this job is truly become too much for me. I think it would be best for the Administration if I stepped down now."

Guidry slammed the palm of his hand on his desk. "God damn it, Hernandez. How many times do we have to go over this? You're going to wait until after the election before you go anywhere. Jesus Christ, you leave now and all kinds of assumptions will be made."

"Don't worry, Kyle, I've not been approached to write a god-damned tell-all."

"The fucking minute you leave the White House you'll have publishers crawling up your ass."

Hernandez took several steps toward Guidry, who turned his back and headed in the other direction, but not before getting off another shot. "Just do your fucking job, Álvaro."

Twenty minutes later, Guidry remained frozen behind his desk, writing five times on a notepad the name of the person most on his mind at this moment. Slamming his pen down, he tore off the page and ripped it into as many pieces as he could before stuffing the bits of paper into his front pocket. He pushed himself away from the desk, grabbed his suit coat, and headed to the Oval Office for his scheduled meeting with the president.

# CHAPTER 9

"It's so good seeing you again, Daniel. It's been far too long."

"Eight or nine years, I believe."

Wells and Carla Aronson spent the next ten minutes bringing each other up to speed on their lives. They spent very little time discussing the death of her father. Carla seemed reluctant to speak about it, except to ask if the police had any suspects or leads.

"None at this time, I'm afraid."

They remained silent while each took bites of their smoked salmon and shaved roast beef at the Crossroads Restaurant in Chapel Hill's Carolina Inn. Wells understood she wanted the both of them to finish their lunch before going over the copy of the material Jack Ketchum had accumulated on Hoyt Reilly.

"Daniel, you don't think my father had anything to do with Reilly's death, do you?"

"My god, no. I can't imagine anyone would think such a thing."

"No, I'm sure some sickos will—especially if any of the material my father had on Reilly gets released to the public." Wells better appreciated her apparent reluctance to honor her father's wishes and give his former quarterback a copy of what was incinerated in the blast.

"I still think not, Carla. It would be more the case that someone will think that Reilly was responsible for... I'm sorry."

"No. I need to articulate the fact that my father is dead—and likely murdered." The statement stripped away any strength she had to speak further of the matter. She dropped her head and began crying.

###

On the drive back to his place across the Potomac, Wells glanced at the papers Carla Aronson handed him when he walked her out to her car. She had locked the material in the trunk, along with a framed photo of the three of them after Wells played his last game for UNEV. "You can see my father's love for you, Daniel. He couldn't have been prouder of you if you were his own son." Wells knew Coach Ketchum's affection was real that day. UNEV had lost that game, in large part because of the fourth-quarter interception Wells threw.

Still emotionally wrought, Carla spoke of how her father reacted when word came that his all-time favorite player had been seriously wounded in Iraq. "He cried when he heard, but soon made phone calls trying to find out where you'd be taken and when you'd come home."

"And there he was—spending most of the team's off-week messing with my hospital bed pillows when I was flown to Germany. He stayed there for three days before going back to practice with the team. I hear he took considerable heat from the administration for that act of exceptional kindness."

"He didn't care—not one bit."

By the time Wells drove through Richmond on I-95 he was fighting the temptation to pull over and read the file Ketchum had on Reilly—still confused as to what damning evidence his old coach possessed. He also shook his head at the irony—or was it coincidence?—that two men, two coaches so different in temperament and class were killed on the same morning, perhaps by the same person. But Wells dismissed the urge to continue pondering the matter and turned his thoughts to the meeting Andrea had with Darryl Roebuck and Roebuck's subsequent murder. During his call to her after Nordenson informed him of what happened, Andrea would only tell him she was never going to walk with Roebuck to his car—and called for a cab instead. Regardless, Wells was still shaken by what he considered a very close call. There was no greater feeling of helplessness than being unable to know ahead of time what might happen or being unable to stop what he felt was sure to happen. He had experienced that helplessness over fifteen years ago in Fallujah, and it was the worst feeling of his life—even more than the loss of his hand and wrist.

At the end of his four-and-a-half-hour trip, Wells reached his apartment and saw a package lying in front of the door.

###

"Andrea Chase here." She just finished the first two paragraphs of her piece on the Hoyt Reilly murder when she took the call. "Yes, Lieutenant?"

After she hung up, she grabbed her coat and headed out towards Metro headquarters. The detective wished to talk in detail about the slaying of Darryl Roebuck and their meeting at Tryst not long before the UNEV linebacker had been slain. Surely they weren't going to include her among any suspects. Nevertheless, Andrea found it difficult to look upon this third murder with a UNEV connection in any objective and analytical sense. She grabbed her phone and called Wells, but only got his voice message. She slipped on a knee-length dress and combed out her lush hair, but then thought better of it and changed into pants and a heavy sweater and put her hair in a pony tail. Looking too feminine might not be wise under the circumstances, she concluded.

###

"The first lady is disappointed she won't be able to address you this morning. Perhaps this afternoon. Thank you." Paula Bradford-Adams, Cecilia Erskine's chief staffer, politely parried all inquiries about the first lady's health. She thought it best not to deny that the first lady was fighting flu-like symptoms or one of her periodic migraines, because Bradford-Adams learned early on that Cecilia Erskine's capriciousness required several avenues of deception to avoid the out-right lie. Today, the first lady complained of neither the sniffles nor a headache, though she was struggling presently with the onset of the latter. She was primarily immobilized by the news of her step-brother's murder out on the UNEV track—yet not so immobile that she couldn't imbibe two of her favorite Sea Breezes. Ordinarily, she claimed that multiple cocktails of this kind weren't dangerous since she had been drinking vodka since she was a teenager, that the cocktail also contained healthy cranberry and grapefruit juice, and that each drink was some 120-140 calories less than daiquiris and margaritas. Whenever she was away from the White House, the ingredients always traveled with her.

When one of her staff persons checked on her, the first lady was staring out of her office window in the East Wing with cocktail in hand, her face frozen in an attitude of contemplation and regret. When asked if she was all right, Cecilia muttered a monotone "I'm fine. Helene, I'd appreciate not being disturbed for the time being."

"Yes, ma'am."

Cecilia stepped away from the window and half reclined on the sofa, still holding the cocktail in one hand and a cold cloth, which rested inside an ice-filled bowl, in the other. Once again she had forgotten to take her preventative medication for her migraines and was left to apply the more habitual alleviation–inside and out. Closing her eyes with the cold cloth pressed into her forehead, she returned to her thoughts, filled with painful memory and regret.

She always felt badly about rejecting Daniel Wells the way she had in the late summer after their graduation from UNEV. She dearly cared for him from the time they began dating in their sophomore year. That he was a campus celebrity, quarterbacking the football team, wasn't his main appeal for her—not even close. She loved most of all his consideration and patience with her hesitations and doubts about herself and their relationship. Her mother had often advised her to find a "gentleman" to love, and for the first time she had understood why. Nor did Wells complain when she initially declined his invitation to go with him for weekend or overnights trips. When they began having sex, eight months after they started seeing each other exclusively, she asked if he would make love to her from behind. From then on, she would only take him inside her in that position or with her sitting on him looking forward. She was also eager for oral sex, and as time went on she seemed more and more intent on reaching orgasm on her own or having him do so orally. When Wells asked about her reluctance to look into his eyes when they had sex, she explained that she had always been told that pre-marital sex was a sin, and as a ridiculous way to honor the wishes of her mother she would wait until she was married to him before engaging in the more traditional sexual position. "I know, I know. I'm a nut case, but I want to save something special so you'll actually go through with the wedding," she teased.

But there was no wedding. After he was cut by the Denver Broncos that summer, he talked to her about his short-term plans and then turned the subject to their marriage. At first she said they should wait a year, but her face told him she had lost all desire to marry him. What had happened during the time they were separated while he was away with the Broncos? She merely shook her head and left the restaurant as she began to cry. She wouldn't take his calls, and after an agonizing week he received his "Dear John" letter explaining she could never make him happy and all the rest of it. His consolation was that she had hand-written it at least and not sent it via e-mail.

When Wells returned to the States after the events in Iraq, he desperately wanted her to visit or at least call him. He felt now that he was maimed, she wouldn't ever want him intimately, but just seeing her or hearing her voice would have meant so much. After he recovered and began working, he heard from Coach Ketchum that Cecilia had called him and inquired about her former lover. When Wells asked how he could get in touch with her, Ketchum informed him that she specifically requested that he avoid doing so because she was now likely to marry someone.

Cecilia moaned softly from the increasing pressure of her migraine and the pain of her memories, which touched her more often in recent months. She would have loved to have been Mrs. Daniel Wells and looked deeply into his eyes as they shared their passion rather than eventually marrying a man she had little passion for—even if she did become the First Lady of the United States. But all of what she wanted and what she was then and was now, had been determined by her step-brother, the recently murdered Hoyt Reilly. Her reflections were interrupted by the opening of her office door.

"Cecilia, I'm sorry. I know you're having a migraine, but we've got to get a picture with the students from Gallaudet."

"I'll check my face and be right along, Stephen."

### 

"Thanks for calling, Daniel. I'm barely able to think straight. I'm meeting with the team in a few minutes and then the press."

Wells tried earlier but couldn't reach Mike Cipriano, who he assumed had been informed of Darryl Roe's murder. Wells felt for Cipriano—just having been named head coach for the bowl game in the wake of Hoyt Reilly's murder and now a day later discovering that one of his players had suffered the same fate. Wells knew the UNEV president and athletic director were presently dealing with other issues relating to the football program and the university at large. Should the football team be sent a day early to Glendale for final practices? How much police protection could they expect to receive if they flew out when originally planned? There were around a hundred scholarship and non-scholarship members of the team, of which over forty were counted on to play on offense, defense, and special teams. And what of the nine coaches and assorted graduate assistants and training staff? How many could be protected and for how long?

Was the killer of Reilly, Ketchum, and Roe a deranged fan of UNEV's bowl opponent, attempting to kill as many of the enemy as possible before kick-off? Even a former member of Jack Ketchum's or Hoyt Reilly's staff? Would the president, AD, and the Virginia Board of Regents make a decision to pull UNEV out of the game? When he spoke with the university's vice-president for academic affairs, Wells raised the possibility that the two murders might well have been committed by two separate killers—neither attempting to attack members of the football team—to which the VP replied, "We have to think the worst here, Mr. Wells. We have the team members, coaches, staff, and even the general student body to worry about."

Wells also remained troubled by the fact that Andrea was with Roe before he was murdered. Could she too have been an intended victim? Or was there another disturbed individual who was enamored of her and therefore resented Roebuck for being with her—enough so to kill him? If true, Wells reasoned, he too could be a target. Wells couldn't help toying with the idea that he might be on some kind of death list—a football dead pool, as it were. There were still too many possibilities for him to accept one of them and act upon it. The best he could do now was to watch his back and that of Andrea Chase.

# Chapter 10

Paula Bradford-Adams was having an early lunch with fellow staffer Helene Eckermire at the historic Old Ebbitt Grill right across from the White House on 15th NW. Paula took considerable teasing from other women at the White House for frequently dining at an establishment with an "old boys club" vibe, its "manly" bar and antique paintings, and "dead animal heads" hanging on the walls. But Paula went for two main reasons. First, she loved the food, especially the Oysters Rockefeller on which she was presently dining and the fact that her mother worked at Old Ebbitt's Grill when she attended Georgetown—several years before Paula's birth. In fact, Sherry Bradford was an employee when the Grill moved around the corner from its previous location on 14th Street.

Helene Eckermire had been to the Grill for lunch twice before—once with Paula and the other time with a male staffer working for the Senior Director of Strategic Communications, whom Helene found too dour for her tastes, in spite of his impeccable manners. Each time she came she ordered the Veggie Lentil Burger, so today she went rogue and ordered the Clams Casino and the *Burrata Crostini*, both highly recommended by Paula. The women spent the first part of lunch sharing work-related complaints and the status of Helene's relationship with the latest man in her life, before turning to the murder of Hoyt Reilly and the first lady's reception of the news.

"Paula, I know they were step-siblings, but I'm not sure how they got along. Are you at liberty to tell me?" Helene was sensitive to the political demands of discretion, although she believed intimate friends and spouses could be told what wasn't for public consumption.

Paula hesitated, taking another bite of her Oysters Rockefeller before she revealed what the first lady shared with her. Cecilia Erskine's mother—Nora Finch—became a widow at thirty-one, when her daughter was five, her husband dying in an auto accident. Three years later, Nora married a forty-two year old divorced man named Reilly, who brought with him a son and daughter.

"He had custody of both the kids because his wife was abusing drugs and prostituting herself."

"Lovely."

"Wasn't it though? So Hoyt Reilly became her step-brother when he was seventeen and she was eight—the step-daughter fourteen at the time. Cecilia told me all this after we shared a bottle of sparkling wine in the White House. Actually, I had one glass—she had the rest of the bottle."

"Did she say anything about how she got along with her new step-brother and step-sister?"

"No—not a thing. I tried to ask at another time, but she put me off with the kind of look that prevented my ever asking again."

"Hmm—most intriguing."

"Helene, I'm trusting you to keep to yourself what I just told you."

"I promise. You can depend on me. You know that."

"Can I also depend on you to give me a few more details about your new fella?"

"Let me have another of my clams and I'll be glad to oblige."

As they conversed, a man stood in front of the triple archway entrance and debated whether to enter. Noticing the two women at the table, he decided. Re-zipping his jacket, he made his way north on 15th Street, heading for McPherson Square.

### 

Wells was anxious to look into what Jack Ketchum had on Hoyt Reilly, but he had made a late lunch date with Chas Overby right before he learned the news of Andrea's meeting with Darryl Roebuck and he wanted to see her before he met Chas. Fortunately, she had a business luncheon scheduled with others from her magazine who came down from New York; therefore, he could be with Chas without anxiety or guilt. There was just enough time to spend fifteen minutes with Andrea before they both met their luncheon dates. Wells headed straight to her apartment.

Following an embrace and long kiss, Wells shared what he'd done and learned at UNEV and from Carla Aronson in Chapel Hill.

"Have you read any of the pages yet?" Andrea's curiosity was also piqued.

"Had no time. I was leery of glancing at anything on the way back up here for fear I'd end up killed in wreck near Fredericksburg."

"That's not funny, my love. But I'm happy you kept your eyes on the road. She toyed with his shirt collar. "How about bringing the papers back here after we both have lunch?"

"Andrea, you have that certain way about you that makes very difficult saying no to anything you ask."

"Why do you think I'm a good journalist?"

"I hope the number of collars you play with is limited to just mine."

"Well, there is Father O'Connell at Notre Dame."

He laughed at her mischievous wit. "Why did they ever let you do your interview up there? Didn't you tell them you were Methodist?"

"I did. I said I was Methodist with strong Catholic tendencies."

"And Gina told me she was a Catholic with strong agnostic ones."

Andrea's choppy laugh quickly turned to a long "Ahh." She went on, "Yes, Gina. Did you know she called me and asked about my relationship with Dylan Nieporte? Any chance *you* told her about it. She mentioned she 'heard' I had one with him."

"Guilty as suspected. Sorry. But I didn't provide any specifics— promise."

No, he hadn't mentioned that Nieporte had just come to work for Chuck Lamont, when Andrea interviewed him regarding his short-lived career in the National Hockey League, as well as the similarities between professional hockey and Washington politics. Before his career-ending injury, Nieporte was one of the NHL's best young centers, noted for his "quarterbacking" the offensive and defensive zones, but he suffered a devastating injury at the end of his second year in the league—when an opposing player knocked him to the ice with a punch in retaliation for a cheap shot Nieporte had taken earlier and then fell with his full weight on Nieporte's neck and skull. Nieporte was hospitalized and retired soon after he was released. By happy circumstance, he was hired by his father's good friend Chuck Lamont and rose quickly up the ranks to be the senator's chief of staff by the time he was thirty-five.

He took an immediate liking to the affable and attractive Andrea Chase, and after three interview sessions and publication of her story, they began to date. But whereas Andrea found his history most unfortunate and enjoyed learning the ins and outs of politics on the Hill, her interest in Nieporte in no way matched his for her. After their fourth date, the good-night kiss and hug were no longer enough for him; accordingly, he insisted that they become more intimate by spending the night at her place. The moment he pushed her back into her bedroom and appeared as though he would force himself on her, she kicked him where she had been taught by a female MMA fighter she recently made friends with. She didn't catch him flush, but the shock of the blow caused him to drop to one knee, apologize quickly, and just as rapidly limp out of her place. They never communicated again, but when she began seeing Daniel Wells seriously, she learned that Nieporte was furious and resentful—a female senate staffer telling her that Nieporte accused Andrea of "betraying" him with a "crippled, never-was" athlete, who wasn't good enough to make it in the NFL. The fact that Wells was a thorn in Chuck Lamont's side made it easier for Nieporte to despise him. Andrea never publicly accused Nieporte of sexual assault only because she still felt sorry for him, since he had never fully shaken his occasional post-concussive symptoms.

"Nothing to be concerned about, Daniel. I told Gina everything."

"Good—now I won't have to." Their teasing ended with another loving kiss. Wells brushed her hair back from her face, admiring her collection of freckles on her upper cheeks. "When I come back after lunch, I want you to tell me more about your talk with Darryl Roebuck."

###

Miles Thompson sipped coffee from a UNEV thermos while he watched his son at the team's practice. This was the first time he was allowed to attend, because Hoyt Reilly refused all requests to do so—from Miles and from his son Carter. Having played the sport, Thompson was aware of coaches who kept practices closed to the public, but often fathers of the players were granted access. During Carter's high school years, his father—then already retired from the NFL—rarely missed a practice. He would sit in the stands where he had excellent sight lines to both the playing and the practice fields. But his friendly overture to Reilly when Carter was a freshman was met with cold and efficient formality. "You can't sit up there. Practices are closed." And such was Reilly's response every season since. But this year Miles discovered that Reilly made frequent exceptions to his hard and fast rule. Carter didn't tell him; rather it was the father of another player who shared that fact. "As long as you're white, you have a shot at watching practice." When Miles confronted his son about what he was told, Carter apologized for not saying anything, but he realized his father, especially the way he was lately, would react strongly to the racial slight and demand to see Reilly privately. "I didn't want anything to get in the way of keeping my starting job, pop." It took Miles a night's sleep before he promised his son he'd say nothing to "that racist piece of shit."

Mike Cipriano called Thompson the night before, inviting him to attend all practices in preparation for the bowl game. "Hell, Miles. You might see something that can help us in Arizona. I regret you weren't allowed to watch before now, but..." The elder Thompson appreciated Cipriano's overture, even though he planned to attend practice regardless. There was justice in the new coach's invitation—just as there was justice in the murder of the bigoted Hoyt Reilly. Thompson watched his son complete a deep pass for a touchdown, which pleased him—but not as much as the fact that Reilly's body was presently lying in the local morgue.

### 

Wells nursed a beer at Equinox on Connecticut Avenue NW, a short walk from the White House. Overby called to say he was running two or three minutes late and asked Wells to order for him "Something different that bleeds red" and a Stella Artois. Wells was tempted to order Chas the Roasted Heirloom Beets with Tabbouleh Salad for something that "bleeds red," but went with the Fennel Spread Lamb Burger for both of them. After a four minute wait, he spotted Overby looking at him through the window facing Connecticut Avenue.

Wells stood as his friend arrived at the table. "How the hell are you, Chas?" Wells pumped Overby's hand as vigorously as he had always done since the two men met while freshman in high school. Wells took an immediate liking to the larger boy, who had shed fifty pounds since his playing days in college. Now he was a solid six-three and 245 pounds, with a muscular physique impossible to hide under the nice suits he wore for his position as an aide to the U.S. Ambassador to Canada.

"You're looking great as always, Dan. You let your hair grow out a bit since I saw you last."

"Andrea likes my hair a little longer." Overby was one of the few Wells allowed to call him Dan. He normally reminded others, like Grant Paulson, that he preferred Daniel.

"That's my friend—always willing to please the ladies."

"Perhaps always willing but not always successful, I'm afraid, Chas."

"I well remember the young lady you brought up to Ottawa two winters ago. She seemed most pleased by every gesture you made toward her." Overby's demeanor surprised Wells, seeing that his friend said nothing about Reilly's murder, which Wells guessed Chas must have heard about by now.

"That was for show—apparently. I didn't know her that long. I shouldn't have asked her to fly up with me. On the plane flying back she grumbled about the weather being too cold and the Ottawa traffic, among other complaints."

"She worked in D.C. and she complained about the traffic in Ottawa?"

"Right—go figure. Almost forgot. She also didn't care for the history lesson you gave us about the embassy. She personally didn't give a fig that Clinton was the first American president ever to dedicate a new embassy—anywhere in the world. She moved right from that to her assessment of the Lewinsky affair and how she herself would never engage in oral sex with a politician. It was at that point that I made up my mind to put some distance between us. On the cab ride from Reagan, she said nothing to me until we reached her place. She crooked her finger and asked me if I wanted to come up. I told her no—I had to get up early the next morning."

"Great line, Dan. Mind if I use it?"

"Long story short—we didn't see each other again—and she started dating someone in the State Department." Overby laughed. When he was done, Wells asked if he'd heard about Reilly's murder.

Overby took a long swallow his Stella before responding. "Yeah, I heard. You don't expect me to mourn his loss, do you Dan?"

"Of course not." Wells thought his old friend sounded defensive, but perhaps that was due to his having long harbored an animus for his old position coach.

When their lamb burgers made it to the table, Overby changed the subject to Wells's appearance before the Senate Committee at the beginning of the month. "I hope you avoided the rhetorical traps the good old boys and girls on the committee likely set for you." After Wells shared some general remarks about how his testimony went, the men discussed living in Ottawa and Chas's apparent interest in a fellow employee at the embassy. "She's twenty-seven, divorced, and—"

"So you and Lisa have called it quits?" Wells referred to Lisa Busby, who was carrying on a long-distance relationship with Overby, broken up by periodic reunions in Washington, Ottawa, and New York.

"No, we haven't. I just look at other women to keep the blood flowing while Lisa and I are separated." Wells thought a cloud of gloom came over his friend's face. The tone of his voice sounded impatient or annoyed. But their discussion was interrupted by a host of pedestrians running past the window, heading north on Connecticut toward Farragut Square.

"What the hell?" both men offered the same question in near synchronism.

###

By the time Wells and Overby paid the bill and made it outside, quite a crowd had gathered along the edge of I Street NW across from the Square. Three cars had collided with each other. One of them, a white Ford Escape, was pointed west in the direction of traffic; another, a red Audi RS 3 was turned so that its front was wedged into the driver's side door of the Escape. The third, a black Toyota Corolla was perpendicular to the Escape, the passenger-side wheels on the sidewalk on the north side of I Street, with the driver's side wheels in the road. The left front tire was in shreds, with the left rear seemingly blown out. Wells and Overby heard one pedestrian say, "It was the loudest blowout I ever heard." The police had begun to take control of the scene as Wells ran to the Corolla. Smoke came from under the vehicle, but it wasn't the kind of smoke the presages an explosion or fire. Rather it was if the explosion and fire had already occurred. "The loudest blowout I ever heard" now took on a more frightening meaning.

"Gina, Gina?" The driver's side window was broken out but he couldn't see her behind the wheel. He put his head inside the car just as a police officer pulled at his shoulder. "Sir, I have to ask you to..." Both men saw her lying on the front seat, her head against the passenger side door. Her seat belt had apparently broken free during the explosion.

# CHAPTER 11

"Here drink this." Andrea handed Wells three fingers' worth of Crown Royal as he dropped onto her sofa.

"Thanks." He downed half of it in one swallow.

"But Gina was talking when they put her in the ambulance, right? So that's a very good sign."

"They wouldn't let me go with her, and I have to call to check on her condition before I go to the hospital."

Wells called Gina's name three times before her eyes opened as she lay in the front seat of the Corolla. He went around to the passenger side door and saw her attempting to lift her body to a sitting position. "No, no, Gina. Just stay still," he shouted. A policeman insisted she listen to him, adding, "An ambulance is on the way. You're going to be all right." Wells was able to touch her hand as she was removed from the car. Her smile was difficult, but it suggested the officer was right to be optimistic. Perhaps she was just badly shaken up. Clearly, she was frightened. Following her removal from the scene, Wells parted from Overby and called Andrea. She had just finished her meeting and told Wells she'd go right away to her place.

Now that he was there, Wells finally began to relax, although the strain was still evident on his face. With Andrea's encouragement, he called the hospital and talked with one of the doctors. The talk lasted a mere half minute. "He said they wanted to hold her a little longer to be sure there aren't any significant anatomical and physiological changes from the blast, but he said it looked good for her. He doesn't think it's necessary for me to come over." He paused for a moment. "Damn it."

"Daniel, I know you're upset about what happened, but everything you've said is very optimistic regarding her condition."

"It's not that. It's the matter of the explosion." Andrea asked if he felt it could have been a malfunction of the automobile's engine. "I think it was a set explosive of some kind."

"My God. But who would want to harm Gina?"

"Probably no one, but..."

"What? What is it?"

"Have you forgotten? She's had her car for just a couple of days."

Andrea sat in the chair across from him and stated the fact without emotion. "She was in your Black Corolla."

"Right, the one I just sold her."

### 

Kyle Guidry completed the staff meeting with other members of the president's legal team, still steaming from the remark made by Erskine before the gathering commenced. "Kyle, if you look back at all the chief White House counsel since the post was created in 1943, there are few names that are recognizable. You had Clark Clifford under Truman and Ted Sorenson under Kennedy. Of course there were others who basically constructed a rogue's gallery. Gonzalez under Bush II and Ehrlichman, Colson, and Dean under Nixon. Even though Dean redeemed himself afterward, I wonder which of these the three groups you'll end up being associated with?"

"Three groups, Mr. President?"

"Yes, the highly respected duo Clifford and Sorenson; the notorious Gonzalez, Ehrlichman, Colson, and Dean; or the forgettable—meaning all the rest of them." Erskine laughed and patted Guidry on the back as he made his way to the Oval Office. Guidry could never be certain, but he guessed such playful insults were proof Erskine suspected his chief counsel's affection for the first lady, which Guidry had hoped to conceal since the beginning of the administration almost three years earlier. In truth, he had become enamored of Cecilia Erskine before she moved into the White House, having then given her legal advice on a "hypothetical" situation involving her step-brother Hoyt Reilly. Guidry vividly recalled her achingly beautiful expressions of concern as she spoke of the situation and matters of anonymity, blackmail, and statutes of limitations. Guidry felt that day and since that he wanted to help this incredible woman, never quite limiting himself in regard to what he would do for her or on her behalf.

Since Erskine's inauguration, Guidry saw the first lady most often only momentarily, as she left or came into the Oval Office or walked through the halls of the White House. But on two occasions they spent time alone—the first time in the Blue Room, after the first lady rehearsed her lines for a short spot on Grover Cleveland's marriage to Francis Folsom in 1886, the one time the White House hosted a presidential wedding. Guidry had knowledge of history that impressed Cecilia Erskine; accordingly she wanted him to hear what she was going to say before the camera. Afterward, she asked if he'd like to share a cocktail with her—the president was then traveling south to campaign for candidates in congressional races. The cocktail quickly gave way to another and the first lady spoke freely of her childhood before her mother married a man named Reilly. The second occasion occurred several days before—at this year's White House Christmas Party. The first lady seemed troubled as she and the president descended the Grand Staircase and headed for the photo line. But her face brightened when she saw Guidry, and she got through her short speech and the many photos and greetings in good shape. Guidry thought she looked stunning, regardless of her initial unsettled countenance. When he approached her, she whispered to him, "Let's get off by ourselves after everyone leaves. I need to tell you something. Did you have the eggnog?" He shook his head no. "Good. I hate eggnog." Her smile charmed him palpably. They met two hours later in the East Sitting Hall—situated on the second floor above the East Room. The first lady had chosen to place two chairs on either side of a low table and the sofa that rested in front of the distinctive fanlight window, which looked out at the Jacqueline Kennedy Garden with the

U. S. Treasury in the distance.

When he arrived at the Hall, which was located between the Lincoln and the Queen's Bedrooms, Guidry found the first lady sitting in one of the chairs, a glass of champagne in front of her and another on the table in front of the chair opposite. She was no less lovely in the black pants and yellow sweater outfit she presently donned. Guidry was nervous, owing to his feelings for her, but also because her husband—at least he believed—was presently down the hall in the Presidential bedroom. He attempted to break his tension with humor. "Did you know that Charles Dickens was in this room waiting to meet John Tyler in 1842."

"I don't believe I knew that."

"Dickens called this 'as unpromising and tiresome as any waiting-room' he had ever been in."

Her laughter was anemic—a sign to Guidry that she had something distressing on her mind. When he left the North Entrance of the White House forty minutes later, he sensed that she hadn't told him everything, but what she did reveal about her step-brother Hoyt Reilly was enough to encourage Guidry to loathe the man. In a brief medieval reverie, Guidry imagined himself a protective knight informed that someone had paid a grave insult to his lady.

### 

"Henrik? Hey, thanks for calling. I was just going to call you." Wells became even more convinced that the Black Corolla was rigged with an explosive and wanted to be sure Nordenson would be checking for that possibility, even though he assumed he would, given his friend's job with the Metro force.

"I'm sorry to tell you this, Daniel, but the Corolla was targeted. When I came to the scene, my heart went to my throat because it looked just like your car and I thought the worst regarding your life—but they told me the driver was a young woman who works for you. Did you lend her the Corolla?"

"No, she bought it from me only two days ago."

"*Gudskjelov.*"

"Bless you."

"I didn't sneeze, you idiot. I said, "Thank God." You haven't been keeping up with the Norwegian lessons, have you?" Wells was grateful for their humorous banter at this time, but Nordenson apologized. "I shouldn't have said 'Thank God,' since your colleague could have been seriously hurt. Is she all right?"

"Yes. She might have to stay at the hospital overnight, and she'll need to see an audiologist to gauge any hearing loss, but it looks good."

"*Veldig bra!*"

Wells laughed. "I know that one. 'Very good!' right? I was just thinking about how I almost killed the both of us in the Corolla when we were driving up to Congressional to see the tournament, and I had that sneezing fit while I was trying to get off the outer loop."

"I'm still having nightmares." The two men had taken in several professional sporting events since late spring.

Well's was the first to drop his smile; he had to face the implications of the planted explosive. "Henrik, you think somebody was trying to kill me?"

"You? Not your colleague?"

"Since the car was mine up to a few days ago, I can't discount that possibility, can I?"

"I'm afraid not, my friend. But we might have to qualify your assessment somewhat?"

"What do you mean?"

"Based on my initial examination, I'm tempted to conclude that killing you or the young woman wasn't the intention of the person who placed the explosive under the Corolla." Nordenson explained that someone attached magnetically a VBIED—which he explained stood for "vehicle-borne improvised explosive device"—and set a timing mechanism to set off the charge. "The placement of the explosive as well as the fire power in it wasn't in line with causing maximum damage to the car or to the driver. This is a far cry from the car bomb used six or seven years ago to kill eight people in Oslo—and injuring over two hundred, including my uncle and cousin."

"Then Gina should be happy the bomber was an amateur."

"No, Daniel. I believe the perpetrator was quite professional. The person got the result he—or she—wanted all along."

### ###

Seeing that Wells had a busy afternoon and she was freed up after her meeting with the staff from New York, Andrea received his permission to take to her place and look through the material Wells received from Carla Aronson in Chapel Hill—before Wells had enough time to do so himself. She found Jack Ketchum's entries both lucid and shocking. Ketchum indulged in no gratuitous or slanderous remarks about Hoyt Reilly, suggesting to Andrea that he kept his personal opinions at bay in order to allow his observations to stand as untainted evidence. Coach Ketchum included a table of contents—incomplete—but still helpful. The first part of the manuscript was printed on light yellow paper and consisted of statements made by players and staff personnel at UNEV and the other schools at which Reilly coached, testifying to Reilly's objectionable remarks—along racial and religious lines--as well as lewd remarks and jokes. Here Andrea found evidence of Reilly's use of racial slanders and stereotypes directed primarily at blacks and Hispanics but also the occasional remark about Canadians, the French, and Asians. She discovered that he talked about the laziness and lack of intelligence of black and Hispanic players in front of his white players—and on two occasions in front of the entire team. One former player remarked, "Coach Reilly gauged the reaction in the locker room, and when he saw it wasn't good, he laughed and claimed he was making a joke—but we all knew better." On one occasion, said another former player, "Reilly told several of the black players that one of our offensive linemen, Raoul Castillo, called them "jive niggers" in front of the white players. As you can guess, there was a big confrontation on the field after practice, and Raoul took one in the mouth from one of the black players. I saw Coach Reilly standing ten feet away smiling and twirling his whistle—the son-of-a-bitch." The player added, "I couldn't believe anyone would punch Raoul Castillo, because he was one of the most popular players on the team. So I confronted Dwayne Isaac—the guy that slugged Raoul—and he told me what Reilly had said. I then asked Raoul, who of course swore he never called Dwayne the 'n' word and never would. I set up a players-only meeting and everything got straightened out. Four guys quit the team, including Raoul—but no one confronted Reilly about what he had done." Andrea detected the pattern clearly enough. Reilly loved pitting player against player and indulging in his own racism through outright lies as well as direct and indirect comments.

Andrea turned to the section of pages printed on light blue paper. Here was evidence of Reilly's sexism, crude remarks to and about women, and other forms of harassment. Ketchum had testimony from Reilly's male players, three women who worked in the athletic department and Reilly's own office, one female administrative support assistant, one female athletic trainer, and two cheerleaders. The players cited frequent incidents when their coach called women "bitches," "campus whores," "sluts," "slits," and "cunts." Reilly was free with is advice not "to fuck the honeys" the day of and the night before a Saturday game, but wasn't at all hesitant to suggest during team meetings that during football season the players should lie back in "a comfortable position and let your old lady suck your cock till you get off" rather than risk pulling a muscle by "fucking in the usual way." He called a player who was less aggressive than he liked a "pussy" who was as "aggressive as a pre-teen virgin."

The women Ketchum interviewed all complained about his "compliments," which focused on their body parts, not their faces or what they wore. His secretary, then a thirty-four year old divorcee, decided to take action when Reilly commenced harassing her for refusing to have dinner with him. Fearing he might lose his job, Reilly saw to it that she was transferred to another position at a slightly higher pay. The young female trainer noted that Reilly had smacked her bottom and kept his hand there for several seconds before she turned around and demonstrated her anger and embarrassment. Reilly claimed that he was hitting the males "on the ass" and hit hers before he realized she was female. Two of the UNEV cheerleaders, then twenty-one year old juniors, were in a local establishment enjoying their skinny margaritas when an inebriated Reilly joined them without invitation and made his pitch to have the three of them go to another watering hole five miles from campus. One of the girls tried to put him off gently, but the other left the table. "Nina said she was going home, but I knew from other experiences we had that she was going to wait it out the bathroom. I then told Coach Reilly I had to go with her, since she was driving. He took my hand and tried to kiss it, but I pulled it away. He left the club and he never approached either of us again that year or so far this season."

The third section of Ketchum's manuscript was printed on light orange paper, and Andrea could see it was not complete. She hadn't examined these pages carefully yet because she wanted to wait until Daniel came before she read further. But this section seemed to deal with matters not relating to Reilly's life as a football coach. As she fanned through the pages, she reached the last one, which was blank except for the handwritten title at the top: "More from Cecilia (Finch)."

# Chapter 12

"Good practice, son."

"I thought so too, pop."

"But Cleon seemed out of it today." Cleon Garver was the team's left offensive tackle—the most important lineman in UNEV's passing scheme. He protected Carter Thompson's blind-side when the quarterback dropped back to pass. "I'm going to tell him to get his head out of his ass." The elder Thompson began to walk toward the limping Garver.

"Wait, dad, wait." Carter grabbed his father's arm. "He sprained his knee at the beginning of practice. It doesn't seem serious, but I think he wanted to protect it today." Once again, his father had reacted impulsively and way out of proportion to his assumption about the lineman.

Miles took a couple of quick breaths and nodded. "Well, that's good. Got to have him one-hundred percent before the bowl game. I don't want my boy taking any unnecessary shots."

Carter knew he was lucky to have a father so involved with his son's athletics. Miles never rode his son the way his father did him—complete with the humiliating and often menacing "advice" he gave Miles from the sideline or the bleachers. Miles grew up believing he was just one mistake away from being disowned. He ended up surprised that the "mistake" took place off the playing field. The occasion was his marriage to a white woman twenty-three years ago.

Jana Maddox, whom he had begun dating in college, announced to him a week after Miles was drafted by the new NFL franchise in Charlotte that she was pregnant. Miles promptly announced they would marry—as that had been the long-range plan anyway. Miles's father wouldn't have it, and the bond between father and son—such as it was—was permanently severed. When Miles signed a free-agent contract six years later with Washington, young Carter began playing organized sports. Miles made as many of his boy's baseball and football games as he could until he retired from the NFL. After that he never missed a single one.

"Dad, can I ask you something?"

"Of course." Miles expected it to be sports-related.

Carter hesitated for a moment. "Is there any truth to... I mean, a few guys mentioned to me that Reilly hit on mom—on several occasions. Did that happen? I mean, did you know?"

Instead of another eruption of anger, as Carter feared, Miles emitted only a labored sigh. "Yes." The memories rushed back. One night two months earlier, Jana informed him that Reilly had seen her at the grocery store several days after addressing the team's parents, at which time Reilly spoke with Miles about his NFL career. At the store, Reilly attempted to exude whatever modicum of charm he thought he possessed with "flattering" remarks about her hair, earrings, and blouse. But he had also given himself away with half statements such as "You must have your hands full dealing with the bigots when they see you arm and arm with..." and "I admire your willingness to risk your family's..." In truth, her parents and siblings, although initially reluctant, quickly warmed to Miles Thompson's personality and heart. They didn't hold it against their daughter that she withheld news of her pregnancy until after she and Miles returned from their honeymoon. They of course doted on their new grandson and wouldn't allow any friend or acquaintance to bring up the matter of having a mixed-raced grandchild.

Less than a week later, Reilly found Miles and Jana at The Smith in D.C.'s Penn Quarter, where he was having a beer with one of his assistant coaches. The Thompsons were there for dinner, and when

Miles was called by fans over to another table, Jana took the opportunity to go to the ladies room. When she came out, Reilly was waiting for her. As she told her husband weeks later, "He didn't appear drunk, so there was absolutely no excuse for what he said. He asked if I'd like to join him for a drink later in the week. I of course refused, reminding him that I would never do that to my husband. He just smiled in a smarmy way and said, 'You are without doubt one of the most beautiful women over thirty I've ever seen.' Half of me wanted to tell him I was now forty and the other half wanted to bash him in his smug face. I tried to get past him, but he blocked my way and whispered, 'I'd give what I got to make love to you, Jana.' I didn't answer, but just pushed past him. I didn't tell you right away because I knew what would happen, and I didn't want my privileges revoked at one of my favorite restaurants."

The light-hearted tone at the end of her admission did nothing to alleviate her husband's fury. After allowing Miles a minute or so to rant, she reminded him that their boy's chances to remain starting quarterback would dwindle to zero if Miles confronted Reilly and punched him out. As much as hated agreeing with her, Miles apparently saw the wisdom of her caution and vowed to hold his tongue—until after the bowl game, that is. Regardless of his assurances, Jana wondered if he would live up to his promise. His behavior in recent months made it clear that it would take little to set him off. What if he ran into Reilly and the coach asked where his wife was? With his more impulsive behaviors lately, she could see Miles flattening Reilly, causing a law suit and putting Carter's career in jeopardy.

After Miles revealed this account to his son, he asked, "Carter, how did the other players hear this rumor?"

"I'm sure the bastard bragged about being with mom or at least that he was after her."

"Just curious, son. Why didn't you tell me when you first heard these rumors?"

"Are you kidding? I knew what you would have done to him."

###

"Maybe you shouldn't read the last part of Coach Ketchum's notes, seeing that you want to go through your guest column for the *Post*." Wells occasionally wrote pieces on veterans' issues for several papers. "You might get too involved in analyzing everything."

Wells considered her advice for a moment. "Right. But I'll just skim through to get an idea of what Jack has there."

Andrea didn't share with Wells what she found by doing the same. "I'll fix us a drink, then."

White Andrea was in the kitchen, Wells gave further thought to the car bomb placed under the Corolla he had just sold to Gina Lorenzetti. If he was the intended victim, was it an honest attempt to harm him or a dangerous practical joke of some kind? Yet Wells kept going back the possibility that the bomb was a warning to him. Whether the intended victim was he or Gina, it could still serve as a threat to him, perhaps in relation to his pursuing the matter of Jack Ketchum's information on Hoyt Reilly. Reilly's now being dead would mean that another person or persons had interest in Reilly's past. But who and why?

Wells glanced through the first sections of Ketchum's collection of papers, noting the evidence of Reilly's behavior while employed at UNEV and two of his other coaching stops. There were apparently damning accusations made against Reilly over the years, accusations Wells would dig deeper into tomorrow. He noted a series of names his old coach believed were relevant to Reilly's actions and reputation, complete with street and email addresses and phone numbers. Surprisingly, he saw the names Hernandez, Guidry, and Bradford–Adams—all of whom worked at the White House. Wells wondered how many of these persons Jack Ketchum contacted. When turning to the sparser third section, Wells froze at seeing the name "Cecilia Erskine (Finch)."

His old coach had jotted down a series of words and phrases as the headings of separate pages in this final section, including "Family crisis," "Late middle school through high school," "Boyfriends/dates," "Paul S. and Robbie C. hospital," and "Travels." There was no information under each heading, although Wells deduced that

Ketchum intended to fill out each one. Was his old coach in the process of collecting the filler when he died in the explosion? Might he already have composed that missing material and not have given it to his daughter?

"Here you are—nice and weak with plenty of ice, so you can have another. Take it from one who knows, you must keep your wits to edit your piece well. But first take this." Andrea placed her mouth two inches from his.

Wells kissed her and took the diluted Scotch, wishing it were a double.

### 

Paula-Bradford Adams stepped into the first lady's East Wing Office to retrieve the draft of the New Year's wishes Cecilia meant to give at a small gathering in the East Garden Room. Paula was pleased the first lady had made but two small changes to Paula's draft. As she picked up the paper on the office's conference table, she looked to the left of the bookcase and saw the landscape painting on the wall was missing. She gazed about the room and found it leaning up against the back of the sofa. But right next to it was a framed print of the famous painting that scared her when she first beheld it in an art book when she was a young girl. There resting next to the landscape was Edvard Munch's famous late nineteenth century work, *The Scream*. Surely, Cecilia Erskine wasn't going to replace the landscape with Munch's frightening painting—not on the wall of the East Wing office—was she?

### 

"Carla, forgive my calling so late. I was going to wait until the morning, but I... well, I need to ask if your father sent you a copy of *everything* he had written about Hoyt Reilly."

"I received the file three days before he was killed." The sound of the horrible fact of his death from her own lips upset her. "But... but I was certain he either had more he hadn't yet sent or he was finishing the document, after which he would send me the rest. But then, I can't really say for sure."

Wells ended the conversation by apologizing for the call and asking again if he could do anything for her. She told him he need not apologize and that she would surely call if she required anything. Since Andrea was already asleep, Wells sat in the living room and pondered the possibility that Jack Ketchum might have made copies of the material he hadn't yet sent to his daughter and kept them in some other location than in his desk at home.

### 

Watching the gold pocket watch swaying before him, the man stuffed the black gloves in his coat pocket and picked up a bright red ski mask, holding it before him as Hamlet held poor Yorick's skull in the majority of theatrical adaptations. The man had read that a red ski mask had an even more intimidating effect than a black one. Black was certainly sinister enough, but the red suggested impending death more readily. He preferred the Kingou model ultra thin full-face Lycra mask with the eye openings slanted more than rounded. With no opening for the mouth, the mask had more of alien appearance to it—that other-than-human quality that always served well in such activities as he now contemplated. But the longer he held the mask in front of him, the more he doubted whether it would matter if his identity was disguised. He deplored gratuitous violence of any kind, but in this instance death was again his only recourse. After staring at the ski mask another several seconds, the man decided he'd take it with him.

# Chapter 13

Álvaro Hernandez sipped from the glass of Alamos Argentinean Malbec his wife set before him when he returned from the White House at 9:50 p.m. Maria Hernandez maintained her pleasant personality while enduring her husband's many late nights for the past three years. But now and then she displayed frustration that their marriage was far too often strained by his long hours. She was presently three-months pregnant, and her husband could see she was dreading the continuation of his schedule after the baby came. For the past four months, Álvaro dropped hints he would resign in a year-- after Stephen Erskine's first term—assuming the president would be re-elected. Erskine dismissed every one of these hints, but Hernandez grew daily more certain he would call it quits and was presently attempting to come up with a good reason to step down earlier than inauguration day, a little less than thirteen months out. His wife would give birth at the end of June, leaving her to deal with the new baby and her husband's insane schedule for another seven months.

"Maria, a toast." He gestured for her to pick up her glass of sparkling water.

"A toast? What for? Did you get a raise?"

"Are you kidding? I already make more than I'm worth—so say the vice president and that lovable asshole Kyle Guidry." Hernandez made just under $175,000 and never complained about his salary. "No, let's toast to the fact that I've just made up my mind that I'm stepping down the first of June of the coming year."

Maria's eyes filled with tears. She hugged him tightly. "I love you so much. So very much." She had wanted her husband out since the end of his first year as press secretary.

After kissing his wife, Hernandez lifted his Malbec and took a long and satisfying swallow. Maria had just brought the sparkling water to her lips before her smile dropped. "Álvaro, I hate to throw *agua fria* on this fabulous news, but have you given thought to what you'll do after leaving the White House?"

He loved the way she threw out Spanish words and phrases as if she were a freshman in Spanish 101. "Of course I have, Señora Hernandez." He apologized for not telling her earlier that he had been in contact with UT-Austin about returning to the university, where he had been an associate professor in the Department of Journalism before becoming Texas Senator Brad Laxley's communications director and then Stephen Erskine's press secretary. He added that although he'd be taking a pay cut, his salary would certainly be partially evened out by a lower cost of living and supplemented by occasional speaker's fees and a book contract, should a major press be interested. In any event, they'd both be happier. "I'd have to give up being press secretary at some point in the future, so this way I can get back to a university for next year's fall term."

An hour and three glasses of Malbec later, Hernandez reiterated his impressions of Kyle Guidry, about whom Álvaro frequently complained—regarding Guidry's curt manner and the way he liked to look over the press secretary's shoulder, often dispensing advice on Hernandez's delivery of statements and unnecessarily detailed answers to press questions. Hernandez extended his remarks to Guidry's apparent fascination with the first lady. Maria listened attentively as her husband spoke about Guidry's habit of staring at Cecilia Erskine when she stood in profile or in front of him. "Twice I heard him sigh upon her walking into a room—you know, the kind of sound a man makes when he's stimulated by a woman."

"The kind you make when I stumble into the kitchen at 6:00 a.m.?"

"Exactly." After they shared a laugh, Hernandez related the several times he caught Guidry touching what the first lady moments earlier held—for example, books, notes, and china cups—and once a cloth napkin with which she had wiped her mouth. "Guidry held the section where her lipstick was visible and brought it to his nose." Hernandez also shared his concern that Guidry would one day go too far and say something to Cecilia Erskine about his infatuation for her. "I wouldn't be surprised if he attempted to steal a kiss or rub her back—something like that. Anyway, Guidry's interest in her seems... well, it seems..."

"Creepy?"

"Well put, my darling."

"Another good reason why you should go. You might otherwise be a witness in a criminal investigation." He could tell his wife was only half facetious.

"I don't know. Perhaps he's just playing a modern day Sir Galahad—serving his lady and all that kind of thing."

Maria frowned. "Or perhaps a Sir Lancelot. And I trust you remember how that story turned out."

###

Carla Aronson was suddenly awakened by a gloved hand pressing hard against her mouth. The room was mildly lit by the nightlight from the bathroom, which she always kept on throughout the night. Her eyes focused first on the hand and forearm that applied the pressure on her mouth. She didn't look up until she heard a voice say, "Shhhhh." She was startled further by the frightful red mask with no mouth but just two eyeholes, which looked like demonic slits. "Quiet. Say nothing and I'll lift my hand. I have no intention of hurting you—unless you force me to." The masculine voice was disguised by a robotic voice changing app run through an iPhone resting under the red mask.

Carla nodded her head, and the man lifted his hand. "I simply want what your father wrote about Hoyt Reilly. That's all I'm here for. Show me where the pages are, and I'll take them and leave. Nothing will happen to you. Do you understand?"

Her eyes broadened. "I don't have the pages anymore." The gloved hand reapplied pressure on her mouth.

"I'll say it just one more time. Tell me where the papers are—now." The man punctuated his order by moving his hand so that both her nose and mouth were covered. He lifted his hand after ten seconds of further pressure."

Carla gasped for air. Her words struggled to escape her mouth. "I just gave them to someone. I swear that's what I did."

"Who?" She remained silent. "I said who?" He began to move his hand back across her face when she nearly shouted, "Daniel Wells."

"Turn over."

"No, please. Please."

"Turn over." She obeyed. "Spread you legs as far as you can." Her entire body shook from dreadful anticipation of what he would do next. She moved her legs outward and began whispering "Oh my God, I am heartily sorry for offending Thee..." She felt his gloved hand grab her right ankle as she continued her prayer.

###

Cecilia sipped her cranberry juice, as she habitually did as a prelude to a classic breakfast, a meal she never missed, although her husband rarely indulged in full morning meals, unless they were politically required. She knew he was in the Oval Office with his coffee and cream-cheese bagel, brushing crumbs from the Resolute Desk. But his wife thoroughly enjoyed her breakfasts alone in the President's Dining Room, located in the northwest corner of the second floor. This morning, Cecilia would have *Eggs Sardou*, the Louisiana Creole dish featuring poached eggs, creamed spinach, artichoke bottoms, and Hollandaise sauce—a dish she first sampled at Antoine's in New Orleans, where it was invented. She would alternate this dish with *crêpes sucrées*—sweet *crêpes*—which she enjoyed in Paris some fifteen years earlier on her trip through Europe.

As had been her preference, Cecilia sat at the round table facing the sofa and the two windows looking out at the North Lawn. She had learned before her husband took office that this room was once known as The Prince of Wales Room, which later evolved into the Lincoln

Bedroom until Jacqueline Kennedy transformed it into a more intimate family dining area. Now it seated four comfortably, although Cecilia preferred to take all her meals alone whenever possible. The room, as she knew, was chosen as a surgery suite when Teddy Roosevelt's daughter Alice needed an appendectomy in 1907. Far more depressing was the fact that this room was chosen by Drs. Janvier Woodward and Edward Curtis for the autopsy of the slain body of Lincoln, which was also embalmed by Dr. Charles D. Brown soon afterward. In addition, Lincoln's eleven year old son Willie died in this room in 1862. Regardless of the tragedy witnessed in these surroundings, Cecilia felt comfortable here. It was an area of the White House to which she came to escape her present reality and communicate with her memories.

The first bite of the *Eggs Sardou* returned her to New Orleans after she left home when she was still seventeen—right after her senior year of high school. Accompanying her was a rising senior at LSU, the older brother of one of her friends whom she had met when he returned home for summer break. She wanted out of her intolerable home life and felt she couldn't wait until she went off to college herself in a few months. Trey Kirkman provided her an escape, and he offered to take her to his Baton Rouge apartment and allow her to stay as long as she liked. Kirkman's sister knew nothing about the plan—nor did Cecilia's family. Cecilia called her mother from the road and tried to explain, without being completely truthful, why she had to leave home earlier than planned. She and her step-father were never in agreement—about her likes, dislikes, philosophy, or future—and often the arguments between them were quite heated. Her mother said she understood and just wanted to know where her daughter was and that she was safe. After getting her mother to keep the location to herself, Cecilia revealed she was in Louisiana and promised to call every week—and that she wouldn't take drugs or allow anyone otherwise to lead her astray.

Kirkman took her to New Orleans and the French Quarter a few days after they arrived in Baton Rouge, and they dined at Antoine's where she first tasted *Eggs Sardou*. They stayed just for the afternoon but returned three weeks later and spent a weekend at the Chateau Hotel on Chartres, just two blocks from Jackson Square and Bourbon

Street. Cecilia had never felt as free as she did walking down Bourbon Street, buying trinkets, tossing coins into the instrument cases of street musicians, and surreptitiously sipping on Trey's alcoholic beverages. When they returned for Kirkman's Monday class, Cecilia saw him off and then laid out several note cards, each listing a summer job she could apply for, including Personal Care Attendant, Telephone Operator/Receptionist at a physician's office, ADA Greeter, Guest Experience Maker, several server positions at Baton Rouge restaurants, and Dog Walker. She remembered putting red asterisks next to the most promising possibilities when she heard a knock on the apartment door.

She looked at the clock and assumed Trey had returned early from his summer class, since it was the first day and some professors merely took roll and passed out course syllabi before dismissing their students. She remembered thinking that Kirkman had his arms full of groceries and books and couldn't put his key in the apartment door.

"Hang on. I'm coming." She took her empty juice glass to the kitchen before she walked to the door and released the security chain. As she turned the knob, the door was shoved open, hitting her on the forehead and on edge of her nose.

"You're getting your ass home—right now, you stupid bitch." She closed her eyes at the sound of her step-brother's voice. Hoyt Reilly was then coaching at a Division II school in east Texas, some 185 miles from Baton Rouge. He informed her that he learned from his father about her location after the senior Reilly forced the information from her mother. "I told them you'd be on a plane back home later today. I have your ticket. Pack your shit and let's go."

Cecilia trembled at the realization she was alone with her step-brother, a situation she vowed never to be in again. Feeling the pain from being hit by the opening door, she gathered courage and lifted her body erect to pronounce that she wasn't leaving. "Here, I'll pay you for the ticket you bought. How much was it?"

She turned to retrieve her wallet, which contained four of the seven hundred dollars she withdrew from her savings account before she left her home in Manassas, Virginia. Before she took three steps, her step-brother yanked her backwards by the hair and flung her onto the living room sofa. "Get your bag packed, Cecilia, or we'll relive some of our more tender moments together." Her breathing ceased and her memories flooded over the barriers she had worked so very hard to construct the past year. "You've got five minutes to throw your stuff in a bag. Move it."

She went into the bedroom, retrieved her bag, and began emptying her drawers as Reilly watched her from the bedroom entrance. She felt a trickle of blood descend from her forehead. "Can... can I leave him a note?"

Reilly laughed. "As long as you tell him your relationship is over and that you don't want him contacting you anymore. I think you know what will happen to the *both* of you if you see him again."

She finished packing her bag and small carry-on but didn't have the strength to write the note to Trey.

# CHAPTER 14

"Yes, I've given my statement to the police, and I'm going to speak further with them about Jack Ketchum later today."

"Did they ask about the car bomb?"

Wells was having breakfast with Henrik Nordenson at Pete's Diner on 2nd Street NE, across from the Library of Congress.

"Yes. They said you talked with them and they agreed that killing me—or Gina—wasn't the intention of the mad bomber or whatever the hell he is."

"When did you talk with them?"

"Late last night."

"I see."

"What is it, Henrik?"

Nordenson put down his breakfast sandwich and shook his head. "I don't know why, but I woke up this morning thinking more about the possibility that the girl was the intended victim rather than you, as I believed yesterday. I wondered if someone was trying to send you a message without targeting you directly. With that thought in mind, I went out to my car and looked underneath with my flashlight."

"Don't tell me..."

"Yes. There was a bomb."

"Same as the one under the Corolla?"

"Not exactly, but yes, with generally the same low explosive quality. I turned it over to one of my colleagues before I came here. I thought it best that someone else look at it. I doubt they'll find any prints. This person's too smart to leave any."

Wells signaled for more coffee. "Jesus. What the hell is going on?"

"I could say that someone is getting at you by threatening your friends and associates, but your former coach was killed deliberately by a charge that had plenty of power behind it—yet the girl and now I have been targeted—or you and I have been targeted, so..."

Wells thought of Andrea Wells and her safety. "Excuse me, Henrik, I have to make this call."

### 

Miles Thompson left his breakfast company stunned. What, they wondered, made him lose his temper and behave the way he did outside the historic Leesburg Diner on South King Street? Thompson met every month with four other former NFL players at the Virginia diner, where they would enjoy good natured bantering about "how badly" the other guy played during his NFL days and who among them was the best at any position over the years. But today, the topic was UNEV's chances in the bowl game in Arizona. The other four men naturally praised Carter Thompson, and one of them claimed the young man was the "best quarterback" the school ever had. Two men sitting at the next table, who had overheard the group's discussion, decided to inject their own opinions into the conversation.

"You guys never saw Daniel Wells or Ben Jankowski play, I take it," said one of the men.

"Thompson's good, but no way he was as good as Wells," offered the other.

The men of course didn't know they offered their assessments in the presence of Carter Thompson's father—nor did they see the looks from the other four men, one of whom put his hand on Miles's shoulder and said, "Let it go." But one of the men at the adjoining table kept shaking his head and smirking. "Wells and Jankowski could throw deeper and more accurately. And they never made some of the mental mistakes Thompson's made this season. But what can you expect?"

The man had no opportunity to clarify what he meant by his last statement because Thompson was up with his fists clenched, partially lifting the table and knocking over all the water glasses and coffee cups. Thompson's friends prevented him from reaching the man, and quickly ushered Miles to the door as he challenged both men to follow him to the street.

Thompson remained silent until they began to cross Loudoun. "That mother-fucker and his fucking Daniel Wells shit." As they walked to their cars, the men tried to commiserate with Thompson, knowing their friend was sensitive about the criticism that his son wasn't the "brightest" on the field—as Hoyt Reilly often told Carter. The elder Thompson also bristled whenever he was reminded that Carter was the first starting quarterback of color in UNEV's brief history, knowing that every poor decision his son made was held against his heritage as well him personally. All year he endured the comparisons made to Daniel Wells and his "brilliant" career at the school and his "intelligence" and "leadership" qualities. He grew frankly sick of hearing Wells's name, one which he couldn't denigrate publicly, given Wells's military record. The elder Thompson would tell his closest friends that he felt his son ran with the ball far more effectively than Wells ever did and that Carter had to overcome so much more than had Wells, who had the correct racial makeup and a coach in Jack Ketchum who praised and encouraged him. It was Carter's ill luck that he was coached by a racist bastard named Hoyt Reilly.

"Just let it go, Miles" said one of his friends. "Think about the bowl game and all the attention Carter's going to receive."

"That fucking Wells never took the team as far as my son has."

The men reached Thompson's car, and when Miles drove off, the others thought their friend had something wrong with him to react in such a manner. Sure, he'd been displaying evidence of quick anger these past several months but nothing like this. Perhaps his marriage was having problems, one of his friends surmised.

###

Wells took his time walking from Pete's Diner to the front of the Capitol. The weather turned colder the previous night, dipping into the high twenties. But today was delightful for someone like Wells, who liked the cold--currently thirty-four degrees and sunny, with hardly a breeze. He made his way up 2nd and crossed Independence, putting him on the east side of the Capitol, where presidential inaugurations were held until Reagan's first in 1981. Wells called Andrea and warned her to check under her car before starting it up.

"You mean I have to get on the ground in this cold and risk ruining my new coat?"

"Are you working from home this morning?"

"I'm afraid so. I have to finish my piece for the magazine by early afternoon."

"All right. I have an interview with a reporter from the *Baltimore Sun* about my testimony before the Veterans Committee earlier this month. After I'm done, I'll come by and check your car for you."

"I can go with you this morning, if you want? I can ask for a three-hour extension on my article."

"No, you'll just make me nervous if you're there."

"Nervous?"

"Okay, aroused."

"Uh, huh. Sure, I will."

They both chuckled, although Wells was only half joking. "You told me you've never filed anything even a minute late—so I refuse to be the cause of ending your streak."

"Okay—if you insist, my love. Bye for now."

Wells crossed Constitution Avenue and headed across the Mall to the Smithsonian Castle, where the older sister of the Sun reporter worked. She had agreed to let her brother use her office to conduct the interview. As he turned west on Jefferson Dr. SW, Wells gave further thought to the explosives under the Corolla and now under Henrik's car. If someone targeted both Gina and Henrik, who besides Andrea might be next to have a bomb placed under his or her car? Was the same person responsible for setting the explosive in Jack Ketchum's oven? If so, what was the connection? How easy it would be to place the responsibility on Hoyt Reilly if he hadn't been murdered. But slain by whom? Would there be a bomb placed under Wells's new car or did the perpetrator believe he was still driving the Corolla? Wells reached the entrance of the Smithsonian Castle. Without thinking, he looked back over his shoulder before he stepped inside and saw a young man in his mid-twenties approach him with hand extended.

"So happy you could make it, Mr. Wells."

"Please. Just call me Daniel." The men entered the building.

"Thank you. Oh, this is my sister Simone. We'll be using her office."

Wells exchanged pleasantries with the woman and once again looked back over his shoulder before he closed the door behind him.

### 

In her White House office, Helene Eckermire rubbed her finger on the lip of her coffee cup as she conversed with the new man in her life. Their last date two nights previously began with a wonderful meal at renowned chef José Andreas's *Jaleo*, a little north of the National Mall on 7th. She had never been there and usually limited her ethnic cuisine to Italian and Asian. The *Reserva Brut Nature* was among the best sparkling wines she had ever tasted, and she was surprised she so enjoyed the *Aceitunas rellanas*, the stuffed olives with anchovie and piquillo peppers. At first she refused to try her date's *Erizos de mar con pirrana*—the sea urchin with trout roe, but after taking a bite, she took two more, marveling at her new man's sophisticated palate. She would never have guessed he was such a foodie. They split a bowl of the delicious Gazpacho, and then awaited the main course—the Lobster rice dish *Arroz caldoso de bogavante*.

She passed on dessert but made the mistake—as she saw it—of drinking a little too quickly an after-dinner *Crema de Alba*, the crème liquor along with her share of the two bottles of sparkling wine knocking her off her bearings. When they returned to her place, she invited her date to stay for another drink, fully intent on making love if he was inclined, but he was the perfect gentleman and refused to take advantage of her inebriated condition, but left after getting her some water and helping her lie on the sofa. She knew many women and men would have enjoyed each other's bodies after the first, second, or surely the third date, yet she wasn't raised that way. But after the fifth date, she decided she was ready to slough off her conservative upbringing.

"So have you chosen where we should go—and when?"

"I'm afraid I'll be tied up the next couple of days, but to make it up to you, I'm taking you to the 1789 in Georgetown. Have you been?"

She thought a lie was in order. "No."

"Wonderful American fare, although the chef is Korean. But he is outstanding. I think you'll love the decor. Early American, like your parents' house." She'd told him her father was a professor of History at William and Mary and made sure his surroundings reflected his academic position. "I'll try to get a table by the fireplace."

Helene couldn't wait to see him again, but hated that she'd have to wait another few days. Already she was struggling with the possibility that he was dating several other women. But she was confident she was the only one who worked in the White House—in the office of the first lady. On their date at *Jaleo* she had spoken of her duties and conversations with Cecilia Erskine. He seemed sincerely interested in everything Helene said and made her understand he had long been fascinated by the White House, first seeing it when he was a young boy, and seemed delighted she was sharing day-to-day details about the first lady and others of her staff, including her good friend Paula Bradford-Adams.

"Helene. We've got work to do." There was Paula, shaking her head and smiling in that knowing way. Helene said goodbye to her new man and prepared herself for the good-natured grilling Paula was about to give her.

### 

"I appreciate that, Jim, and I'm sure the first lady will as well." The president concluded his morning meeting with his Secretary of Health and Human Services, James Porter. Porter had praised Cecilia Erskine for her recent speech about pre-natal care, especially the effects of alcohol consumption by expectant mothers, adding that fathers might cut back on their beer and cocktails to lessen the temptation on their wives and partners. Porter added, "Mr. President, this country is so fortunate to have such a caring first lady."

After Porter left the Oval Office, the president sighed in

exasperation. If Porter and the nation only knew of the first lady's frequent reliance on alcohol, particularly when she dwelt on the past and, as she put it, her "many mistakes." Erskine never pressed his wife for specifics, and she never volunteered them—with one exception. He assumed the mistakes were alcohol- or drug-influenced, and tried to avoid thinking of her sex life before they met. But often his attempts failed, and occasionally his thoughts drifted into the more distressing possibility that she had a lover or lovers even after she claimed to be his alone. Erskine knew she traveled to Europe and Canada before and after college, even after they were married, and his imagination was rife with images of her meeting handsome or wealthy men and giving herself to them as an expression of freedom or an act of revenge against her mother, who married an older man named Reilly. Twice the press asked Erskine why the first lady had not officially traveled abroad on her own, as had other presidential wives. He passed off the question with an attempt at wit—"I don't want her leaving me alone in this big house"—and he reminded the press that she always traveled with him on his foreign trips.

But she did tell him something of her relationship with her stepbrother, although she only admitted the older man harassed her throughout her teens about her budding femininity and boyfriends, always turning the topic to sex. She also confessed that she came to hate her mother for defending her step-son by excusing his boorish and vulgar side and advising her daughter "just ignore him," even after Reilly left home for college and just returned periodically for family events. But Erskine knew she hadn't told him everything—and it was impossible not to imagine something worse than what he knew. On two or three occasions, Erskine spoke frankly about these matters with his chief legal counsel and college chum, Kyle Guidry.

# Chapter 15

The recounting of his appearance before the committee in the interview with the Sun reporter left Wells both bemused and agitated. It was still fresh in his mind—every detail from that morning in Senate Room 418 in the Russell Building.

"On behalf of this committee, I welcome your testimony today, Mr. Wells." Chairman of the Veterans Affairs Committee, Charles D. (Chuck) Lamont wore on his face what Wells judged as a contrived look of pleasure. "For those who may not know, Daniel Wells is an authentic American hero—a former Marine who risked his life to save one of his unit, saving him but also losing his hand in the bargain. He is the chairman of FVETS—Forgotten Veterans—an organization that is committed to bringing attention to our brave men and women who served honorably in defense of this country. Let me also say for all of us that we not only honor your service, Mr. Wells, but we especially honor *you* as well." Twelve other heads nodded in agreement—two of the committee had not yet appeared, although Wells assumed they would eventually. During Lamont's opening remarks, each member wore at least a semblance of a smile on their faces. The scant one who frowned was Lamont's chief of staff Dylan Nieporte. It was obvious to anyone who bothered to notice him that he found unpalatable his boss's high praise of the witness. Nieporte trained his eyes on Wells until Wells met his gaze. After some fifteen seconds of mutual staring, Nieporte whispered something to Lamont and left the committee room.

"Once again, we are delighted to have before us someone of your reputation, Mr. Wells."

"Thank you, Mr. Chairman, but honesty compels me to offer this correction of your generous remarks. Sadly, I was unable to save my fellow Marine, owing to the blast that killed him and wounded me."

Lamont stared at Wells as though he had been kicked in the groin. He recovered quickly enough to say, "That takes nothing away from your being a true American hero, Mr. Wells."

Wells often surprised friends and acquaintances by finding the country's more recent appreciation of the military somewhat disconcerting. He noted frequently that the acknowledgment of each man and woman in uniform as "brave" and as a "hero" was a little much, for after all, shouldn't the designation be reserved for someone who truly shows bravery and heroism. Wells could make that point without any indication that he was one of the privileged ones who deserved the status. He had since boyhood made sharp distinctions in the way he categorized groups of saints and sinners and found it illogical and lazy to paint groups with the same brush—positively as well as negatively. He deplored any who committed the act of "stolen honor" with lies about their military experiences—even finding objectionable older men who claimed to be "Vietnam Veterans," when they had served during the war years but not actually in Vietnam. Respecting members of the military and thanking them for their service was gratifying, especially after hearing tales from his father and uncle about the hostility or disregard they and others in the military experienced in the late 1960s and early 1970s. Even so, Wells wondered if these current expressions of appreciation were but part of a fad destined to expire in the years ahead.

Neither was he a fan of the connection sports teams made to the military, in that such "tributes" were most often for show, reflecting the current trend of military appreciation. Wells didn't like it, but he felt as though so many of these gestures were substitutes for commitment to ending the national atrocity that was the treatment of the country's combat veterans. Whether it was in the form of military-camo alternate team uniforms and hats or the gratuitous focus on men and women in uniform by television cameras, Wells couldn't help thinking it was all pandering and self-aggrandizing. "Hey, look at us. We're all about the military." And he bristled at the money the Department of Defense paid sports teams to stage military-themed events and moments—to the tune of up to $700,000 given to one NFL team. A recent estimate was that the DOD paid in excess of fifty million dollars to "honor the military," which was seen by many as merely a recruitment tool. Wells had already spoken publically about the "abomination" of paying off billionaires instead of providing returning veterans with adequate care and employment.

But what disturbed him most was the failure of men in power to act on their effusive compliments of the veterans and declarations that they needed better care. Wells was determined to call the committee to account and resist any temptation to soften his stance in the wake of each member's flattering to gushing expressions of respect and appreciation for the men and women who came back home in dire need of assistance. "Talk is both cheap and insulting," his mother once told him—and Wells took the words to heart. His audience today would be the American people and veterans, who he hoped would put some pressure on the committee and full Senate for changes and reform. He was delighted the media was widely represented at the hearing.

In his opening statement, Wells noted that "only twenty percent of the Senate served in the military and just three members of the committee sitting here today are veterans." Wells's statistics left all members of the committee frowning, except for the newest member, Senator Heather Gellman, who served and was wounded in Iraq in 2004-05. Although he spent four years as a Naval officer from 1979-83, Chuck Lamont wasn't at all happy that Wells had made his point at the committee's expense. Without pondering the implications of what he would say, Lamont interjected, "The committee's percentage is the same as the full Senate, Mr. Wells—twenty-percent—and only 7.3 percent of all Americans have ever served in the military."

"Yes, that is true, Mr. Chairman, but the percentage of the men and women this committee is responsible for is *one hundred* percent."

Lamont glowered at Wells, "Please continue with your statement."

Daniel knew the rest of his time before the committee would be devoid of further praise of his heroism. Without losing a beat, Wells brought up the issue of fraudulent Veterans Organizations, who either sent to veterans a bare portion of the funds they received or hardly any at all. "I would like to see a stronger statement from this committee, the entire Congress, the VA, and the White House about these fake or qualified charities—all with 'Veterans' in their name." Wells spoke of one "affinity fraud" case in which a single person embezzled close to a hundred million dollars from generous souls who wished to help needy veterans. "In most instances, the amount of direct aid from these fraudulent charities ranges from nothing to a mere eleven percent of the money contributed. At worst, ninety percent of the funds donated were aid to solicitors and for 'fundraising costs,' whereas the average for these so-called charities was between seventy and eighty-five percent for solicitors and costs." After taking a swallow of water, Wells looked at the committee members one by one, "Of course, we've all heard the excuses that these charities don't have the resources or staff to do their own soliciting, as well as the shameless and shameful view that 'Hey, a little percentage is better than no percentage at all.'"

Following a reiterated call for more public education about the truth behind these charities, Wells turned his attention to the scandalous treatment or non-treatment in VA hospitals. "It's fashionable these days to praise these men and women as heroes, and yet far too many of them are ill-treated, if treated at all, by a system that is bloated with bureaucracy, often incompetent in its diagnoses, and too dismissive of the psychological damage caused by combat. I sometimes feel as though many in the Congress without battlefield experience have had their impressions of war shaped merely by action films of the 40s, 50s, and 60s."

Wells noticed several of the committee members squirm in their seats, while four stared coldly. The three veterans, most notably Chuck Lamont, gave him all their attention, and one Senator rudely conversed with a member of his staff.

Wells delivered further grim statistics and accounts. Over three hundred thousand vets were estimated to have died in this country before their applications were processed. The VA lost almost two million dollars due to executives carving out job openings with higher pay for themselves. "Almost two million that could have been spent on vital assistance to veterans. And those who wished to make public the abuses were intimidated by their superiors at the VA, who maintained through fear the sweet financial situation they created for themselves." Wells continued by noting the priority "service connected" health issues received over combat veterans—from sports-related injuries to medical problems stemming from unhealthy habits and risky behaviors. "We are all behind the use of more solar energy, Mr. Chairman, but the VA spent over four hundred million to equip their hospitals with solar panels, while so many veterans were on wait lists, suffering from their combat-related injuries and illnesses. One California hospital alone lost one hundred patients in a ten month period while they waited for care."

Wells punctuated his remarks with the tale of one veteran for whom a health provider recommended a late January date to begin care. "This veteran told me—and I checked the record—that the scheduler entered a desired date as October 2nd, and the patient was seen on October 17th. The VA asserted that fifteen days wasn't an inordinate amount of wait time, but the veteran actually waited some 260 days to *begin* care. There are too many of these failures to chalk up to 'inadvertent errors' or 'cracks in the system.' The cracks are more like chasms, Mr. Chairman. Remember that research has shown some half a million claims for VA assistance pending for more than four months. Every one of us should be appalled by these statistics."

Wells next offered a sampling of letters and emails he had received, including several which praised the VA. "I don't want to suggest that the VA has done noting worthy of praise and appreciation. They just haven't done enough on one hand—and too much harm to the men and women they claim to serve on the other." There was one letter from a soldier who developed PTSD from his two tours in Iraq, who spoke of the drugs he needed, as well as the necessity of controlling what he watched, read, and drank. "It took the VA two years to respond to his disability application. The letter from the VA informed him that his PTSD was not connected to his military service." Wells added that one soldier who fought in Afghanistan finished his medical treatments, the bills for which, he was assured, would be handled by the VA. "He wrote that he owed over a hundred thousand dollars for his treatments and that he went through all the proper VA channels to get the bills paid. He sent the VA his statements, and they informed him there should be no problem with the payment. After three months, the former soldier began receiving the bills from the individual providers, who said they hadn't yet been paid. He called the VA, and they informed him they needed the tax codes from the providers before they could pay—never having informed the veteran about that requirement, of course. The vet called the providers and had them send the tax codes to the VA. But the bills kept coming. The VA assured him everything was still processing. Eventually the vet received a letter from the VA informing him they would not pay any of his bills because ninety days had passed since he was in the hospital. The vet had to call his representative's office, and they got in touch with the VA. As a sad and inexcusable end to this sorry tale, the VA said they'd pay the hospital but not the providers because ninety days had passed. So this veteran, who had risked his life in Afghanistan and been wounded—one of our true heroes—had his credit destroyed and doesn't know what to do to make matters right."

Wells final example was a letter sent from a former Marine, who informed Wells about his buddy who had done three tours in Iraq and who had severe reactions when he returned home to loud noises and constant memories of what he had witnessed in country. "The Marine told me his friend became addicted to sedatives while he waited for VA counseling, which he was informed had a long backlog. The friend's wife left him owing to his screaming almost every night in his sleep and her husband's inability to control his anger, which resulted in jail time on two occasions. When they wouldn't let him take his children for the weekend after he was released the second time, he shot himself to death in front of the house where his wife and daughters were then living."

Wells concluded, "Mr. Chairman and Members of the committee, I know measures have been recently taken and negligent employees of the VA have begun to lose their jobs, but much more needs to be done—and quickly. The treatment of our veterans is a national disgrace and can no longer be tolerated. It's not enough to praise everyone in the military as 'heroes' or to wear camo at sporting events. Private hospitals should be reimbursed for veterans care. The wounded and disabled returning from war not only deserve excellent and prompt attention—they are also owed it by this government, who says daily, 'Thank you for your service.' Not much thought is given to the matter of morale, and few gestures can be as helpful to morale as the assurance that the wounded—physically and psychologically—will receive the *very best* of immediate care. I know of the arguments that say there are just too many who need assistance and not enough employees to handle the demand for care. Instead of leading to capitulation and hand wringing, these arguments need to be overcome rather than acceded to. I ask that your committee, the entire Senate and House, and the executive branch work together to improve—drastically and quickly—the horrendous situation so many of our veterans find themselves in after doing what they were asked to do by the Congress and the last several presidents. I promise you that history will not forgive you if you simply honor the veterans with mere compliments rather than action."

# CHAPTER 16

After thanking the reporter and his sister, Wells checked his cell phone. There was a text message from a number with a 919 area code. As he made his way from Smithsonian Castle and across Jefferson to the National Mall, he called Andrea.

"Yes, it went real well. He was good—a nice guy. I'll tell you all about it when I see you. Look, can you break free for the rest of the day? Because I want you to go with me to Chapel Hill. Something's happened to Carla Aronson—Jack Ketchum's daughter."

### 

"Damn it, Carter. That's three in a row you've underthrown to me. What's going on in your head, man?"

Carter Thompson and his favorite receiver Lamar Durden walked off the field as interim coach Mike Cipriano blew the whistle ending the morning practice session. "Coach is going to give me hell, Lamar."

"No. He's not that fucking asshole Reilly. See. He's not even looking at you." In truth, Durden caught the coach's eye after the last underthrown pass. It was obvious Cipriano wanted him to talk to Thompson and find out what was wrong. Unlike Reilly, who micromanaged as much as he possibly could, Cipriano preferred delegating and trusting the other coaches and the team leaders. Thompson and Durden re-hydrated and splashed their faces with water.

"Getting nervous about the game, Carter?"

"Hell no." He stared for a moment into Durden's eyes. "Don't tell anyone else this—not coach, not anyone—but I got a letter this morning in my box at Bly House." Blyleven House was the athletic dorm on UNEV's campus.

Durden waited for his friend to continue, but Thompson looked around as though he were debating whether it was wise to reveal the contents. "What did it say, man? Wait. Someone ask you to throw the fucking game?"

"That's what I'm not sure about. It said that UNEV owes "the piper"—whatever that means. The guy who wrote it—I assume it's a guy—also said he wanted me to "play my heart out" so that no one will suspect me. He asked me to remember that it's the 'small losses in life' that do most damage to the heart, not the big ones—or some shit like that. That's all he wrote. He never said to throw the game or keep it below the point spread. I don't know what the hell he was trying to say."

"Was the letter signed?"

"No."

"Hand-written?"

"No, it was printed out."

"Just forget it, Carter. Someone trying to fuck with your mind, that's all."

"I can't just forget it."

"Why not?"

"Because they found Darryl's body in the trunk of his car—that's why not."

###

Chas Overby arrived at the Canadian Embassy on Pennsylvania Avenue, just north of the National Gallery of Art. He was picking up Lisa Busby, the Canadian who worked in the Embassy in roughly the same position Overby held at the American Embassy in Ottawa. They had known each other for more than two years and over that time they met in both cities and in Manhattan for short and long weekends. But neither spoke of marriage or any long-term arrangement, although each time Chas saw her, he desired her more and fancied her as his wife. Overby reminded himself not to mention he'd been in D.C. two days before he claimed he was. He hadn't mentioned that to Daniel Wells, either.

As he sat waiting for Lisa, Overby noticed a small boy grabbing his crotch in an obvious signal that he needed to use the bathroom. His father took him, as his older brother buried his head in his hands in embarrassment. Yet it was more than simple embarrassment Overby felt as a freshman when Hoyt Reilly humiliated him in the locker room by sharing with the team that he had seen Overby's penis in the shower area and it "wasn't as long as my god-damn pinky finger." But the team didn't know that a day later, Reilly grabbed Overby's scrotum while the player was wearing only his underwear, about to put on his clothes after practice. "I just want to see if you have a pair or at least one, Overby. You play like you don't have anything down here."

Raised by his parents to sound the alarm if he were ever molested, Overby made an appointment with the Athletic Director and reported what happened. The AD said, "You okay—I mean physically?" Overby assured him he was, but he expected the AD to be concerned about his state of mind. But the AD merely assured him that "I'll take care of it. Just don't speak about this, okay?" Foolishly, Overby assumed Reilly would be called into the AD office the next day or two and then come forward with an apology. Reilly never approached Overby again but he kept riding him until Overby, realizing that nothing would ever be done to Reilly, eventually left the program. He never told anyone what happened, and as the months went by he developed a self-loathing for not making a bigger case out if it. Along with self-castigation grew hatred for the man who had ridiculed and humiliated him. He fancied meeting Reilly and slugging him both in the face and in the crotch. But he never sought Reilly out. By then, he had a career to think about, although the hatred continued to grow. Hatred for his old coach and deep resentment for UNEV, the university that hired the bastard after Reilly wore out his welcome elsewhere. All this would have been enough to justify despising the man, but there was also Reilly's history with Overby's mother.

"Chas, are you ready?"

Overby quickly cleared his head. "As ever, Lisa. As ever. Where are we going for lunch?"

"I don't care. You choose."

"All right. I'm in the mood for Indian—so it's Rasika."

"On D?"

"That's it. I'm hungry for some delicious **Chicken Biryani**."

Lisa didn't let him see her smile. It was at Rasika that she treated Daniel Wells to lunch in appreciation for his putting her in touch with a man who had Golden Lab puppies to sell.

###

"Thanks Rod. I'll call you when I learn more." Wells went over what he had told Rod Pritchett about this afternoon's schedule. He wanted to be certain he didn't leave anything out. Pritchett was usually one step ahead of him in any event, and was always ready to take Wells's place when his boss was tied up elsewhere.

Wells and Andrea shifted over from I-95 to I-85, having just gone through Petersburg. They discussed the status of the investigation into the recent killings, with Wells summarizing, "I've spoken with both the police in Virginia and D.C.—and of course with Henrik. They're having a hard time connecting all the deaths and the bomb plantings under my old Corolla and Henrik's car. But the bombs under my old Corolla and Henrik's car were low-grade, and besides, how could I be connected to Reilly and Darryl Roe—who were both murdered?" Yet Wells didn't tell Andrea that Reilly was the step-brother of a woman he had once loved deeply—the present First Lady of the United States. He had never spoken to Andrea of his feelings for Cecilia Erskine—then or now—except to say they had dated in college. He didn't like to think much about it, but he was grateful Andrea's appearance and temperament were so different than Cecilia's. The first lady had deep blue eyes to go with her black hair and a contemplative manner, whereas Andrea's eyes were brown and her hair sandy blonde, with an outgoing personality and a ready smile—qualities that served her well in her career as a sports reporter and writer. Cecilia's voice was soft and often alluring and her clothes always fashionable, but Andrea could push the meter with her hearty laugh and animated voice. Both women were passionate but Cecilia was so in a darker and quieter way, which was in stark contrast to Andreas's overt and vigorous displays of affection. Loving Cecilia was the most difficult experience he ever dealt with—combat and a serious wound didn't come close. On the other hand, everything with Andrea Chase could be characterized as a breezy easiness.

"And now there's Carla Aronson to add to those who know you and who had a connection to UNEV." Andrea's observation pulled him from his thoughts.

"I'm just wondering who's next." He didn't have to look at Andrea. She knew as well as he that she might soon be victimized. "That's why I want you to look under your car before you get into it. Henrik promised to get us each one of those inspection mirrors used to look under vehicles."

"The ones with handles on them, I hope."

"Yes."

"Good. That will keep me from ruining my pants and scraping my knees."

For the first time since he heard the news about Jack Ketchum's daughter, Wells was able to laugh.

"Daniel, can we talk about something else for the next two hours. That trip we're sort of planning to Vegas, for example." Andrea was going to cover a major female MMA event at the Vegas Hilton in early January and wanted Wells to accompany her for a three day stay at the Wynn.

"Sounds like a plan. First tell me what your daily gambling budget is going to be."

"I don't know. Depends on how much you give me."

"Ha."

###

"I love that sweater. I really do." Paula Bradford-Adams felt free to compliment the first lady on her clothing choices, ever since Cecilia Erskine expressed her appreciation of Paula's taste and invited her opinion on what might be worn on various occasions. This afternoon, the first lady would be on the South Lawn greeting some of the best girls' high-school cross-country runners. The temperature hovered at the freezing mark, but Cecilia tolerated the cold well—far preferring the coldest days to summer in the sweltering capital city. The sweater she chose today, a knitted half dark blue and half gray, would be all she'd need for the event. It was one she picked up in Manhattan right before she married Stephen Erskine. Now thirty-six, Cecilia weighed only two pounds more than she had when she bought the sweater. She slipped a long silver tassel necklace over her head to finish the look.

She glanced in the mirror and remarked to Paula, "I wonder if this sweater would look as good if the gray were on top of the blue. What do you think?"

"I'm sure it would look nice, but with your blue eyes, the blue above the gray is really striking."

"Thank you, Paula." That special delight in being appreciated. Cecilia cherished the compliments she received as a child, for her appearance and talents, but after her mother remarried, any compliment became something to earn, if not solicit. Not simply from her mother, who always provided them, but from her friends and teenage boys, and then men. She tried to check her susceptibility to flattery, but she never listened to the inner voice that warned of the vulnerability that accompanies the desire to be praised. And she had fallen victim in the worst way—to her step-brother Hoyt Reilly, who initially attempted to ingratiated himself to her with unsolicited compliments. Soon enough she would learn how flattery could be masterfully employed by a devious and cruel mind. In his hands, the initial praise simply made his subsequent behavior more devastating.

"Are you ready to meet the cross-country lasses?"

"I believe so. I've been much looking forward to this." The first lady once told Paula of her own experience running cross-country and track in high school and cross-country at UNEV her freshman and sophomore years. But she hadn't shared her view that running was a pervasive image she developed during her teens, an action that dominated her dreams and many painful waking moments.

# Chapter 17

As soon as they arrived in Chapel Hill, Wells drove straight to Carla Aronson's house, where they were met by the police. A male and female member of the Investigative Division asked Wells to sit in the kitchen, preventing his going further into the house. After Wells introduced Andrea, the investigators, one of whom recognized the sports writer, permitted her to stay, inquiring if she planned to write a story on what had happened. Andrea couldn't say for sure. "It's up to the editors, but I will inform them, since Coach Ketchum was her father, and therefore the story may be considered sports related."

According to the investigators' account, Roseanne Manfredi, a friend of Carla's, arrived to take her to their scheduled breakfast date, but no one answered the door when she rang and then knocked loudly. Roseanne called on her cell and heard the landline ringing in the house. She couldn't imagine Carla left for any reason, seeing that the car was in the garage. Roseanne suspected the worst and went around the house looking into windows and making sure the shower wasn't running. The next window belonged to the master bedroom, and Roseanne peered through a sliver of an opening in the drapes. She saw one of Carla's ankles tied to the bottom bedpost. After she called 911, a police cruiser arrived within two minutes, and the one of the officers put his hand on the doorknob, which turned easily. Roseanne had never tried the door, assuming it was locked and bolted, as was Carla's habit whenever she was inside.

Wells listened to the rest of the investigator's account, learning that when the two officers entered the bedroom, Carla's friend remained in the kitchen, too terrified to confront what she was certain she'd see. "I think you can go in now, Mr. Wells." Andrea didn't wait for permission to follow him. As soon as they entered the living room, Wells looked toward the open door to the master bedroom.

"Oh, Daniel." Carla rose from the sofa, where she sat holding hands with her friend Roseanne. Wells embraced her. "Are you all right?" He was told on the phone that she was fine, but nevertheless he couldn't help asking.

"I'm just shaken up—and hungry." Carla smiled, but it was an effort. After Daniel introduced her, Andrea took Carla's order and headed out to the nearby Dunkin Donuts for a box of Carla's favorite cinnamon donuts. Carla took a sip of Scotch and related her story, beginning with the description of the assailant in all black except for the demonic-red ski mask without a mouth opening. She told Daniel the man had some kind of device which altered his voice. "He wasn't rough with me, but he didn't have to be—I was so scared. He made me sprawl on the bed on my stomach, and I just knew I was going to be..." Daniel squeezed her hand firmly. "He tied each of my ankles to the bedpost, and I was trying to get my body ready to fight with him when he grabbed my wrists, but he never touched me further. He just left me there on my stomach with my legs tied to the bedposts while he looked through my bedroom drawers and closet. I was too terrified to say anything—not even to beg for my life. When he was done, he said, 'Sorry to have inconvenienced you. Someone will find you tomorrow. Just get a good night's sleep.' I was sure he would kill me then, but he left and never came back. After waiting half an hour, I tried to turn and reach the phone near the bed, but it was too far away from my hands. I was so exhausted from fear that I just put my head down and fell asleep. I woke up near dawn and tried to reach the rope to untie my legs, but I couldn't move my body far enough to do it. I have a queen-size mattress so I was stretched out really wide. The officer told me that the rope was made of polyester, which is harder to untie than nylon. I yelled for help a few times, but my room is in the back and my neighbor's houses aren't close to mine. I thought I'd end up starving to death before anyone could find me. But then I remembered my breakfast date with Roseanne, and I just knew she would break down the door if she had to and find me." Roseanne lowered her head in embarrassment over the door's being unlocked—left that way Wells surmised by the "gentleman assailant."

"But, Carla, you haven't yet told me what he wanted from you."

Carla's eyes filled with tears. "I'm so ashamed, Daniel. Please forgive me."

"There's nothing to forgive."

"There is. The man wanted to know where my father's papers were. I... I couldn't help it, I was so scared. I told him I gave them to you."

### 

Kyle Guidry left his second floor office in the West Wing and headed down to speak with the president regarding a nominee Erskine was considering for a judicial appointment on The U.S. Court of Appeals for the Federal Circuit. When he made it down to the hallway leading to the Oval Office, Guidry observed Álvaro Hernandez being shown in, holding what was likely a copy of the speech the president was soon to give in Atlanta at the MLK Center. Guidry was hopeful Hernandez would act on what Guidry learned was his frustration over his answers and statements to the press being contradicted by the chief of staff, several of the president's advisers, and the president himself. Guidry also knew Hernandez's wife wished her husband would leave the White House, and perhaps her argument had won the day. But in spite of what he told Hernandez about the need to stay on until the election, Guidry wanted him gone for one compelling and unrelated reason. The press secretary had twice witnessed Guidry demonstrating his fascination for the first lady. In late August, Guidry remained in the Oval Office after the president excused himself for a moment. Guidry walked to the Resolute Desk and picked up the framed photo of Cecilia Erskine and held it in his hands, even rubbing his finger against the first lady's beautiful face. Hernandez walked in and caught Guidry doing so. The men looked at each other, but said nothing as Guidry placed the framed photograph back on the president's desk.

The second occasion was even more embarrassing for Guidry. The first lady had stepped from the West Wing and into the Rose Garden, accompanied by her staffers Paula Bradford-Adams and Helene Eckermire. Guidry saw them when he was heading for the Oval Office. He stopped and watched the women walk around the garden, the first lady pointing to where all the lovely blooms had been the previous spring and summer—the area now devoid of the joyful reds, yellows, blues, and whites of the many varieties of tulips, grape hyacinth, and lavender cotton—and also empty of the dozens of folding chairs set out for the joint press conference of the president and China's premier. As the women made their way to the back of the garden, Guidry noticed that Cecilia Erskine tentatively took her last few steps. She sat on the white bench and removed her shoe, apparently removing a stone or a twig. The two other women took their seats on the outdoor chairs nearby, as the first lady turned over her shoe and rubbed her foot. She wore sheer brown tights with her fall outfit, the hemline of her dress coming just below her knees. Although she was at a distance, Guidry couldn't take his eyes off her as she continued to rub her foot as she spoke to Bradford-Adams and Eckermire. Guidry placed his right hand deep into the pocket of his trousers.

"The president is waiting, Kyle." Álvaro Hernandez stood several feet away. Once again, the men simply looked at each other without speaking, although Guidry saw something on Hernandez's face that let him know the press secretary had found him voyeuristically watching the first lady. In the month that passed, Guidry had spoken to Hernandez more aggressively, expressing impatience whenever he could. Guidry fully realized he was attempting to encourage the press secretary to resign, and he feared more than ever that Hernandez would inform the president of Guidry's inordinate concentration on the first lady.

###

Wells and Andrea pulled over for coffee on the trip back to Washington. Wells called Henrik, who relayed what he learned from the police in D.C. and in northeast Virginia—that they were both disinclined to believe the murders and bombings were done by one person. "They're thinking at least two, maybe three, and that there may be no connections at all." He also found out that the Virginia police considered Miles Thompson, Carter Thompson, and new UNEV coach Mike Cipriano as persons of interest. After Wells told him about Carla Aronson's intruder—but not about what the man wanted from her—Nordenson asked, "Did she say or think the man was black or foreign, at least in his accent?"

"I didn't ask." Surely the police in Chapel Hill had already done so and would share all such details with the police in D.C. and Virginia. At least Wells encouraged them to do so before he and Andrea left Carla's house. "Anything on these low explosive bombings, Henrik?"

Nordenson paused. "Henrik?"

"Found one under Andrea's car—but don't tell her. Same kind as the one under mine. I don't know what kind of game is being played, but we can't assume any more of these teases will be just that. Please be sure you and Andrea check every time you get into your cars." Wells realized he hadn't done so when he left Carla's house. "I'm going to try and get your cars set up with a TALOS sometime tomorrow." Not long ago, Nordenson informed Wells of the sophisticated TALOS vehicle bomb detector.

After hanging up, Wells called George Washington University Hospital to check on Gina Lorenzetti's status. She was released earlier in the afternoon, prompting him to call her place. Gina's mother answered the phone, having driven down last night with Gina's younger brother from College Park, Maryland. Wells tried his best to explain that the bomb "prank" was intended for him, although he wasn't yet entirely sure, but Mrs. Lorenzetti was still considerably upset. He heard Gina in the background insist that she be given the phone.

"I'm okay, Daniel. Really I am. Just shook up. More scared than scarred, you could say. I didn't need to stay in the hospital." Relieved that Gina elicited her usual playfulness with the language, Wells reminded her to check the bottom of her Corolla before she started it and was about to offer to rig up a mirror-device for her, when she interrupted. "I'm afraid your Corolla won't be driven again for quite awhile if ever. The bomb went off—remember?"

### 

"Fuck you, Freeman. Wells couldn't do half what my kid can do on the field." Miles Thompson was in the middle of another argument with one of his former NFL teammates, LaRoy Freeman, about past and present NFL and college players. Freeman, whom Thompson hadn't see in several months, always took the position that on the whole today's players lacked the guts and commitment to the game reflective of those who played before 1990—even though his and Miles' pro careers began in 1996. When he was in a particularly puckish mood, Freeman waxed eloquently about the earlier days of UNEV's football program and the talents of quarterback Daniel Wells. Freeman enjoyed Miles Thompson's reaction when he argued that Wells was the best quarterback the school had yet produced. Normally, the elder Thompson would laugh before cursing his friend, seemingly aware that Freeman was merely attempting to get a rise out of him. But Thompson's profanity at this moment, as the men were sharing a few drinks at their favorite tavern off the 270 Spur in Potomac, Maryland, wasn't prefaced by a smile. Rather, Thompson seemed to have judged Freeman's teasing praise of Wells at the expense of Carter Thompson a direct and personal insult. Freeman believed his old friend was ready to punch him out, and accordingly jumped in with a "Hey, man. I'm just playing with you."

But Thompson was too deep in his anger to be mollified. He finished his drink and left the tavern without another word to Freeman, although his teammate heard him mutter to himself as he walked away, "Fucking Wells."

# Chapter 18

White House Director of Public Liaison Grant Paulson reread President Erskine's memo regarding his desire for Daniel Wells to join him at the bowl game in Arizona in a few days. Erskine added to the memo, "Why hasn't Wells made a statement about Hoyt Reilly?" Paulson understood the question was really "Why haven't you convinced him to do so?" Paulson could tell from Wells's earlier reaction that he wouldn't agree to the president's request. As for Wells attending the bowl game, Paulson was intent on convincing him to do so. After all, he long ago convinced his college friend to approach the achingly lovely Cecilia Finch for a date when they were students at UNEV. Paulson thought the two of them were destined for marriage, an opinion shared by others in their circle of friends. At the very least they were what Hollywood called an "It" couple. Wells was the envy of many young men at the university. Cecilia had the aura—the factor—that made men desire her but also fear her power over them should they find themselves in a relationship with her. It was as if they all sensed she would break their hearts and forever crush their spirits. Paulson was one of those young men, who even now fifteen years later felt no differently about her. In weaker moments he would admit to his friends that he feared for the president and by extension the country if the first lady lived out the destiny fate had assigned her of damaging if not destroying the men in her life. As for Daniel Wells, Paulson kept enough in touch with him after graduation to realize that his school's starting quarterback left his relationship with Cecilia Finch more wounded emotionally than he was physically after returning from Iraq. Paulson never knew what precipitated the break between them. All he knew was that after college Wells didn't accompany her when she traveled to Europe, where she remained for some fifteen months. The next thing he learned was that she had married older UNEV alum, Stephen Erskine. That Paulson ended up working in the White House, where he would see and occasionally speak to her remained a coincidence and an irony he still couldn't get over.

As he approached the Deputy Chief of Staff's West Wing office, Paulson recalled further his recent visit to Wells's apartment and his old friend's reaction to hearing the first lady's desire that Wells accompany the president to the bowl game. It was clear to Paulson that Wells was still not over Cecilia—that the pain of their break-up remained—even though he seemed happy with sportswriter Andrea Chase. Wells's curious opening of the UNEV yearbook suggested he was searching for the candid picture of the two of them, taken inside the school's library—the one that showed Wells "studying" with his nose in a book while Cecilia Finch looked straight into the camera's lens with an enigmatic smile on her lips. Friends teased Wells that he appeared so out of place—an intruder in what everyone considered a photo of a stunning young woman, secure in her beauty and appropriately aloof. Paulson would have given much to be instilled with enough nerve to talk to the first lady about her relationship with Daniel Wells, but he knew that was simply impossible.

### 

As Andrea showered, Wells read though Ketchum's research on Hoyt Reilly—especially the final few pages. There were obvious hints as to the other areas his old coach wished to explore, but Wells found nothing new upon a second reading. The thought bedeviled him. Had Ketchum come up with something else, written it down, and planned to send or deliver a copy of any new material to his daughter in Chapel Hill? Did the explosion destroy that additional research? If so, did it contain information of considerable significance, perhaps unlocking a mystery that would have finished Reilly's career and perhaps led to charges against him? Wells couldn't let go of the possibility that Reilly had somehow set the charge in Ketchum's kitchen but then in an unrelated event ended up being murdered while running on the UNEV track. But what then of the intruder in Chapel Hill and his interest in the pages Ketchum had given his daughter shortly before his death? The planted car bombs, though not intended to kill anyone, had to be related in some way. Wells was forced to decide what to do with the pages Carla Aronson handed him. She had told the intruder she had given them to Wells, and logic dictated that the man would eventually come for them at Wells's apartment. Should he keep the material here at Andrea's or place it in his safety-deposit box at the bank? Andrea. How much danger was she in?

"I'll be ready in ten minutes—just as soon as I figure out what to wear." She came into the living room wrapped in a towel, with her hair down and make-up applied.

"I wish the Redskins, Nationals, and the Wizards could see you like this."

"Don't forget the Capitals."

Wells adored Andrea's displaying her ultra-feminine side when they went to dinner and occasional parties. And yet he also found her desirable when she wore her hair in a pony tail and wore shorts, a tee-shirt, and ball cap. In between was the "Interview Look"—a mid-thigh dress, flat shoes, and her hair up. As she returned to her bedroom, Wells couldn't help recalling that he never saw Cecilia Finch's hair in a pony tail—not for the entire time they were a couple and never since in any of the hundreds of photographs of her.

### 

"I'm having second thoughts about this."

"What do you mean? Not enough? All right, I'll up it to twelve hundred."

"It's not the money." The attractive young woman shivered in the cold in spite of the heavy coat she had on. "I've never been here before," she aimlessly mentioned. She was with the man in Rock Creek Park in the Northwest quadrant of the city. The last time she had seen him was in a hotel room near the Potomac. This meeting was the fourth she had with him, although this time there would be no sex. She just received a thousand dollar offer to make a call and tell the woman on the other end that Daniel Wells had impregnated her and paid for an abortion in the early fall and that she didn't want any other woman used the way she had been.

"Why the hell won't you do it, Joni? Haven't I been good to you?"

"Yes, you have. And I appreciate the way you... I mean that you aren't rough or cruel in any way. But I'm not comfortable telling lies to someone—even if it's someone I don't know. Besides, she probably wouldn't believe me."

"I'll give you fifteen hundred."

"I'm sorry, I can't. I better go now." She headed toward her car as Dylan Nieporte shook his head in frustration. He wouldn't push the issue because he wanted to continue his bi-weekly trysts with the beautiful long-haired blonde, who worked for one of D.C.'s most discreet and classy sex agencies. As for Andrea Chase not believing what Joni would have told her, he expected she wouldn't, but it would still put enough doubt in her mind to cause uneasiness for Wells. And besides that, this ploy was nothing more than a juvenile prank compared to what else had come into his mind lately.

### 

"Give this to one of the White House staff, and have them store it." The first lady handed Helene Eckermire the landscape painting that previously hung in her East Wing office. After Helene took it away, Cecilia picked up the print of Munch's *The Scream* and placed it on the conference table in the middle of her office. She had been intrigued by the work ever since she studied Scandinavian art in her Art History class at UNEV. The piece spoke to her then, but especially so following her return to the United States after her European tour following college. In the years since, she frequently examined it in the large folio art book she bought at the Strand on Broadway—the money for the purchase provided by one of the men she met during her European travels, who was spending the weekend at an absent friend's apartment on West 85th. Although she fully expected the offer, she refused to spend that night with him, giving him instead the twelve hours from breakfast through dinner.

Cecilia looked at the print and replayed the facts she had learned about the piece. The goal of his 1893 painting, Munch remarked, was "the study of the soul, that is to say the study of my own self." He said he'd been walking with friends down a road when the sun set: "suddenly, the sky turned as red as blood. I stopped and leaned against the fence, feeling unspeakably tired. Tongues of fire and blood stretched over the bluish black fjord. My friends went on walking, while I lagged behind, shivering with fear. Then I heard the enormous, infinite scream of nature." Munch added, "I was almost mad... stretched to the limit—nature was screaming in my blood.... After that I gave up hope ever of being able to love again." Cecilia never told a soul, but she not only understood what Munch expressed, but she believed she also felt all of it from the time she was a young girl.

Cecilia turned her head to her right, toward the white book shelves in her East-Wing office. She raised her eyes to the top unit of four shelves, and once more the memory touched her. She was eight, too short to reach the book she wanted on the top shelf of the book case in her room. Turning around to locate a chair on which to climb, she came face to face with her new step-brother, the seventeen year old Hoyt Reilly. His words she would never forget.

"Need to reach a book up there?"

Cecilia nodded. She didn't like talking to this new member of her family, although she initially felt comfortable with Reilly's fourteen year old sister. In fact, she hated the sound of Hoyt's voice the first time she heard it, as though it served as a warning—a harbinger of bitter unhappiness.

"Want me to lift you up a bit?" Before she had a chance to answer, her step-brother placed his large hands around her waist. He lifted her so that her lower back rested against his face. She grabbed the book, but he didn't lower her. Instead he lifted her even higher until she felt his head against her buttocks. When he lowered her to her feet, she without a word ran out of the room with her volume clutched tightly in her hands. She found it impossible to read the book, which she then discarded in the kitchen trash basket. At dinner, Reilly smiled knowingly as he asked how she liked the book, a seeming gesture of interest that pleased Cecilia's mother. Cecilia looked at her step-sister, who wore a disinterested expression on her plain round face.

The first lady found Helene down the corridor in the calligraphy office. "Helene, will you see that *all* the books on the top shelf in my office are moved to the third one down and that the statuettes and music boxes on the third are placed on the top shelves?"

"Will do."

Cecilia smiled and touched Helene on the shoulder. "Thank you. I'll be downstairs in the East Garden Room if you need me."

As soon as the first lady left, Helene looked at the deputy calligrapher, who shared her puzzled look.

### 

"Much obliged, Henrik." Wells nodded as Nordenson finished checking the underside of both Wells's and Andrea's cars.

"Just remember to check before you drive away from dinner—and then in the morning."

"Thanks, Henrik." Andrea planted a kiss on his handsome cheek.

Nordenson quickly filled Wells in on the current state of the investigations in D.C and northeast Virginia. There was still little agreement on the number of persons involved in the recent homicides and intimidations. As he finished, Wells's cell phone rang.

"Hello. What? Who is this?" Wells paused, listening carefully. "What the hell?" He turned toward Andrea and Henrik. "You won't believe this. It was some kind of recorded message in one of those robotic voices. It said, 'Mr. Wells, boom, boom. Soon enough we'll meet and all will be clear to you. But there's more work to do first.' Nothing more was said."

Nordenson took the cell phone and checked the number. "It's a 303 area code. I believe that's Denver—but that doesn't mean anything."

"A hoax of some kind, Henrik?" Andrea asked.

"Probably, although..." His qualifier let her know he didn't believe it was.

"Daniel...?" She grabbed his hand.

"If we take this seriously, it seems I'm going to meet someone who knows what the hell's happening."

"I can arrange someone to watch you."

"Thanks, Henrik. But I have a feeling I'll be receiving at least another call before the meeting is to occur. I'm not worried about me, given what was said, as much as I am about the 'more work' that's planned. Can you have someone keep an eye on Andrea?"

"Consider it done." Henrik looked at Andrea, who was in no state to protest. "Once more—watch your back. Or what is the American football expression you told me, Daniel."

"Keep your head on a swivel."

### 

Wells and Andrea did their best to enjoy dinner, and neither worried about Wells's car, seeing where it was parked—near the entrance to the Partisan on D Street NW. Wells and Andrea called such a space "a Constanza" in honor of one of their favorite *Seinfeld* episodes. While they indulged in their delicious charcuterie choices, the couple speculated on what else Jack Ketchum might have discovered about Hoyt Reilly—and his step-sister Cecilia Erskine. Wells once more chided himself for not opening up to Andrea about his relationship with the current first lady when the two were at UNEV, but he didn't think the present moment was right for a full confession.

"Here's a copy of the last page. I copied it on my printer while you were in the bathroom before we left my place."

Wells took the paper. "And you put the rest of the pages in your safe—right?"

"Yes. In the same one you have—remember?" Wells had recently purchased two of the thirty-pound, eighteen-inch-high safes—giving her one as an "unromantic" Christmas present. He rubbed her hand and examined the copy of Ketchum's last page, which noted **"Family** crisis," "Late middle school through high school," "Boyfriends/dates," "Paul S. and Robbie C. hospital," "Calls to police," and "Travels"—as relating to Cecilia.

"What's that near the bottom of the page, Daniel?"

Wells had noticed the markings earlier but assumed they were merely his old coach's doodling. As he studied the markings further, he could make out a name, tentatively written. "Lew—Lewis?—Kreese???" There were also seemingly unrelated doodles or perhaps letters modified by other swirls of the pen. Or might these swirls be disguised letters? "We need to look at the original pages when we get back."

Andrea agreed but suggested they concentrate on their meal until then. "I'll pour you some Hennessy when we get to my place and we'll examine the original."

"And just where did you get the cognac?"

"Write a feature piece on France's most dashing football—excuse me, soccer—player and you get appropriately rewarded."

"I'm jealous."

"Don't be. He's not sharing my bed tonight. But you are."

"In that case, we better drop by my place so can pack my toothbrush."

###

When they entered Wells' apartment, he detected that someone had been there. Although hardly ransacked, his drawers were partially open and his throw rugs were slightly displaced. The intruder was rather neat, he thought. Wells only hoped he wasn't successful. Nothing seemed amiss in the living-room and kitchen areas, or in his bedroom. But when he opened the closet in the guest room he saw his new safe was missing.

# Chapter 19

Helene waited half an hour at the 201 Bar for Paula to get free of her duties at the White House. Helene waved her friend to her two-person table near the semi-circular bar and grinned at Paula's being bundled up in a heavy coat and pull-down hat—her usual wear when the weather dropped below forty degrees. Resting on the table were two Manhattans and an order of **Four Roses Bourbon Apple Wings, the** favorite cocktail and light fare of the two women, who had been coming to the 201 near Capitol Hill at least once a week since mid-summer.

Each woman shared the day's frustrations and humorous moments, before the subject shifted to Kyle Guidry's fascination with the first lady. Paula savored her Manhattan. "I don't know what he'd do if he found himself alone with her for any length of time."

"I know. I just wish my new man felt that way about me."

Paula laughed. "You need to wear skirts more often, that's all." Helene Eckermire favored sharply tailored pants with her collection of colorful blazers.

"Can't do it. I have ugly knees. Anyway, I wonder if Kyle shares his feelings about her with any of his friends."

"Doubt that. Wait. Are you implying that you've spoken about him to friends other than me?"

"Well..."

"Pillow talk with the new man?" Paula flashed an impish grin. "And by the way, you haven't spoken yet about what you two... do."

"Maybe we haven't done anything yet." Helene drew on an impressive poker-face whenever she needed it.

"Okay. I'll wait for the details. Perhaps after another one of these." She held up her empty cocktail glass.

"Okay, Helene—it's time to share what I saw and heard today—that is, regarding Kyle."

"Our dear Cecilia knows he's enamored of her, certainly—right?"

"I'm sure she does, but then, who isn't smitten with her? No, I mean to say that I came from the Entrance Hall into the Cross Hall as the first lady came out of the State Dining Room with the Chief Usher. She smiled as they passed me, heading toward the East Room. She stood at the entrance for a moment and brushed her hair back with her hand. When she stepped into the East Room, I saw Kyle at the entrance of the Green Room. He walked to where Cecilia was just standing and bent down to retrieve something. I can't be totally sure, but I think it was one of her earrings, which she may have knocked loose when she brushed her hair back. Kyle looked for a moment at the East Room entrance and then placed the item in his coat pocket and went back into the Green Room."

"Did he see you?"

"No. I was tempted to ask him what he found, but, you know me, I thought better of getting involved in what would be an embarrassing moment for him. I just know he's going to keep that earring—if that's what it was—until the time's right to give it back to her."

"Or maybe he's going to keep it and wear it in her honor." The women laughed and Helene signaled for a refill.

###

Wells and Andrea stayed at his place until the police arrived and examined the apartment. "Do you know why this person left everything where it was and only took your safe?" This was the third officer to ask him the same question.

"I think he must have believed I had money or something else valuable in the safe."

"Did you?"

"As I told your colleagues, I had two hundred dollars of various denominations for emergencies. I also had my will and passport in it—and a copy of my most recent tax return." Wells didn't reveal what he knew the intruder was looking for—Ketchum's papers now in Andrea's safe. It was too complicated a matter to mention to the police—at least for the present.

After the dusting for prints and asking about various items in the apartment, the police departed at 9:00 p.m., leaving Wells and Andrea alone to consume a stiff drink before they went to her place for the rest of the night. But before they took their second swallow, the doorbell rang. Wells opened it cautiously. It was one of the officers.

"Excuse me, but we found these on the front seat of one of the patrol cars." He handed Wells the two hundred dollars, his passport, and the copy of his tax return.

### 

Carter Thompson pressed the ice bag where a teammate's helmet had collided with his knee during today's practice—the last before they left for Arizona. Thompson felt badly that the defensive lineman suffered the verbal wrath of Coach Cipriano for getting too close to his quarterback—who was not supposed to be touched during the passing drill. But Carter had more on his mind as he drank a cold beer in his room. He was thinking of his father, whose agitation over the course of the season had increased to the point of embarrassment and deep concern. Miles Thompson had shown signs of vigorous annoyance ever since Carter could remember, but these were always somewhat justifiable, relating to matters of politics, racial inequities, or perceived personal slights. Yet over the past several months his father's reactions and complaints seemed often inordinate given the actual seriousness of the situation. On the other hand, Miles Thompson restrained himself when it came to Hoyt Reilly because he understood that a confrontation with the coach would surely affect his son's position and by extension his chances in the NFL, which weren't outstanding as it was. Carter's mother did her best to keep her husband's temper in check, but more and more her influence waned.

Carter had been reluctant to read anything on Chronic Traumatic Encephalopathy because he didn't wish to put into his mind any argument that cautioned against playing the sport he loved. But now he typed "CTE" into his web browser, curious about the signs and symptoms of the disease. His gut tightened when he saw impulsive behavior, irritability, aggression, and emotional instability as effects of head trauma, especially frequent head trauma over an extended period of time. His face grimaced as he read that one of the reasons to consult a physician was "personality and mood changes. See your doctor if depression, anxiety, aggression, or impulsivity occur." His father had always dismissed the new research on CTE, pointing to former teammates and other ex-players who revealed no signs of the physical and mental damage evident in others. Over the years, Carter saw many video highlights of his father's violent collisions of the field—four of which knocked Miles Thompson woozy or completely out.

Carter exited the site and grabbed his jacket. He had to walk around campus to clear his mind of what he just read. But as he walked in the chilly night air, another thought forced his way into his mind. Could his father have shot Coach Reilly? The desire and opportunity were certainly there, but...

### 

Wells checked Andrea's apartment before he allowed her to enter. Her safe was seemingly untampered with—and nothing else in her place was disturbed. While Andrea made a call to Ignacio Suarez, a member of D.C. United, from whom she wished a few quotes for her piece on the east-coast MLS teams, Wells fixed them drinks and took his to the kitchen. He was adamant about solving the mystery. Three men had been murdered—Hoyt Reilly's, his player Darryl Roebuck, and Jack Ketchum. The connection among the men was that they all were part of the UNEV football program. What did they do to become targets of a murderer or murderers? Wells had no problem seeing Hoyt Reilly as a potential victim of violence; he surely made many enemies in Virginia and the other states in which he had coached. Had he called Roebuck his favorite player, therefore dooming the young linebacker? But why Jack Ketchum—who clearly despised Reilly enough to dig into the man's past? Wells couldn't help going back to the possibility that Reilly had set the bomb in Ketchum's kitchen, never imagining he himself would be shot to death on the UNEV track.

But was that explosion tied in any way to the low-level charge that went off under Gina Lorenzetti's car and those found under Andrea's and Henrik Nordenson's vehicles? Gina and Henrik were of course connected to Wells—as employee and good friend. Wells took another swallow of Scotch to steel against the fear that Andrea might be a victim, not of a low-level explosion, but one that could maim or kill her. And what of the intruder in Chapel Hill, who learned from Carla Aronson that Wells had a copy of Ketchum's pages on Reilly? Surely he was the same man who pilfered Wells' safe. Could he be involved in any of the other criminal activities—or some of them, at least? That the intruder left Carla tied up but unharmed and returned Wells's money, passport, and tax documents suggested what exactly? That the man was at heart a decent guy and merely interested in the information on Reilly? Or did he have a peculiar sense of humor or a plan to leave everyone off balance? If he was the same man who murdered Reilly, Roebuck, and Ketchum, he might have a mental condition that would defy any prediction of what he might do. If he was the same man who killed Reilly, what did he care about Ketchum's pages—after the fact? Wells finished his drink and headed to Andrea's small stand-up bar to pour another. He listened to her speaking with Suarez in impeccable Spanish, recalling that she also spoke excellent French and could at least read German and Italian. Dropping fresh ice in his glass, Wells was impressed by her proficiency. He took French in college and could read it well enough but not speak it. And of course there was the smattering of Arabic every Marine and G.I. picked up in the field, particularly the profanity and expressions such as *"Kess Ommak,"* *"Ayreh Feek,"* and *"Ya Khara."*

Thoughts of Iraq invariably led to his feeling with his right hand what was left of his left arm. He never felt sorry for himself because he was strong enough to realize self-pity would do him no good. Nor did he wear a prosthetic hand, even though he was shown the advanced "Terminator" model during a reunion of the members of his Marine outfit. When he was a boy and he asked his favorite uncle, who had just lost his job, how his family would make do until he secured new employment, his uncle told him, "We'll just get by with what we have until I do." The reply stuck with young Danny, and he came to embrace it as a personal motto. Yes, he missed not being able to play softball and golf or go canoeing the way he once did—and cutting a steak could be a real pain in the rump—but he could "get by" very well in tennis, bowling, shooting baskets, ping-pong, and pistol shooting, even though in the last he was no match for Andrea Chase, who had a deep box full of medals and trophies from her competitive days. He did regret being unable fully to embrace her, but their lovemaking was uninhibited by his disability, though he never called it that. Andrea met him long after Fallujah and she never expressed sadness or pity because he was missing one hand and most of a wrist. Wells found it hard to articulate how much loved her for that. As he heard her wrapping up her phone call, he gave another thought to what Cecilia Finch's reaction to his wound would have been had they still been together when he went off to the Middle East. It would be easy and satisfying for him to believe she wouldn't have stayed with him, but he could never bring himself to think the worst of his former love.

# Chapter 20

The president fell quickly asleep after an evening of meetings and discussion with his main speech writer, which lasted until 11:15. His wife entered the Oval Office during one of the meetings to excuse herself for the evening—kissing her husband on the cheek, as she always did if others were present. She wasn't concerned if they falsely assumed she would be waiting in bed when the president finally retired for the night.

She decided this evening would be devoted to reading time, of which she had too little since becoming first lady. She had good teachers in her primary and secondary schools, who encouraged reading of the classics, at first in sanitized and abridged form and later as they were first published. Cecilia most loved nineteenth-century novels, in spite of their length, and particularly enjoyed Shakespeare, becoming familiar with all of his works, even acting in three of his plays when she was in high school and then at a local community theatre while a student at UNEV. She played the Fairy Queen Titania in her high school production of *Midsummer Night's Dream*, even though she wasn't as tall as she felt the character needed to be. During her college years she performed the aloof and desirable Olivia in *Twelfth Night* and the wise and lovely Portia in *The Merchant of Venice*. But there was another Shakespearean role she was asked to take on that she could not in the end perform—Isabella in the problem play *Measure for Measure*. The director hadn't required her to audition, since he had directed her in *The Merchant of Venice.* She took part in the read-through with the rest of the cast, but when it was over, she excused herself and left the theatre, coming back twenty minutes later to inform the director she couldn't play the part. When he asked why, she gave no satisfactory reason.

Tonight Cecilia wished to continue her examination of Shakespeare's famous speeches, which she had recently started reading again. She read Hamlet's four soliloquies and looked forward to Romeo's "O, she doth teach the torches to burn bright" speech and Macbeth's three soliloquies, "If it were done when 'tis done," "Is this a dagger which I see before me," and "Tomorrow, Tomorrow, and Tomorrow." She sat in her favorite chair in the East Sitting Hall, sipping on a small glass of amoretto as she read these pieces. Her eyes moistened at Romeo's impassioned words of love and her senses were heightened by the contradictory feelings of admiration, contempt, and pity as Macbeth considers the reasons and consequences of assassinating his king. She took another sip of her cordial before turning the pages to the next of Macbeth's soliloquies. Cecilia warmed to Macbeth's imagination as he sees the dagger before him: "I have thee not, and yet I see thee still." She always prided herself on her ability to visualize most vividly the events and characters in the stories she read. Her early daydreams were also distinct and dramatic, and always delightful and adventuresome. That is, until they began to change when she was nearly nine and when they became overwhelmingly horrifying when she reached thirteen.

Periodically she had to remind herself, as Macbeth did in the soliloquy, that any terrifying imagining was "a false creating, / Proceeding from the heat-oppressèd brain." How often had she shared Macbeth's sense that "o'er the one half-world / Nature seems dead," as she fought her depression and fears, listening hungrily to the advice of friends and even casual acquaintances before giving her mind to a man she met while traveling through Europe, who seemed to comprehend her innermost thoughts and repeated to her that refusing to give in to her despair would be rewarded "by the gods." Cecilia found stimulating his poetic cadence and literary manner—evident in his often calling her "his lady" — as he claimed that with her beauty and depth of heart she would always be loved, occasionally teasing that accordingly she was destined to be wealthy. He told her that she could weave magical spells and that she was powerful enough in her charms to be the cause of war.

Memory of being able to weave magic was heightened by Macbeth's view that in that dead nature "Witchcraft celebrates / Pale Hecate's offering." Macbeth speaks of the wolf's howl in this exhilarating and frightening moment of the soliloquy: "this with his stealthy pace, with Tarquin's ravishing strides..." Cecilia stared at the words she had just read, unable to obey what her mind demanded she do. All of her fears flooded over her spirit. Only after several moments was she able to flip the pages to another section of the text. When she looked down to which other Shakespeare work she had turned, she released a plaintive gasp and let the volume fall to the floor.

### 

Watching the local news, Helene finished rubbing her hands and wrists with scented lotion, feeling serene after having just talked with the new man in her life. Yet at other times she found the budding relationship disconcerting as well as gratifying. Since she came to the White House, she had dated five men who worked for the government, falling hard for one she didn't date — a member of Stephen Erskine's Secret Service detail, a man who had no idea he had such a fan in Helene Eckermire. Paula Bradford-Adams set her up with three of these five men, all "one and dones." As for the other two, one had three dates with her, and one lasted a little over two months before they both accepted that their differences were irreconcilable. Therefore, her track record suggested that her new relationship, which had just passed the three-week mark was no guarantee of happiness, but what most troubled her was the commitment her heart had already made to her new beau. He certainly was handsome enough to make her feel insecure about keeping him, but at least he didn't work at the White House, where she would witness daily the attention other women would pay him.

She hadn't expected her phone to ring this late. Unfortunately, it wasn't her man, but she couldn't be sure it wasn't work related, so she answered. "Hello?"

"Helene, I hope I didn't wake you."

"Kyle?" What could Kyle Guidry want from her? "No, no. I'm just watching the news. Something wrong?"

It took several moments for him to answer. "I'd like to talk to you, if I can."

"That's what you're doing now, isn't it." Her voice failed to hide her aggravation.

"No, no. I mean in person. It's just too... Well, I'd rather talk to you face-to-face."

"About?"

"It's nothing bad. Just... I guess you'd say it's a bit awkward. That's why I want to see you. There's something I need to ask you, and I can't do that on the phone."

"Kyle, how much have you had to drink tonight?" She wanted to laugh at his cloak-and-dagger phrasing.

"Maybe not enough. It's been a tough day."

His witty reply relaxed her enough to be more responsive to his request. "We can meet in the White House Mess tomorrow morning if you like."

"No, not at the White House. The tables are too close to each other."

"Where then?"

"Can I come over now?"

"I'm in bed, Kyle." She winced, expecting him to answer with a bawdy or otherwise inappropriate remark.

"Sorry. First thing in the morning, then. Is that okay?"

"All right. Let's meet at Greenberry's. If it's too crowded, we can walk into Lafayette Square and you can ask me whatever it is you want to ask me." She had seen him once in Greenberry's Coffee Company a couple of blocks from the White House. "I have a meeting in the first lady's office at 8:15, so I can meet you around 7:30. All right?" Guidry took his time answering. "Kyle?"

"So you'll leave your place around...?"

"Around seven, I guess. Why do you want to know that?"

"Thanks, Helene. I'll see you in the morning. Bye."

###

It was her first time in the First Degree Burn in southwest Baltimore. The bar was opened by two former firemen from the city, who retired in their fifties and decided to live out a longstanding dream. Initially very popular, the business suffered as soon as these owners left owing to health problems, the bar being taken over by one of the owner's sons, who drank as much as his favorite customers and let the place deteriorate to the point that it was bought for a song by the new owner—a retired Air Force colonel. Improvements were being made, but the old crowd had not yet returned. The service was inconsistent at best and the drinks either anemic or muscular, depending on who was tending bar. But Martha Tillman was grateful to be anywhere with a man who showed interest in her. Now forty-four and twice divorced with what she termed acceptable though not attractive looks, she hadn't had a date for over three years and a satisfying sexual encounter for nearly twelve. She married first at nineteen, had two children in the next three years, and was divorced at age twenty-four. Six years later she wed again—to a man fifteen years her senior, who wanted her in spite of her ten- and eight-year-old daughters. Her second husband, whose hobbies included selling heroin and cocaine, was shot to death by a dissatisfied customer three years into the marriage. It was only after the funeral that her facial bruises were allowed to heal. She had been struck three or four times by her first husband, but she chalked that up to his immaturity. The more regular beatings from her drug-dealing second spouse she accepted as fit payment for her earlier sins.

Charlie Warren met her at work. He took his sweet time asking her out because, as he admitted, he was afraid she would think of him as too young to date. She laughed. "You're just six years younger than me, right? Remember Demi Moore and Ashton Kutcher? She was sixteen years older. Jennifer Lopez? Seventeen years. Mariah Carey? Thirteen years. Need I go on?"

Martha felt Charlie would be gentle and attentive, respecting her intelligence and decisions. He wasn't handsome by any stretch, but neither was she Demi Moore, Jennifer Lopez, or Mariah Carey. Charlie could use some training on the best places to meet a woman for a cocktail, but she felt he would quickly learn. Although at work he had shown an interest in her past, he never pushed to learn what she was unwilling to discuss. That was most important to her. As for her daughters, the elder--a graduate of Villanova--was now twenty-four and living in Philadelphia with her boyfriend. The younger was twenty-two and finishing her last semester at the University of Delaware. Neither of Martha's husbands had physically harmed the girls, but most of their years at home were miserable, prompting their desire to leave the Baltimore area as soon as possible. Fortunately, their drug-dealing step-father had left enough money at his death to pay for the girls' educations. Martha was looking to marry again, and although this was their first official date, she thought Charlie Warren would make a good husband. She'd be more than happy to shed the name Tillman and live the rest of her life as Martha Warren.

"I hope it was okay to meet here for our first date. Since this place is just six tenths of a mile from your house, I thought you would feel comfortable here. Did you like your fish and chips?"

She thought him charmingly naïve. "Yes, the food was good." She couldn't resist. "Have you been to the Owl's Bar or the Brewer's Art near 83—on North Charles and East Chase?" He shook his head no. "Next time we'll go to one of those places. My treat." At these Baltimore establishments she found the interiors, food, drinks, and ambiance much more satisfying. Across the street where Charlie had parked, were three empty lots, pock marked with holes in the concrete and loose chunks of cement. A rusty fence topped off by barbed wire stretched across the three lots. She hardly felt comfortable in this area, even if it was just about a half mile away from her house.

They conversed for another hour about their interests and previous work experience, until she asked that Charlie take her home. She thought it best not to invite him in for a night-cap this time. She sardonically evaluated her "good girl" decision as in part ludicrous— but then Charlie was such a gentleman he wouldn't ask to stay the night. She would make sure they had plans for a second date before they reached her house, so that he wouldn't feel rejected.

They walked across the darkened street to Charlie's SUV, which was parked along the rust fence, some twenty feet from the one working streetlight. As soon as he opened the door for her and headed around the front to the driver's side, a voice came from the door of the tavern. "Are you Charlie Warren?"

"Yes."

"There's a phone call for you. The guy says it's important."

"Oh, gee. I wonder who... Okay, okay. I'll be right there. Martha, you want to come back inside with me?"

"Sure." She walked only half-way with him before changing her mind. "No, I'll just wait in the car."

"Okay. Here are the keys. Start it up and turn up the heater so you're comfortable."

"Thanks, Charlie."

"I'll go see who the heck's calling me. Probably somebody at work." He was near the door of the bar when he realized that his interior light didn't come on when she opened the doors of the SUV. He stepped inside to take the call.

Martha started the engine and adjusted both the temperature and the rear-view mirror to check her lipstick, but there was hardly enough light from the lamppost to see her mouth. But she was able to see the man rise from the rear seat of the SUV. He wore a dark wool ski cap but his face was visible. His expression was cold; the gun he lifted over the rear seat was pointed right at her. Her mouth opened to scream, but it was too late. The sound of the shot was muffled by a silencer.

"Hello? Hello? Hello?"

"Did they hang up?"

"There was no on the line. Charlie looked at the bar counter and a basket of wings left by an exiting customer. Seven wings were left untouched. "Hey, can I have the rest those wings if you're going to throw them away? I can pay you for them if you want."

# CHAPTER 21

Carter Thompson arrived at the team meeting ten minutes early—at 6:50 a.m. Later this afternoon the team would make the five hour flight from Washington to Phoenix and begin on-site preparations for the bowl game on New Year's Day. Carter called to say goodbye to his mother, who would be flying out on the 31st for the game. His father promised to be at the airport to meet the team and then take an early evening flight on another airline so he could be there for the practices, to which interim coach Mike Cipriano invited him. But since Carter couldn't reach his father by phone, he was worried. Might the elder Thompson's recent displays of temper and illogical thinking have caused some kind of violent confrontation, which resulted in his arrest or worse—a hospital visit? Carter was tempted to call his mother back to ask specifically if his father contacted her during the night or early this morning. But Carter could tell by her voice that his father wasn't home and probably hadn't been all night. Painful recollection reminded Carter of the time his father left home for eight months when he fell under the spell of another woman. Jana Thompson forgave her husband then and for other flirtations he had with women, and Miles had seemingly remained faithful and attentive since Carter entered UNEV. If he was afflicted with CTE, as Carter feared, would a desire for another woman be part of the pattern?

Carter considered what he'd do if his father was a no-show when the team bus arrived at Dulles. Would he call the police? His mother?

The hospitals? Then another possibility shoved its way into his thoughts. Could his father have discovered what his son had done and was planning on doing? No, it was impossible. Carter had told no one else about it. Still, he felt his stomach tighten as he pondered what his father would do if he had indeed found out.

"Carter, let's go, buddy. Take your seat." Mike Cipriano was ready to start the meeting.

###

"What time is it, Andrea?"

"7:20." She had just come out of the bathroom wearing nothing but a red "Keep Calm and Carry On" tee shirt, complete with a British crown.

Wells sat up. "You know, you're sending a mixed message with that shirt. I can't *carry on* if I *keep calm*, you know."

"Then perhaps it should read *you* carry on while *I* keep calm."

"That's easier for you to say, lovey."

"Just kidding, my darling. Do you want to stay in bed another hour?"

"No. I need to get up and showered. I have an interview at CNN this morning at 9:00."

"Who with?"

"Stella Voorman."

"Stella the Storm Woman?"

"The one and only." Voorman had earned her nickname due to the decibels produced by her voice and torrential nature of her interviewing style. Wells added that she wished to speak with him about the fallout from his recent Senate Committee appearance and the general state of the VA.

"I can drive you if you don't mind going a few minutes early. I'm interviewing Senator Kalionis about his glory days with the Orioles."

"Ken Kalionis. Five years leading the American League in strikeouts until he took a line drive in the face. Poor guy. The left side of his face is still caved in a bit, but there probably isn't a more popular lawmaker on the Hill."

"Well, I'll be going to his office in the Russell Building, so we'll just be a short distance from each other. Maybe a late breakfast or early lunch at Lucky's Café?"

"Sounds like a plan." Andrea's cell phone interrupted their conversation.

"Hello?" Her expression brightened. Good morning, Henrik. Yes, he's here." She handed the phone to Wells, who said hello but then not much of anything else for close to a minute.

"Okay. Keep me posted. See you later. Right, right. I'll check our cars. Bye."

"What is it, Daniel?"

"Seems that Henrik decided to play guardian angel and drove by here last night. He saw someone on the steps looking at your front door. "Henrik pulled over and watched until the person turned and walked down the street, disappearing between other buildings and heading for Wesley Heights."

Andrea's voice quivered. "A man?"

"Henrik thought so, but the head and face were covered up by a hat and the collars of the person's long winter coat. Could have been a large woman, but more likely a man. Henrik parked nearby for half an hour to see if the person came back, but he apparently didn't."

For the first time, Andrea was visibly frightened by the events surrounding her and Daniel. "What does Henrik think I should do?"

"Stay with me, first of all. He suggested we go to my place tonight at least, and he'll ask someone at Metro to keep an eye out for anyone who seems out of place."

"But you live in a complex on an elevated floor."

"All the safer, then. Henrik will also try and get someone to watch your place to see if that person comes back tonight."

"We better check the bottom of our cars."

"That's what Henrik said. And we need to open the hood and trunk and look in there too. Don't worry too much, Andrea. It may have been someone searching for another apartment in the area. He's likely never coming back, since he didn't ring or knock on the door."

"Hope so."

Wells didn't reply, but he had little confidence the visit to Andrea's front door had no relation to all that had happened the past few days.

### 

Helene arrived at Greenberry's right on time. Guidry was waiting for her and had been there since 7:15. He rose to greet her and shook her hand. She found the gesture odd, since he had never offered to shake hands with her before. When they sat, Guidry took a sip of the coffee he had already ordered.

The server came to the table. "What can I get you to drink?"

"Coffee with cream would be fine." She took the menu and perused it while Guidry struggled to begin the conversation.

"Thanks for meeting me, Helene. I really appreciate it."

"Sure, Kyle. What's so important?" She knew she sounded off-putting, but her tone was cover for her fear he'd request something she wouldn't or couldn't do. When he called the previous evening, she thought he was going to ask her to spy on someone in the White House. But when she woke up this morning, her suspicion shifted to the possibility he was going to plead with her to be some kind of go-between between him and the first lady. The server returned with Helene's coffee and took their food order. Helene stifled a grin as Guidry looked to his left and right before commencing.

"Helene, I feel a little funny asking you this, but I was wondering if you could pave the way for me by asking the first lady if she'd like to have lunch with you, Paula, and me this coming week."

Helene was dumbstruck at his desire for lunch at the White House with her and Paula. She knew he long wanted to have lunch with the first lady, but why a foursome? "Why would you want to have lunch with us?"

"I wouldn't feel at all comfortable asking the first lady to have lunch with just me. And I'm sure you wouldn't agree to ask her in that case."

"Kyle, what do you hope to gain by your infatuation with her?

You're putting your job at risk—you know that, don't you?"

Guidry's features seemed menacing to Helene as he leaned across the table. "Quiet, will you? I don't have an infatuation for her, for Christ's sake."

Helene rolled her eyes before she replied. "Then what is it, Kyle? You only find her intellectually stimulating?"

Her dismissive tone proved too much for Guidry. "Be careful how you mock me, Helene—you and Paula both." He stood and reached for his wallet. As Helene had seen in so many movies, Guidry threw a twenty on the table before walking out.

### 

Wells enjoyed his interview with Stella Voorman of CNN. He reinforced the points he made before the Senate Veteran's Committee and was able to share a story he didn't get around to when he was in the Russell Building. He spoke of two close buddies, who served together in 23rd Infantry Regiment in the summer of 1952 during the Battle of Old Baldy in West-Central Korea. Their friendship grew when they were recovering from their wounds after taking mortar shrapnel fired by the Chinese during the battle. After being discharged, the men lived a mere six miles from each other in Akron and Cuyahoga, Ohio. Now at ages eighty-six and eighty-seven, the men had lost much of their mental sharpness. Each received calls from a reputable veterans outreach organization—or so each man thought. They had both reached the age where, having accumulated a healthy savings, the men decided they would donate ten thousand dollars each to the organization—having talked at length with representatives who called them asking for money. Volunteering to pick up the donations to prevent the money from being lost in the mail, the scammers arrived at both residences and spoke with considerable respect to each man, lauding their service in the Korean War. When personal information was gathered, along with the checks for ten thousand each, the two proud veterans met in Akron and celebrated their generosity. It was two months later that one of them read an article written by Daniel Wells regarding veteran scams. The men called Wells's office and learned that they had been swindled. Wells asked Stella Voorman to include his warning about phone scams when she aired her piece—a request she promised to honor.

As he waited for Andrea to conclude her interview, Wells checked to see if he had received any messages while his phone was turned off. There was just one. From Gina Lorenzetti. "Back at work. Please call me ASAP. Important call for you."

Wells dialed Gina's cell. She told him a man named Tyler Boselli called and wanted to talk with him. "He sounded very insistent."

"Did he leave a number?"

"No."

"Did she say what he did or why he wanted to talk to me?"

"Sorry."

"If he calls again, give him my cell number. Oh, check online to see if you come up with his name and hopefully a number."

"Already done. No luck. No one by that name in the area."

"Did you try alternate spellings of the last name."

"He spelled Boselli out for me—so..."

"Okay. So are you sure you're feeling up to being at work?"

"I'm fine—really I am. As I said, I didn't need to spend the night in the hospital. I'm just nervous about getting in my rental car and starting it up. Did you know that Mr. Nordenson called and reminded me to look under the rental?"

"That's my friend. He worries about all of us. But you better do as he says until all this is settled."

### 

"I'm fine, but can't say the same for my Passat."

"Did you call Daniel?"

"I tried, but the call went straight to voice mail."

Andrea again asked Nordenson what happened.

"I wasn't in the car when the bomb went off, thank goodness, but I wasn't that far away from it either. I don't know whether the bomber timed the explosion or triggered it by remote." Nordenson informed her that the blast was more destructive than the one that damaged Gina Lorenzetti's Corolla or the ones found under Andrea's vehicle and the first one discovered under his. "This one could have killed me, I'm afraid. But that's what I get for not following my own advice and checking before I drove it this morning."

"Henrik, I'm really getting frightened now. Who is doing this and why? Is he targeting Daniel's friends—just waiting until he attacks Daniel? And why would he do that?"

"It's still a puzzle, Andrea. But we're working on it from several angles—trust me."

Andrea didn't articulate the possibilities hammering into her mind. Were all these events—the murder of Hoyt Reilly, the large explosion killing Jack Ketchum, the murder of Darryl Roebuck, the intruder seeking Ketchum's information on Reilly, and the small bombs under her, Gina's and Henrik's cars—related? If so, what was the common denominator? How could it be Daniel?

After checking under her car and under the hood, Andrea drove to Lucky's Café. Upon entering, she noticed a table with a cup of coffee and Daniel's flannel-lined jacket on the back of one of the chairs. She assumed he was in the men's room until she heard his voice walking up behind her. He was on his cell.

# Chapter 22

Chas Overby came out of the International Spy Museum on 9th and F Streets NW—not far from Rasika, where he and Lisa Busby had lunch. Overby had never visited the museum, even though he was a fan of spy thrillers—on screen and in print—and a James Bond aficionado. Lisa told him that soon the museum would be moving some eight blocks south to L'Enfant Plaza—so he decided that if he wanted to tour the distinct old building with "SPY" on the corner juncture of the structure, he best go now, seeing that he might not make it back to D.C. before the museum moved to its more modern digs.

He enjoyed touring the exhibits of spy paraphernalia—some which he had seen in movies and television series. He laughed when he came upon the shoe with the heel transmitter and thought of Bond's in *Goldfinger* and Maxwell Smart's shoe phone in *Get Smart*. Overby also took delight in viewing a fountain pen, lipstick tube, and cigarette lighter cameras, as well as tobacco pipe and glove pistols and ring and flashlight guns. But what intrigued him most was the more sophisticated items allowing for hidden surveillance and recording. The subject never failed to intrigue him, and he often lamented turning down an overture from the CIA when he moved from North Carolina to Charlottesville to do his graduate work at UVA. His mood turned sour as he recalled how close he had come to dropping out of college after his experience playing football under Hoyt Reilly.

Reilly fully exploited the fact that Overby's attractive mother was divorced but also that she was sexually active, a contributing factor to the break-up of her marriage. Chas never told Daniel Wells, but Tessa Overby was even more interested in Wells than she let on during her flirtatious and, to her son, embarrassing interactions with the star athlete when the boys were in high school. Overby never understood why his mother frequently inquired about his friend Daniel—what he liked to eat and listen to and what kind of girls interested him. "Does he have a steady girlfriend," she asked on several occasions. When Overby brought home his friend home for the weekend after they graduated, the boys sat poolside when Chas's mother, in a flattering two-piece bathing suit, snuck Wells a gin and tonic and rubbed the young man's arm as she spoke with him. Feeling humiliated, Overby jumped into the pool's deep end, never wanting to come up again. When he did, he saw his mother kiss Wells on the cheek, but close to the lips, while Wells showed no embarrassment over the kiss, or so it appeared to Overby, who had never totally forgiven his friend for what he considered a demonstration of disloyalty.

Somehow Hoyt Reilly learned about the history of Tessa's sexual looseness soon after meeting her before Chas's freshman season in college ended. She drove to campus to spend a surprise weekend with her son—her only child—and while eating at a local restaurant, they ran into Coach Reilly, who was on his way out. After addressing Overby as "Overton," Reilly offered a perfunctory, "We're glad to have him on the team," and spent half a minute staring into the eyes of Chas's mother. Distressed by the attention his coach was paying to his mother, Chas was unprepared for Reilly's next remark. "Are you going to be here tomorrow?" The question was not addressed to him.

"Yes, I'll be driving back home on Sunday."

"Mom?" Overby was stunned that her answer had not even a hint of shyness or hesitation in it.

Reilly pushed forward. "I'd love to show you around the campus tomorrow afternoon."

Tessa looked at him briefly as though she were considering the nature of the offer. "I'd love that. Chas has a movie date tomorrow early afternoon that I don't want to interfere with."

In truth, he did, but had told his mother he would call his date that night and reschedule since his mom was in town. Chas was still too shocked to argue with her and so remained silent while she gave Reilly the name of her hotel.

"I'll be in the lobby at what time?" she inquired of Reilly.

"Wonderful, I'll pick you up at two. So nice meeting you,...?"

She offered a broad smile. "Tessa." Chas had simply introduced her as "my mother."

The next afternoon, as soon as he returned from the matinee, he called his mother's hotel room. No answer. He tried again at 5:00 p.m. and every fifteen minutes after that until she answered at 7:15. The sound of her voice informed him that something had happened between her and Coach Reilly. He just couldn't tell what.

"Mom, we were supposed to have dinner across town at 6:30."

"I know, baby. I'm sorry. I'll take a quick shower and meet you downstairs at eight."

### 

"You seem concerned. Who called?"

Wells pulled out the chair for Andrea, who sat without taking her eyes off him. "It was someone who worked in the athletic department where Hoyt Reilly coached before coming to UNEV. Her name is Carolyn Yarrow and she's just retired as of August first."

Andrea was puzzled by Wells's inability to explain the reasons for the woman's call. "So what did she call about?"

"I'm sorry. You know me. I'm just processing."

Andrea surely did. She'd invariably tease him whenever he broke off in mid-sentence or didn't pick up the first part of her conversation. Occasionally, he would hesitate to sit, while pondering what he'd just heard or was focused on—as he was doing at this moment.

"Come on, my darling. Sit and tell me all about it."

Wells laughed and sat, but before he could begin, the server came to take their order. Finally, he was able to commence. He looked across the table at Andrea, who sat with both her hands, in modified fists, curled under her chin, as if she were the most patient woman in the world. It was no wonder she was such a successful interviewer of athletes and other sports personalities.

"Carolyn Yarrow wants to talk to me about why Reilly was let go. She wanted to wait until she was retired because the athletic department insisted on "less said about him the better."

"Have you set up a meeting?"

"Yes. She's in Washington with her husband and asked to meet today around four at the hotel lounge. Her husband will be at a business meeting in town, so she'll be alone."

"Can I trust you to be faithful to me?"

Andrea's grin didn't soften the effect of her question on Daniel Wells. His expression dropped. He couldn't help it. The question was exactly the one he had asked fifteen years earlier.

### ###

The president kissed his wife on the cheek before he started down the stairs for a Rose Garden speech and photo op with a combined Girl and Boy Scout gathering of 120 eleven to eighteen year-olds. After watching him reach the bottom of the stairs and head toward the West Wing, Cecilia headed for her East Wing office. It was the couple's habit. Except for larger events, which required them to descend together, or coming off Air Force One, Cecilia Erskine preferred to come down all stairs by herself. It was to others a quirky habit, although some thought it was even a superstition of hers. But only one person knew that at Christmas time, when she was twelve, she had bolted up the stairs when her step-bother Hoyt, then in college, told a crude joke about one of his university's cheerleaders, as his father and step-mother were heading out the door for some last minute Christmas shopping. Reilly's football team had ended its season with a losing record—and therefore had no bowl game to prepare for. Cecilia's mother found nothing amusing about the young man's joke, while his father laughed boisterously. Also in the room was Reilly's eighteen year-old sister, also back home during her college's holiday break. She too found amusing her brother's joke about the reason why the cheerleader was quite adept at full splits. Cecilia told the both of them they were "disgusting" and fled up the stairs to her bedroom. Shorty afterward, there was a knock on her door.

"What?" She assumed her step-brother was going to torment her with another example of his disgusting sense of humor.

"Let me in, Cecilia. I want to apologize. I shouldn't have told that joke in front of you. I'm sorry—really I am."

"Sure you are." At this point she could barely tolerate Hoyt's presence, made unpalatable during the years they had lived under the same roof. But he had gone off to the university three years earlier and she was left to deal with her step-sister's praise of Hoyt, which Cecilia believed was deliberate harassment of her.

"No, really. Besides, I brought you back a *Delta Gamma* sweatshirt. I know you wanted one."

Cecilia was projecting herself six years in the future when she would pledge the sorority. She was a big fan of *Delta Gamma* Julia Louis-Dreyfus, then starring in *Seinfeld*. "What color is it?" Perhaps her step-brother didn't know the Greek letters and had brought her a *Chi Omega* or *Sigma Kappa* sweatshirt instead.

"It's pink." He tried the door, but it was still locked.

"And what's on the front? Describe the letters to me."

"All right. It has two letters. The first is a triangle and the second is like a weird R. It almost looks like a faucet. Both letters are outlined in blue."

The door opened. Cecilia's eyes widened at her apparent gift. Hoyt handed her the sweatshirt.

"See, it goes with that cup and the pennant you have over your bed."

She was too enamored of the gift to be cautious. "Thank you, Hoyt."

"You're welcome. I see you've changed your room since I was here last."

She nodded and kept staring at the sweatshirt. "Why don't you put it on? I'm sure it's the right size, but let's check to be sure."

Without responding, she obeyed his request. As she put her head through the sweatshirt and raised her arms to slide the sleeves through, she had inadvertently lifted out of her sweatpants the shirt she was wearing. While her hands and head were in their vulnerable positions, her step-brother pushed her back on the bed. His hands felt for her breasts, which were in the budding stage. Reilly swept his hands from them and turned his right hand over while his left pulled down her sweatpants and panties. Before she could cry out, he licked his right index finger and inserted it partially into her vagina. She screamed for her step-sister, but she remained downstairs.

Hoyt returned to his feet. "Put on the sweatshirt and let's go downstairs and show your sister." He jerked Cecilia up and pulled up her panties and sweatpants and the new sweatshirt down. He half carried her to the doorway and whispered, "Walk down with me and act like you're thrilled by your gift. Say nothing about what happened or I promise I won't stop with my finger the next time."

Terrified, she came down the stairs with Hoyt's arm around her shoulders. She saw her step-sister half reclined on the sofa reading a copy of *People*. Cecilia would never forget the look on the eighteen year-old's face. Her features suggested that she was fully aware of what her brother had done and would take his side if he was ever accused of sexually assaulting his step-sister.

###

"No, we're getting ready to pay now. I'm going to my office. Andrea's dropping me off. Okay, I'll see you there. Bye."

"Your friend Chas?"

"No. It was Henrik. He has some 'news' he wants to share with me right away."

"A suspect in all this mayhem?"

"Hope so. You have time to drop me off at the office?"

"Yes. But we better go. I have to get back to my place and call Denver by 1:30 their time."

"11:30 here. Yes, let's move."

They reached Andrea's car ten minutes later. Wells checked the under carriage and had Andrea pop the hood and trunk.

"Looks clear. He opened the door and kissed her as she slid into the driver's seat. As he moved around the back to enter on the passenger side, he saw a yellow post-it note attached to door right below the handle. It contained but one word. "Boom!"

# CHAPTER 23

"Paula, come on. Let's get some lunch."

Paula Bradford-Adams looked at her watch. "It will have to be quick, Helene. The first lady wants to go over some Icelandic history and geography in preparation for the Icelandic first lady's visit next week."

"Is she enthusiastic this time?"

"Shhh. Do you want to get us both fired?"

The women suppressed laughter, each recalling Cecilia Erskine's reaction when she and the president met all the Scandinavian First Ladies and Queens, during which Cecilia struck up a friendship with the Icelandic and Finnish First Ladies but remained somewhat cool to one Crown Princess in particular—the reason for which the press didn't know.

"So where do you want to go that's close by?"

"We can try the Hamilton."

"At this time of day? Should be slammed by now."

"Let me make a quick call and see what I can do."

Helene grinned mischievously. "So you've slept with the head chef?"

"He's way too busy for that. I'm friends with one of the managers. *She* and I go way back to our freshman year at Cornell."

"I'll get my coat." As soon as Helene left her office, Paula called the Hamilton and was assured she and Helene could be squeezed in. She gathered her coat and recalled the number of times she helped the first lady on with hers. Cecilia Erskine was the kind of woman both men and women strove to assist in whatever way they could. But Paula knew that no other person—man or woman—was ever entrusted with the secret Cecilia bestowed on her. And Paula was sure the first lady was confident she could trust her favorite staff person to keep that secret forever. After all, Paula cared deeply about her and loved the woman enough never to betray her. Besides, there were other issues to consider—primarily, the effect on so many should she reveal what she knew, let alone the effect on the history of her country.

###

"Before you tell me anything, look at this." Wells handed Nordenson the yellow post-it note stuck on the passenger-side door of Andrea's car. Wells retrieved two bottles of Diet Coke, Nordenson's preferred beverage when he was on duty.

"Jesus. Did Andrea see this?"

"No, I didn't think she'd appreciate it."

Nordenson took a long swallow of his soft drink. "You notice that each letter is slightly different and in different ink, don't you?"

"Sorry, I only paid attention to the message."

Nordenson explained that whoever wrote "Boom!" used a different pen for the four letters and the exclamation mark and that each letter was written differently. Wells examined the post-it and saw that indeed the width of the pen points was different and that there was a combination of black and dark blue colors. He also detected that each letter slanted differently—with a mix of block printing and cursive.

"Do you think more than one person wrote it, Henrik?"

"No. I think it was written by one person."

"Then why all the differences with each letter?"

"Good question." Nordenson laughed. "Appears to be the work of a naïve teenage boy."

"But you don't think it is, do you?"

"Not with everything that's happened—no. If you don't mind, I'll take this and have our handwriting expert look at it and see what she thinks. Just continue to be vigilant when you or Andrea get into your cars."

"Don't worry."

"I lost my Passat because I was careless, you know."

"Just thank god you weren't driving it when the bomb went off."

"I'm just wondering if the bomber knew I wasn't in the car when he set it off. I'd like to think he did."

"I hope you're right about that."

"But let's not take any chances. Check your cars."

"We will. Now what's the news you have for me?"

"Have you ever heard of a Martha Tillman?"

Wells thought for a moment. "No, don't think so."

"She was shot to death at close range last night in Baltimore."

Wells was perplexed by Henrik's desire to share the news.

"All right, so...?"

Nordenson took another swallow of Diet Coke. "She was Hoyt Reilly's sister."

### 

Miles Thompson reached his son's cell phone and informed him he would be in Arizona "just as soon as I finish some business I have here."

Concerned, Carter asked if his father had called home. When Miles said he hadn't, his son implored him to make the call. "Mom's gotten in touch with me four times wondering if I've heard from you today. She said you never came home last night. We're worried about you, dad."

"I'll call her now." Miles did as he promised and listened impatiently, after his wife expressed considerable relief, to her anger and frustration at his increasingly uncharacteristic and disturbing behavior over the past several months.

"Just tell me where you were last night?"

"I went out of town."

"Where?"

"It doesn't matter where."

"Are you seeing someone—another woman? Don't lie to me, Miles."

"You mean, am I seeing someone of my own race?"

"No, I don't mean that. What a strange thing to say to me. When have I ever even hinted at such a thing?" Jana heard no reply before he hung up on her.

Thompson parked his car at a chain sports bar in Columbia, Maryland. He had been to another one of these establishments in Sterling, Virginia and enjoyed the fish and chips and a special cocktail, which included Irish whiskey and Finland Vodka. As it stood, he planned to have the beer-battered fish and chips and several of these cocktails before deciding what to do with his evening. He took the stool at the end of the bar, ordered, and began watching ESPN on one of the screens above the bar.

Thompson was half way through his first drink when he stopped watching and attempted the kind of self-analysis he resisted for months. It was more than merely allowing so many thoughts to annoy him. It was rather that he took almost everything as a personal insult. His wife and son couldn't question his actions or decisions without being accused of disloyalty or disobedience. Any reference to the success of other linebackers during his era caused him to be defensive and vigorously argumentative. The same held true when others compared his son to the current crop of college quarterbacks. Miles came dangerously close to punching a bartender who in fact praised Carter's skills and said he would go no later than early in the third round of the NFL Draft. Miles took the estimation of his son's draft position as a deliberate insult, justifying the near coming to blows by arguing that if the man respected him he would have predicted Carter would go in the first or early second round. And Miles had come to loath Daniel Wells not merely because many "old-timers" felt Wells was the best quarterback in UNEV's history but also because so many praised Wells's heroism and commitment to wounded veterans. To Miles's mind, these men were disrespecting him and his son, both of whom never spent or would ever spend a day in military uniform. It didn't matter to Miles when his wife and son reminded him that he made a career in the NFL, whereas Wells was cut in training camp and never played in a regular season NFL game.

By the time Thompson finished his meal and ordered his third cocktail, he was wrestling with the possibility that his increasingly uncontrollable temper, suspicious mindset, an hypersensitivity to insults real and imagined could be the result of the many blows he took to the head—several significant concussions and the innumerable collisions with other players' helmets—which may have taken their toll on his health. CTE. Something he never heard of or imagined when he played, when concussions and the lesser blows to the head were dismissed as "getting your bell rung." He recalled the battles he had with a powerful blocking fullback of a divisional rival, who collided violently with middle-linebacker Miles Thompson two games a season. Thompson didn't learn until this past summer that his adversary had died at age forty-six. When his brain was studied it was clear the man had a severe case of CTE, which surely contributed to, if not caused, his early death.

The effects of the alcohol eventually drove the fear of having CTE out of his mind, which was replaced by gloomy and anger-filled thoughts of Hoyt Reilly. He was dead, but Thompson felt that death was an inadequate punishment for what the man said about young Carter and his mother, let alone the way he treated, ridiculed, and humiliated so many other black players he coached. Surely there was more Thompson could do to satisfy his revenge and sense of justice.

After finishing his third and convincing the bartender he could handle a fourth cocktail, Thompson once more turned his attention to ESPN, then in the middle of a feature on UNEV and its big bowl game. Carter's face appeared on screen for a moment and was then replaced by that of Daniel Wells from his playing days, followed by another in his military uniform with his medal for heroism displayed. Thompson couldn't hear what the reporter was saying about Wells, but then he didn't have to. ESPN was disrespecting his son and by extension him. After the bartender placed the fourth cocktail before him and suggested tactfully that he would be happy to call a cab or an Uber if needed, Thomson waved him off and brought the cocktail to his mouth. "That mother-fucking Wells."

### 

Helene sighed upon viewing the clock in her office. It was 3:45, not 5:30 as she had hoped. Just one of those days where time crawled—stopped—and then crawled again. Her feet were sore and her calves ached from the walking she had done during the day. A hand-delivered birthday card from the first lady to Senator Jillian O'Connell, who was not in her Hart Senate Office Building but instead at the Capitol forced Helene to cross a busy Constitution Avenue, walk down First, and then bound up the steps on the east side of the Capitol. It was halfway up the steps that she felt a twinge in both calves. She also made two full tours of the White House from East Wing to West, upstairs and down. Paperwork, phone calls, and a short lunch with Paula led her to bemoan the sluggish time. She had just left selected pieces of correspondence on the first lady's desk and was debating a coffee break when Kyle Guidry stuck his head in to say hello. She easily determined he was still embarrassed over their morning meeting and his request that she and Paula set up a lunch with Cecilia Erskine. Helene thought it wise to say nothing about it to him, although she had mentioned his request to three others. Guidry asked how her day had been so far.

"Busy, Kyle. Very, very busy. She felt for her shoes with her feet and managed to slip her foot into one of them.

"You getting off early?"

"5:30." She winced. What if Guidry wanted have a drink with her so he could talk about the first lady? "I have to meet my boyfriend for an early dinner as soon as I leave here." She feared Guidry would ask to join them.

"Well, have a nice dinner. See you tomorrow."

Good, she thought. Guidry didn't ask where she and her man were going to eat, which would have forced her to lie further. She in fact had no date for tonight.

As she shifted some papers from one side of her desk to the other, she came upon one of the pieces of correspondence she wanted the first lady to read. Putting on her other shoe, Helene walked to the first lady's East Wing office and made her way to the side table where she always placed these bits of correspondence. Her eye caught a display of color on Cecilia Erskine's desk. A dozen Kaleidoscope Roses—each one carefully and impressively dyed red, blue, lavender, yellow, and green—placed in an attractive lavender vase. Helene checked to be sure no one was near the office door. She made her way to the bouquet and saw an unsealed card in its envelope. She pulled the card out enough to notice the message. "A belated Christmas offering. Your devoted, Kyle."

### 

The long five and a half hour flight to Phoenix was over—a little less than an hour of flight time left. Carter Thompson took off his headphones and stared out the window of the charter jet, after being told by the captain that the temperature in Phoenix was a warm seventy-five degrees. The game would begin with the temperature still in the seventies, which alleviated any concern that it would be unseasonably cold. Carter had played three games this season with the weather below fifty degrees and never felt he had a comfortable grip on the ball, which was evident in several of his anemic throws downfield. But one problem remained. He debated whether to call Daniel Wells again after he landed or to simply forget about calling him at all. Perhaps his father's disdain for the former UNEV quarterback wouldn't lead to any harassing calls or visits to Wells's office or residence. If he called Wells about his father and nothing occurred, then he'd feel utterly foolish. But worse, he'd felt as though he betrayed the man who was always there for him, a man who truly loved his son. Carter settled back into his seat feeling gratified that Wells wasn't in his office when he called earlier under the name Boselli.

# Chapter 24

Wells entered the Hay-Adams Hotel across from Lafayette Square and near the White House at 3:55 p.m. He made his way downstairs to the Off the Record Bar and noticed a woman sitting alone in the red plush seating under the caricature wall in this attractive and timeless establishment. As he approached, the woman nibbled on some wasabi peas with a glass resting before her of what Wells recognized as the bar's Fill A Buster—which included Hendrick's Gin and champagne—a favorite cocktail of Andrea's. She stood as soon as he reached the table and extended her hand.

'You're Daniel Wells. I recognized you from television. He assumed she watched a snippet from his committee testimony four weeks earlier. "I'm Carolyn Yarrow." He thought both her appearance and manner belied her age—later fifties to early sixties, he guessed. "Let me buy you a drink, Mr. Wells."

"Please call me Daniel. And I should pay for the drinks, seeing that you might provide me with information."

She smiled. "But the drinks aren't cheap."

"No, but they don't hit their customers with a cover charge—and they should, seeing how delightful it is down here."

"My husband and I come here whenever we're in Washington—which lately has been five or six times a year."

The server arrived at the table, and Wells ordered a Tito's Agave Mule. He could tell Yarrow was hesitant to get to the point of their meeting. When she looked to the ceiling as if to make an observation,

Wells jumped in, "So you have some stories about Coach Reilly you might like to share. I'd be most anxious to hear them."

She nodded and sighed. "I'd been working in the athletic department office for seven years when they hired him. The day we met, he tried to exude charm but I could tell he was insincere. And that's the way he was with others in the office—even the athletic director himself. I gave him little thought for part of his first season, but in late October the assistant women's volleyball coach came in to talk with the A.D. about something Coach Reilly had apparently done. She came out of the office quite upset and really angry. I don't know why but I followed her out and asked what happened. She told me that Coach Reilly—listen to me, I still call him Coach. Too many years at that job, I'm afraid."

"More than understandable, Carolyn." Wells believed see she was comfortable in his presence and no longer hesitant to speak about Reilly. "So what did the volleyball coach tell you?"

"Well, she told me that one of her girls claimed Reilly watched the end of practice one afternoon and then came up to her and praised her playing. The girl said she was surprised yet flattered that one of the football coaches would take the time to compliment her play. But Reilly didn't let it go at that. He came by the next day and handed a sealed note to one of the other girls and asked her to give it to Hanna—I think her name was. As soon as she read it, Hanna gave it to her male head coach, who sat on it until the female assistant coach questioned him about the note. He was troubled, he said, but wasn't sure what he should do with it. The female coach shamed him enough so that he handed over the note and encouraged her to take action if she felt it was warranted."

"Did you see what was in the note?"

"Yes, the assistant volleyball coach showed it to me. Reilly said he wanted to talk to her about helping out with the football team during the upcoming spring practice. He offered to meet her at a tavern about a mile and half from campus and talk about it."

"Excuse me for interrupting, but was she twenty-one?"

"Yes. She was a junior and just twenty-one. I'm sure Reilly knew her age before he asked."

"I can see why the assistant coach wanted to turn him in."

"But that's not the half of it. Reilly also praised Hanna's looks by calling her one of the most beautiful athletes he had ever seen and remarked specifically about her long and curly sandy-blond hair, which he had viewed in 'all its glory'—his phrase after seeing it at the end of practice when she took it out of a pony tail. He signed the note 'Yours, Coach Reilly.' Anyway, when the assistant coach came into our office with the note, the AD didn't want to see it and handed responsibility to the assistant AD—a woman, who had zero tolerance for this kind of thing. She had apparently received at least six other written complaints about Reilly, which I soon learned came from two female members of the football support staff, three recently graduated football recruit hostesses, and the wife of our then golf coach, if you can believe that. As you might imagine, everything snowballed until Reilly was asked to leave. Fortunately for him, the powers that be kept everything quiet by paying off some of the women and threatening us with firing if we talked publicly about what we learned. 'We must protect the university and its reputation' became the mantra of the day. It's bothered me all this time that I was just too intimidated to say anything."

"You shouldn't beat yourself up over that, Carolyn. You had your career and retirement to consider."

"I know. But now you understand why I wanted to see you. I heard you were no fan of Reilly's and that you resented your old coach's getting pushed out in order to hire someone with such a checkered past." She hesitated.

"Is there something else, Carolyn?"

"Coach Ketchum called me two weeks ago and asked if I'd tell him what I just told you. I said I would think about it—and I was thinking about it when I learned that he was killed. You see, he asked me to contact you if anything happened to him. It sounded to me as though he *expected* that something would."

### ###

The first lady gently rocked in a cushioned white wicker chair out on the Truman Balcony just off the second floor Yellow Oval Room. It was almost five o'clock and the sun was setting to her right, its dying light bleeding onto the balcony. She wore a heavy pullover sweater to ward off the effects of the forty-three degree temperature. Her hands were under the sweater, which she pulled out only to take a sip of the hot tea recently brought out to her. She felt alone, even though there were several sets of eyes watching her every move. She faced the South Lawn with the Washington Monument in the near distance, but her eyes were closed. Yet her mind was open to vivid memory of other monuments she observed in another country.

Six years earlier, Cecilia and Stephen Erskine took separate vacations—he to Tokyo and his wife to London. Then formulating a possible run at the presidency, Erskine was determined to avoid having his marriage dissolve at such an important juncture in his career. He and Cecilia had been married a mere five years, but the relationship was already stale and passionless. Erskine reconciled himself to the fact that whereas his marriage was imperfect, his beautiful spouse could do much for his political future and, if all turned out well, she would revel in being America's first lady. For her part, she was resigned to remaining with her husband but only if he permitted her freedoms other political wives wouldn't require. Besides that, she suffered from considerable guilt over having caused so many others pain through her rejections. She also felt undeserving of the good things that came her way and saw no other man she could remain with who could provide her with what Erskine was capable of. She would not add to her guilt by damaging his political prospects. Yet she gave no thought to becoming first lady, and when the reality presented itself during the campaign, she felt more dread than excitement over the prospect.

She had just turned thirty when she flew to London and checked into the delightful Draycott Hotel in Chelsea, close to where an old college friend had a small apartment. Nora Hampson had married a Brit and moved to London, falling in love with the city and deciding to remain—even after her divorce decree six months earlier. Nora took Cecilia to several restaurants and pubs in nearby Sloane Square—including The Botanist, Royal Court Bar, and *Côte Brasserie*. It was at The Botanist that Nora introduced Cecilia to Paul Samuels, a handsome young physician who was best mates with Nora's brand-new boyfriend Robbie Chilvers, an assistant hospital administrator. It soon became obvious to Nora that both Paul and Robbie were enamored of Cecilia, who did nothing to encourage or discourage their attentions. Her modesty and slight aloofness made her even more attractive, Nora reasoned. And her ring-less left hand gave the men the false impression that she wasn't married or engaged. Before the meal, Samuels sprung for the first bottle of champagne—a Louis Roederer, Brut Premier—followed by Chilvers's choice of a Laurent-Perrier, Ultra Brut. Each diner thought the champagne went with their fish and beef entrees and sticky toffee pudding with black treacle ice cream dessert.

After dinner, the foursome walked to the nearby Royal Court Theatre to see the latest offering by the English playwright Simon Stephens, which appealed most to Cecilia, who found the ambiguity and depth of the play especially intriguing. The combination of sensitivity, black humor, bleakness, and terror touched her the way it did not her theatre companions. Throughout the play, Samuels looked at her every thirty seconds it seemed, at times staring down to her lovely legs, which were enhanced by her shortish skirt. Nora sat on the other side of Cecilia, thereby denying her date Chilvers the same opportunity to ogle her American friend.

The group had one more drink before they parted, but the glances given to her by both men suggested to Cecilia that she would hear from them again—and likely soon. Nora took the rudeness of her date in stride, teasing Cecilia about the not-so-subtle "courting" techniques of British men.

Robby Chilvers rang her up first—calling the Draycott at the exact moment Cecilia was at the desk speaking with a member of the staff. He wanted to have lunch.

"Are you sure Nora won't be angry—because you know I'll tell her." Cecilia's voice suggested she was at least amused by the offer.

"I like Nora, but we're not—"

"Intimate or serious, right?"

"Uh. No, no. That's right, no."

Cecilia had always enjoyed the power she developed in her twenties over well-meaning though somewhat skittish men, especially if they were older. "Where and when would you like to meet for lunch?"

Again caught off guard, Childers stuttered his reply and suggested the historic Cheshire Cheese on Fleet Street, to which Cecilia said she wanted to go before she left London. The date was made for the following day—with Cecilia insisting they meet there rather than have Childers pick her up at the Draycott. When the Black Cab let her out, he was waiting at the entrance. She took pleasure being served in the windowless "Cellar Room"—which made her feel more secure than vulnerable. She encouraged Childers to tell her about the pub's history, which included its construction in 1667 following the great London fire of the previous year and its literary associations. Famous writers who dined and drank at Ye Olde Cheshire Cheese included most notably Dickens, Tennyson, Conan Doyle, Twain, Wodehouse, and most likely Samuel Johnson, whose house was close by. But following his discussion of these and other matters relating to the pub and the general area, Childers put aside his fork while Cecilia continued to eat her fish and chips with mushy peas and lemon and made it clear that he found her "the most beautiful lady" he had ever "had the distinct pleasure to have known" and that he wanted to spend all the time he could with her, even suggesting that he could accompany her to the continent when she left in a few days.

Cecilia found his attention and general manner much to her liking and she agreed to have dinner alone with him the following night. He bowed his head as if he had a received a gift from royalty and looked at her with moistened eyes. The following night after an impressive meal at Min Jiang on the tenth floor of the Royal Garden Hotel in Kensington, she agreed to go to Childers's apartment for a night-cap. After that, the next drink they shared was coffee the following morning—still in his apartment. For Cecilia the sex was a release of frustration and a gesture of self-assertiveness. But it was also a form of revenge against her politician husband, whose interest in her, she believed, was just that—political.

Paul Samuels also called and asked her to join him for dinner, but she put him off with a hardly satisfying "I'm going to be just too busy for the next few days before I leave. Perhaps when I return to London." Even though she assumed Samuels would soon learn from his mate Robbie that she found the time to spend the night with Childers, she refused to dwell on any consequences, including the likelihood of losing Nora as a friend. Being in London, Cecilia saw no reason to worry about her husband's being informed of his wife's infidelity.

When she arrived in Brussels, she headed to the Airport Sheraton a short distance away, checked her luggage, and made her way to the hotel's Club Lounge to await the arrival of another hotel guest, whose flight from the east arrived just minutes after hers. She hadn't seen him in over seven years, having met him when she first travelled to Europe after graduation from UNEV, but time had only added to his handsome appearance. The moment she kissed him, she knew he still adored her. Because they could not postpone reveling in each other's embraces, they decided to spend their first night together at the airport hotel. This night she received her lover warmly yet passively, allowing him to adore her fully.

They spent most of the following morning reminiscing about their initial meeting seven years earlier, and after checking out of the Sheraton, they rented a car and headed to the city for lunch at *Le Volle Gas* and site-seeing before checking into *Le Chatelain* and having dinner at the hotel's restaurant. The following day they repeated the pattern of the day before, and after dinner at *Fin de siècle* on the *Rue des Chartreux*, they walked to their rental car just as two young men were attempting to break into it. The men apparently wished to steal Cecilia's late afternoon purchases, which she had in bags on the floor behind the front passenger seat. By the time she yelled "Stop!" her lover was racing toward the thieves. He grabbed one of them in a headlock and wrestled him to the ground. Instead of running, the other young man brought the iron rod used to break the rental car's window down on back of the intruder's neck, catching part of his head and knocking him unconscious. Both thieves ran off, leaving Cecilia's purchases untouched.

Cecilia spent the night at her lover's bedside at one of the city's public hospitals, Earlier, when he came around, he was disorientated to the point he couldn't recall what had happened and asked how Cecilia learned he was in the hospital—which he believed was in another country, not in Belgium. The next day, she sat with him until his head cleared enough to comprehend all that occurred. The day after that he was released, sporting a wide bandage on the back of his head to cover the stitches. It was just enough of a glancing blow, the doctor informed Cecilia, that the damage would not be serious. Otherwise, he added, the result might have been fatal. They parted at the airport, vowing to be together again soon.

Her memories of these events were interrupted by a gentle cough. "You want to see me, Álvaro?" Cecilia offered a weary smile upon the appearance of the press secretary.

"Yes. I just received word that..."

"Of what?" She stood assuming the news wasn't good.

"Your step-sister was murdered in Baltimore."

# Chapter 25

Andrea opened Wells's door with her key and heard him in heated discussion. "I *have* given the committee and Congress credit for what they *have* done, but I can't ignore what they *haven't* done but by now *should* have done." Andrea put down her bag and walked into the kitchen as Wells continued to make his points about the suicide rates for returning soldiers being over twenty percent higher than for other civilians and the higher unemployment rates for veterans being around twice the average of others. Wells also listed to the caller the appalling backlog of claims at the VA, the high homeless rates of veterans, and the fact that one out of three Iraq and Afghanistan vets suffer from PTSD, some form of traumatic brain injury, or a combination of both. "You know damn well that they're still not receiving adequate medical or psychological evaluations or assistance. So you'll have to excuse me for not being more supportive of the committee's efforts."

By the time Wells ended the call, Andrea pushed a glass of Scotch into his hand. "Who was it this time?"

"One of Chuck Lamont's henchmen."

"Dylan Nieporte?"

"No, Nieporte's recent hire, Bill Lingenfelter. I'm sure Nieporte wrote out every word he said to me, though." Wells took a sip of his drink. "So how was your afternoon?"

"Good. The magazine wants me to go a day earlier to Arizona, so we can print my interview with Carter Thompson before the game. But I'm happy about it."

"Because you'll spend one less day in my company?"

"Well, that plus the fact that it lessens the chance of Thompson's talking openly about Hoyt Reilly. He'll be encouraged to keep the focus on the game. I've already received a long email from UNEV's athletic director about it. In his best patronizing manner, he advises that I not risk my standing in the profession by asking any thing about Reilly before a 'great moment' for the school and its football team. He ended with 'You don't want your magazine to regret giving the interview to someone of your... to you, do you?'"

Wells nearly spit out his Scotch. "And what did you say to that?"

Andrea took a sip of Wells's drink. "I said, 'Not any more than you want to regret hiring someone—namely Coach Reilly—who brought shame to your sex, sir.'"

"That's my Andrea. Did you talk to the magazine about doing a two-part interview with Thompson—the first pre-game about the team and what the bowl appearance means to the program and the second coming out the following week about Carter's relationship with Reilly, and what you've recently learned and still may learn about him?"

"Now you're thinking like a female sports writer, Daniel. That's my plan—exactly."

"Well, my beautiful sports scribe, I may be able to provide you with some really good stuff for that second piece."

"What do you mean?"

"Just like you, I received an email this afternoon."

"Oh, from whom?"

"Carter Thompson's father Miles. Seems he wants to see me tonight at 10:30 up in Petworth at the Red Derby. After dinner, I'll take you back to your place—then I'll go up and come back when I'm through talking with him."

"What does he want to talk to you about?"

"What else could it be but Reilly? He knows I'm a booster and former player at UNEV. He might want to talk first about his son's NFL chances, but I'm sure the discussion will eventually get around to his son's former coach. I'll make sure it does at any rate."

"Any chance I can go too?"

### 

"Thanks for understanding, Helene. I was going to wait till tomorrow afternoon, but I want to surprise them by coming up right away—so I'm driving up tonight. I'll stay maybe two days. Hmm? Probably around eight to eight thirty. But as soon as I get back, I'll treat you to a lunch at the Willard. How's that? Good. Okay, must go and finish a little work and get packed. I need to leave in an hour. Give my best to that good-looking boyfriend of yours. Don't run off and elope before I get back to the White House, okay?"

Paula Bradford-Adams loved the always-cheerful outlook of Helene Eckermire, even when things didn't go her way. Because Helene had suffered a string of failed relationships, Paula found it more than delightful that her best friend seemed to have found Mr. Right, although Paula still worried she'd have her heart broken again. But no borrowing trouble as her mother preached to her and her younger sister, now about to give birth to her second child in nineteen months. She was sure Aunt Paula was needed to tend to her already rambunctious young nephew Will for a couple of days before her sister's mother-in-law arrived and relieved her of duty. Paula would make it to Falmouth, Virginia—around an hour's drive south—by nine thirty if she got her work done and packed without any interruptions. She wasn't comfortable driving any distance at night, but she was so looking forward to seeing her sister and doing what she did best— keeping her calm.

### 

Álvaro Hernandez thoughtfully called his wife and asked if he could have a couple of beers with his colleague Grant Paulson at Elephant and Castle between 12th and 13th on Pennsylvania Avenue. Maria was amused rather than put off. "Are you and Grant going to talk about

Kyle Guidry's crush on the first lady or are you going to tell Grant that he needs to talk to the president about a new press secretary?"

"You never know. I just might get around to bringing up the latter subject."

"Don't make promises you can't keep, *mi esposo*. Call me when you're on your way home. I'll order from Sanphan Thai and have Grubhub deliver it at 9:00—so you better be here or I'll eat all the spring rolls myself. So don't consume too much of that British pub food or I'll be forced to feed your Nua Ka Ta to the neighbor's dog."

"I'll have a couple of chicken wings and some of their Truffle Parm Potato Crisps—that's all. Can't resist those. Oh, and the beers, of course. Love you. Bye." Hernandez rubbed his stomach as a reminder that he really did need to lose ten to fifteen pounds.

Hernandez and Paulson realized before they entered the establishment that timing was all—and for them it was all good. Several couples left the booths near the bar within two minutes of each other, and the men were quickly accommodated. Fortunately for their conversation, the patrons weren't at full volume. Neither a pro football nor an NBA game was presently showing on the televisions above the bar.

After exchanging with Hernandez a few observations about craft beer and the forthcoming NFL playoffs, Paulson turned to the main topic. "Álvaro, I'm not expecting you to betray any confidences, but have you heard anything from anyone in the West Wing about Kyle Guidry's inordinate—what shall I call it—crush on the first lady?"

"No one has spoken to me about it directly in any official manner, but it's pretty obvious that it's becoming a subject that's on the mind of several in the White House besides those in the West Wing, although I haven't heard anything from cabinet members or the national security team—mostly just from staff and a couple of interns. I try not to put too much stock in everything I overhear, because some of it is just plain ludicrous."

"Such as?"

Hernandez smiled, understanding that Paulson wanted to probe as deeply as the press secretary would allow. "Well, some—and I'm not naming names—are talking about Kyle's gifts to the first lady— including jewelry. I've also heard he's been writing her daily love letters using some kind of code—but that seems far-fetched to me."

"Anything else?"

"Yes. According to the more outrageous scuttlebutt, Kyle has informed his ex-wife that he was in love with someone new and might marry her in the future."

"That's utterly ridiculous—but should be easy to check."

"Perhaps, but not by me." The men laughed at the absurdity of the rumor.

The server arrived and took their order—an order of chicken wings and fried pickles—much to Hernandez's chagrin, Paulson wasn't interested in the truffle crisps—and two pints of Guinness.

"In any event, I don't believe much if any of this speculation—and especially not that Kyle and Cecilia Erskine are having or have had a recent affair."

Paulson's dropped his head. "Are you prepared to respond to any of these rumors at your next press briefing or gaggle?"

"Why would I have to? Wait. Are you telling me that the press has heard about any of this gossip?"

"If I didn't know you better, Álvaro, I'd accuse you of being naïve."

"Jesus Christ. Well, all I can do is say something about the kinds of bizarre rumors that come out of every White House since John Adams moved in. I would deny the validity of the wilder speculations—which wouldn't at all be inaccurate—and ask that such rumors be quieted out of respect for the president and especially the first lady."

"Yes, that sounds like the best course. Just one problem, however. It's going to be much more difficult to deny categorically that Kyle Guidry isn't enamored of Cecilia Erskine. It appears from two of my sources that a female staffer working for the first lady let it slip that Guidry is stepping way across the line in his communications with her. I think I know who she is but I'm not ready to say—sorry. So, on one hand, the story couldn't lead to any major scandal, for after all, who denies that Cecilia Erskine is a stunningly beautiful woman fully capable of eliciting *inadvertently* the attention of many men in and out of government. But on the other hand, it's no secret that less responsible members of the media have pointed out there is emotional distance between her and the president and wonder out loud and in print whether their marriage will end once Erskine's presidency does. Tell me, Álvaro—again if you can—has the president mentioned any of this to you? I'll tell you up front that he has never spoken of any of these rumors with me."

"No. He hasn't brought the subject up with me—not even hinted at it."

"I can't believe he's unaware of what's being said and written. And if you get a question about it from the press, he won't be able to ignore it."

"Of course, if he fires Kyle, it might make things even worse."

"Tell me about it. Perhaps someone should convince Kyle to resign."

"Again, not me."

"No, not you. I know you two have issues."

"And what if Kyle refuses to resign?"

The beers arrived before Paulson could answer. But Hernandez could see in Paulson's eyes that he was thinking of something beyond Guidry's resignation.

###

Cecilia ate dinner alone at the round table in the East Sitting Room while she looked through the fan window into the darkened vista to the east. Her mind refused to rest after hearing the news of Martha Reilly's murder. She never knew Martha had married and divorced a man named Tillman. Cecilia's thoughts shifted dramatically from sheer satisfaction and a feeling of justice done to a deeply painful memory. Martha had made her young life miserable in so many ways, subtle as well as overt, from blaming her for broken drinking glasses and missing money to the theft of Martha's lipstick and tampons. But until Cecelia was seventeen, nothing Martha did was as devastating as refusing to take her side after her brother Hoyt had placed his finger into her vagina when she was only twelve, clearly enjoying the fact that her young step-sister had been sexually abused.

When Cecilia first became interested in Shakespeare, after appearing as the young lover Hermia in her high school's production of *A Midsummer Night's Dream*, her mother bought her the collected edition of the Bard's thirty-seven plays and his sonnets and other poems. By the time she turned seventeen, she had read thirty of the thirty-seven dramas and comedies and all of the sonnets. Martha, then back home for the summer after finishing her first year of graduate school, teased her about spending her time reading such "outdated crap." But Cecilia ignored her and found satisfying the scolding Martha received from Cecilia's step father, an incident that further hardened Martha against her step-sister.

It was early that June when Hoyt Reilly paid a visit during a break from his coaching duties at a small college Division III program in Illinois. Now twenty-six, Reilly joined the coaching staff the previous year and lamented that he wasn't offered another position at a Division I program after his first season. His mood was therefore more sour than usual upon his arrival home. It took no time for his sister Martha to inform him of Cecilia's interest in Shakespeare—which she of course ridiculed. At first Reilly put her off, choosing instead to watch his step-sister with a leering eye. It was his first trip home in over a year and a half, and she had plainly grown more beautiful. He thought it amusing she was surrounded by high-school boys every day at school—that is, those who couldn't handle her sexual essence and aura of independence. He didn't say it to her but mentioned to Martha that Cecilia needed the attention of a man, not a boy. Martha grinned and walked away as though she were going to formulate a plan.

Still looking at the darkness through the fan window in the East Sitting Room, Cecilia pushed her plate away and took another sip of her cocktail. Resting on the table was her complete edition of Shakespeare, which she now opened, with hands trembling, to page 1580. That June when she was seventeen, she had discovered in her bedroom a folded note on top of this edition. She opened it and easily indentified the handwriting as Martha's. "The best way to understand poetry is to fully experience it." At first, Cecilia thought Martha was attempting to apologize for teasing her—often cruelly—about reading Shakespeare. The remark was perceptive and thought-provoking. But then Cecilia saw the page number 1580 following the remark about poetry. She turned to the page and saw one of Shakespeare's long poems, which she had yet to read. *The Rape of Lucrece.*

# Chapter 26

Paula slipped into the driver's seat twenty minutes later than she planned. Still, there was no need to rush—that is, as long as the traffic on I-395 and later I-95 cooperated. She pulled out from her place off H Street NW to travel on H a short distance to the 395 pickup. As she pulled out into traffic she had to avoid a car jumping onto H ahead of her. She hit her brakes fairly hard and, as she always did on busy streets, looked in her rear-view mirror to be sure no one was going to slam into her from behind. There it was—a black truck right on her tail. Sighing with relief, she knew she was fortunate the vehicles did not collide. As the truck dropped back to a normal distance, she could see first the GMC logo on the grill and then the driver, who she felt looked like a terrorist, in that he wore a dark green or brown hoodie with sunglasses, even though it was now dark. Paula's father was a Richmond, Virginia cop who taught her to take in as much detail as she could whenever observing anyone or anything suspicious. Moving her eyes quickly back and forth from the road ahead to the rear-view mirror, she noticed that the man was wearing dark gloves and his right hand was lifted above the dashboard. After slowing down to prepare for her turn on 395, she peered into the mirror again and saw that the man was swinging something in his hand—which looked like a gold pocket watch on a chain.

That the black truck followed her onto 395 for the run south past the Capitol to where 695 would merge for the turn west frightened her—especially since the truck remained in its position directly behind, in spite of the frenetic traffic. Paula slowed down so the truck could pass her—but it remained where it was. She glanced at her cell phone and decided to call 911 if the truck didn't deviate from its position when she made the bend toward the Jefferson Memorial. Finally, when she passed south of *L'Enfant Plaza*, the black truck pulled out and moved two lanes over, accelerating its speed.

She kept looking for the truck until 395 gave way to 95 in Springfield, Virginia. Soon she pulled off 95 to use the bathroom at the Cracker Barrel near Dumfries. It was just twenty minutes or so from Falmouth, but she couldn't wait. Still upset by the experience with the black truck, she parked in front of the restaurant and checked the area for any black trucks or suspicious-looking men. She made her way inside and took comfort in the number of customers examining trinkets and gifts in the country-store section of the restaurant. After coming out of the ladies room, Paula caught sight of the stuffed animals on one of the display tables and decided to purchase two for her nephew and brand-new niece. As she paid, she caught sight of small model trucks displayed near the counter. She tensed when she saw a black one. But feeling a sudden rush of embarrassment over constant worry during the past forty-five minutes caused her to burst out laughing, prompting the cheerful cashier to laugh as well.

Now more relaxed, she headed to her car parked close by the entrance.

"Hey!"

As she saw the figure coming from the cars parked on her right, Paula's first instinct was to run back into the store, but there were some seven or eight persons who were about to go through the door. By this time the man reached her. He wore a dark hoodie garment, but his head was uncovered. Paula was so visibly frightened that an elderly male patron coming out of the door asked what was wrong.

"He..." was all she could say, pointing at the young man.

"What are doing to this woman, son?" The gentleman was surely in his later seventies and would have little chance against the solidly-built male, but the elderly man wasn't intimidated.

"Scotty, what's going on?" A middle-aged woman put her hand on the young man's arm.

"I'm sorry," he sputtered. "I recognized Ms. Bradford-Adams from CNN's recent feature on the first lady's staff. I'm so sorry if I scared you, Ms. Bradford-Adams."

All she could say in her flustered condition was "Please call me Paula."

Scott Murray explained that he was home from college for the holidays and was a Journalism Major and an "unapologetic political nerd." His mother verified the accuracy of his statement, and it was then Paula noticed that his black hoodie had "Wake Forest" on the front in gold lettering. After wishing him success in his chosen endeavor, Paula signed her name to the back of the mother's credit card receipt and offered hugs to the lad, his mother, and her elderly champion.

As she got back on 95, Paula couldn't stop smiling. She wanted so much to regale Helene with the events of this evening, but resisted the urge to call her. She'd wait until she returned to Washington. As was her habit whenever she visited Falmouth, she exited 95 at Courthouse Road due west of Stafford, picking up U.S. 1 for the final eight miles of the trip. But when she made the route shift she remembered she had never before driven down this way at night. The road was four lanes but hardly as congested at 95; therefore and because it was night, she felt far more vulnerable than when she traveled on it previously.

She passed a small auto repair and used-car lot, taking a quick glance at the offerings. She chuckled when she saw the exact model of the car she had owned while in college—a grey 1998 Ford Taurus. She wondered for a moment if that was it—since she traded it in at a Falmouth dealership two years after she graduated from college. She rubbed her hands on the steering wheel of her brand new, royal blue sedan with all the trimmings. She took another look through her rearview mirror at the dilapidated roadside car lot, but she could only make out the headlights of a vehicle behind her. Since she was on an otherwise lonely stretch of U.S. 1—called the Jefferson Davis Road—

she was relieved to see another vehicle. Before she had gone a mile, she sensed something wrong with her car. Her speed quickly dropped, and pressing on the gas pedal failed to accelerate the vehicle. The engine simply quit. Fearing damage to her transmission, Paula put the sedan in neutral and coasted to a stop. Remembering the vehicle behind her, she glanced into the rearview mirror and saw the other car's high beams. She estimated she was four miles or so from Falmouth and would have to wait ten minutes for her brother-in-law to get her. She reached for her cell phone when she heard the rap on the left rear-side of her car, but was unable to see the other driver in either her rear or side-view mirror. Appreciative that the person had stopped, Paula wanted to inform him or her that she was calling her brother-in-law and would only have to wait a few minutes at most. She unbuckled, opened the driver-side door, and stepped out of the sedan. The high beams of the other vehicle prevented her seeing anyone behind the wheel. She had just realized that the high beams were more elevated than they would be for another car when she was rendered unconscious by the blow to the rear of her head. She momentarily regained some awareness when she felt her body being pulled by her arms through the pine straw and dead leaves into a cluster of trees.

###

"You're not telling me something. What is it?"

Carter Thompson spent the previous five minutes on the phone with his mother, whose voice and manner failed to hide her anxiety. She tried to make him believe she was still very upset about her upcoming breast biopsy. He had done his own research on the subject and discovered that a BI RAD category four, her diagnosis, had a two-third's to three-fourth's chance of being benign. Of course his mother concentrated more on the one-third to one-fourth chance her lesion was cancerous. But there was something else upsetting her. Finally, she confessed.

"Your father has been especially angry today. He is talking crazy about how they won't appreciate you and evaluate you highly even if you lead the team to an upset in the bowl game. He says he hates all of them but will be satisfied settling the score with one of them."

"Who, mom?"

"He just said, 'Never mind,' and that I should shut up about it. I'm scared. Really scared. What's happening to him?"

"Mom, we'll talk about all of it right after we get back from Arizona. Is he there? Can I talk to him?"

"No, he's gone out. Said he won't be home until midnight or later."

"Out drinking?"

"I'm sure, but..."

"But what, mom?"

"Oh, Carter. He took his gun with him."

### 

Crossing the Potomac on I-66, Chas Overby felt calm enough to think of a future with Canadian Lisa Busby. She was the kind of woman who didn't want secrets between them. She had come clean regarding her past affair with her high-school French teacher, which led to his dismissal but didn't affect her academically. She told Chas that when she was accepted at the University of Toronto, she vowed to reject the advances of men at least until she graduated. She made it until midway into her senior year, but it was a monogamous relationship leading to an engagement, which the young man broke a month before the completion of the term. Lisa was involved in a lesbian relationship that summer, but realized she was doing so on the rebound and offered an apology to the other young woman for leading her on. Still leery of another intimate relationship, Lisa casually dated until she met Overby two years earlier. Although she agreed that they see others since they lived 570 miles apart, he believed she provided him enough hints that she was willing to make their relationship permanent.

For his part, Overby couldn't overlook the fact that Lisa possessed some of his mother's mannerisms as well as the same pale blue eyes he looked up at when as a boy his mother tucked him into bed every night and later when they betrayed her as she lied to him about not being interested in Daniel Wells and about having sex with Hoyt Reilly. Overby was often unable to stare into Lisa's eyes when they spoke, leading her to tease him about hiding something from her. He could apologize and make the adjustment, but when they made love he also avoided staring into her attractive eyes. He felt doing so would upset him and make impossible their seeing each other again. He felt he loved Lisa and could envisage them being married with children, but he still had ghosts to banish before he would be free enough to commit fully to her.

As he drove north past the Kennedy Center and approached Foggy Bottom, Overby glanced at the sign for George Washington University. He was helpless to stifle the memory of Hoyt Reilly coming up to him between classes and asking him to say hello to "that gorgeous mother of yours."

Overby remembered looking Reilly in the eye and asking, "Just what did you do to my mother, Coach?"

"Well, since you asked—I, like George Washington, cannot tell a lie. I fucked her. I fucked her real good, boy."

That he merely stood there and didn't smash Reilly in the face crushed Overby's self-esteem and prompted his leaving the school. It wasn't principle that made him transfer. It was plain cowardice.

# CHAPTER 27

"Thank you, Mrs. Heggins. I'm sorry if I interrupted the festivities."

"You haven't done any such thing, darlin'. He's already opened up all his presents. I'll get him now."

Andrea paced in front of her refrigerator and stove, waiting for Todd Heggins to take the phone from his mother. A close teammate of Miles Thompson in the NFL, Heggins had kept the friendship current since the men retired. Andrea believed Heggins would know if anyone would.

After Wells convinced her it would be better if he met Thompson alone at the Red Derby, adding that he would talk to him about doing an interview with Ms. Chase of *Sports World*, Andrea agreed to stay behind and work on one of her projects. But after Wells left, she began to ponder the reason Thompson wanted to see her Daniel. And why at 10:30 at night? Couldn't the men have lunch the following day? She knew from Daniel that Miles wanted for so long to view practice and was given permission by interim Coach Cipriano to come out to Arizona to observe his son getting ready for the bowl game. Then why hadn't the elder Thompson left by now? But what most alarmed her was something she heard on a conference call three days earlier. One of her New York colleagues asked for her input on a piece the magazine was constructing on the effects of CTE, including violent acts and tendencies. She wrote down the five names she would check on, given their history of concussions, but while doing so she overheard another colleague mention that he was looking into the entire starting linebacking corps of the team Thompson played for, noting that all of them were rumored to be showing signs of CTE, even at a relatively young age. Given her preoccupation with the names on her own list, she just hadn't considered Thompson as being one of those linebackers.

Growing more concerned, she called Thompson's teammate Todd Heggins, whom she had twice interviewed. His mother had answered his cell phone.

"Is it important, Ms. Chase? We're having a little celebration here. Todd's baby boy turned three today."

Andrea apologized for interrupting the festivities, promising to take up but a minute or two of her son's time. Heggins was in full party mode—friendly and seemingly fortified with whatever he was drinking. Andrea again begged indulgence for intruding on his son's party—and then came to the point of her call.

"I'll tell you, Andrea, since you must have your suspicions. I've seen Miles's patience disappear on a number of recent occasions and his anger and frustrations increase. The last time I was with him I tried to have a heart-to-heart, but he would have none of it. He cursed me out and I left, telling him I'd be there for him if he wanted to talk. It was only then that I wondered if he was showing the effects of CTE. Duanta Booker—you remember him, our starting free safety—called me two days later and expressed his fear that Miles was showing signs of the disease.

Andrea rejected her initial inclination to contact Wells on his cell and inform him about Thompson's state of mind. Daniel would surely attempt to lessen her concerns and challenge conclusions that were anecdotally based. But she could still make another call.

###

Cecilia slid under the covers of her canopy bed in the Queen's Bedroom across and down the hall from her husband's bedroom on the second floor of the Executive Residence. That they slept in separate beds wasn't shocking to the White House staff, since historically the precedent had been set. It was common to explain that the president's schedule, with a number of late-night meetings, made having separate bedroom easier on the first lady, who in this case preferred to crawl into bed no later than 10:00 p.m. and was since girlhood a light sleeper. She and the president had engaged sexually with each other a mere three times since they moved to the White House—the last being so fraught with tension that Cecilia vowed there would never be another. She had a half finished cocktail resting on the bed stand table farthest away from the window looking north. Her habit was to begin the cocktail while she sat in the East Sitting Hall and finish it once she was propped up in the canopy bed with a book in hand. Before reading, she would often look around the bedroom and recall its history and the notable guests who slept here, including Queen Elizabeth II; the queens of Norway, Greece, the Netherlands, and Spain; Winston Churchill; his daughter Anna; many presidential relatives; and the occasional film star. The bed she now rested in had reportedly been used by Andrew Jackson, but Cecilia found most satisfying the fact that she was allowed privacy and distance from her husband during the night.

An avid fan of non-fiction as well as classic works of fiction, she read in order to learn as well as to escape, and tonight she had on her lap a book relating to figures from mythology. Both fifteen years ago and more recently she was told she was like a famous goddess, who was drawn to physical love, beauty, and material possessions. This goddess sought pleasure and excitement and was proficient at manipulation and magic, introducing the art to both the gods and mere mortals. But as she read further about the mythological figure, Cecilia discovered that the deity was accused both of cheating on her powerful husband and having sex with all the male gods and even elves, as well as her own brother. In addition to being associated with sex and fertility, the goddess was moreover linked to war and death. The Christian leaders took a more jaundiced view—labeling her a "whore" or "harlot."

Oddly, this goddess was later feared by farmers because if she sat on a plough it would no longer be of any use. Cecilia moreover learned that the goddess rode into battle and took away half of the slain, bringing them to her "house with many seats." Finally, Cecilia read that in more recent years in one country the goddess's name and its derivatives had been given to infant girls.

Cecilia put the book down and reached for the rest of her cocktail. Her hand trembled as she considered herself in relation to the qualities and associations of the goddess—especially illicit and immoral sex, war, death, and magic. Since she was twelve, she heard often that she would have many boys fighting over her—which they had in fact done. She had a "magical" aura and appeal, others noted. But none had predicted the nature of her passionate experiences—nor the war—nor the death that would come with all of them.

### 

Wells stepped inside the Red Derby a couple of minutes before his scheduled meeting time with Miles Thompson. The place was hopping as it had been whenever Wells came. He and Andrea liked to sit outside when the weather allowed it, but everyone was jammed inside on this chilly late December night. Deciding to look for Thompson or a couple of empty seats if he hadn't yet arrived, Wells made his way down the bar and saw all stools and tables taken until he spotted Thompson where the bar made its ninety-degree turn, where the last four stools were situated. Thompson apparently saved the last stool, which was against the red wall with brick work partially exposed, on which was a chalk-board with beer selections. Usually, Wells avoided seats against walls or in corners, but there was no choice of seating now.

A near empty beer glass rested in front of Thompson. Whether it was his first of the night Wells couldn't be sure. From a short distance, Thompson looked like a typical lonely drunk.

"Miles?" Thompson looked up at Wells and patted the stool between him and the wall—demonstrating neither pleasure nor disdain at Wells's arrival. Wells squeezed past him and sat. "Crowded, as always. You come here a lot?"

Thompson shook his head but didn't make eye contact. "Two or three times in the last two years," he blandly noted.

Wells was surprised by Thompson's demeanor. He drove up to the Red Derby expecting the man to speak to him about Hoyt Reilly's treatment of his son and the team he coached. Instead, Thompson seemed put off that Wells had arrived at all. The bartender asked what he wanted and if Thomson desired a refill. Wells ordered a pint of Pinner before Thompson shook his head no, another gesture that confused Daniel.

"Well, Miles. I thought you'd be in Arizona by now."

"Going tomorrow."

Wells tried another approach. "I can just imagine how proud you are of Carter. He's had quite a year."

"You think so?" Thompson asked as though he were challenging Wells's assessment, rather than appreciating it. Wells accepted that Thompson wasn't interested in small talk.

"Miles, what did you want me to come here and talk about?"

Thompson finished his beer and watched the bartender deliver Wells's Pinner. He turned and locked his eyes on Wells. "My son."

Wells wasn't sure if Miles answered his question or was about to say something regarding the younger Thompson. Wells waited for Miles to go on, but the man continued to stare at his confused drinking partner.

"What about Carter? His relationship with Reilly, you mean?"

"That fucking bastard is dead," Thompson snapped—the malice in his voice causing the woman sitting on his other side to grab her date's arm.

Wells assumed Thompson was about to blow. "Miles, let's go outside and talk."

Thompson didn't respond verbally; instead he reached for his wallet and threw down a twenty to take care of both men's tabs.

"Here, let me pay for mine, Miles." Wells hadn't taken a sip.

Thompson ignored the offer, getting up from his seat and moving toward the exit. Wells followed, believing Thompson was aware his apparent anger at Reilly shouldn't be expressed inside the premises.

The men exited the red entrance door, and Thompson buttoned his coat and started walking to his left on 14th Street NW, the traffic on which was fairly brisk for this time of night. Thompson held for a van coming down Quincy and then crossed, turning to his left. "We'll sit in my car, and I'll turn it on so there's heat." The men made their way to a parked SUV alongside Twin Oaks apartment complex, and Thompson gestured for Wells to get in the passenger side, which Wells couldn't negotiate owing to a short brick wall less than a foot away from the SUV's passenger door. Thompson got out of the driver's seat. "Get in this way." Wells crawled across to the passenger seat, feeling more enclosed than he did at the end of the bar. Thompson started the car and soon Wells felt the rush of heat, which rapidly became oppressively uncomfortable, seeing he had on his zipped black leather jacket, whereas Thompson had taken off his coat before sitting in the vehicle. The man had retained the impressive physique of his playing days—six three, 245 pounds. His size made Wells feel even more claustrophobic in the front seat of the SUV.

"Miles, I wanted to talk to you about Hoyt Reilly's treatment of Carter. I'm assuming you didn't approve." Given the elder Thompson's reluctance to begin the conversation, Wells also wished to forgo the small talk.

"That son-of-a-bitch is dead. Got only part of what he deserved." Thompson had both hands on the steering wheel. He looked straight ahead, not adding to his remark. Wells easily sensed that whatever Thompson wished to share was going to be difficult to express.

"Miles, just tell me whatever you want." He didn't know how else to encourage the man to speak further. Thompson once more trained his eyes on Wells, who was concerned by the hatred expressed in them. The look suggested that someone other than Reilly was on the man's mind.

"I have something for you." Thompson reached across Wells's lap and opened the glove compartment. He withdrew a 9mm Glock and quickly leaned back to his sitting position while turning his body slightly so that his back was against the driver's-side door.

Although stunned, Wells kept his composure. "Wait, Miles. What are you doing?" The thought hit him. Thompson had shot Reilly. "Look, what you did was understandable. There's no need for you to—"

"Shut the fuck up." Thompson had the Glock in his left hand, his forearm resting across his stomach—the barrel pointed at Wells. Any attempt to wrestle the pistol away from him would be futile and leave Wells with a bullet buried in his chest. Thompson's accelerated breathing and the sound of the engine idling were all Wells heard. "I held back killing that racist mother-fucker because I didn't want to fuck up Carter's career and his chance to get into the league. I kept telling myself that I'd get Reilly after the season. I knew my son was the best QB UNEV ever had—*ever had*, and I believed everyone else knew it as well. But you know what? I started hearing that no, someone else was better. And you know who that some else was?"

Wells knew. "Miles, your son is—"

"I said *shut the fuck up*, didn't I? Thompson lifted his left hand off his chest and pointed the Glock at Wells's head.

Wells nodded slowly, trying to keep from being shot but now thoroughly confused as to what Thompson was doing—and had done. Was Miles responsible for Jack Ketchum's death and the setting of low-level car bombs? Did Ketchum have something on him?

"My boy was the 'best *since* Daniel Wells' was what I heard. Wells could throw it further, harder, and more accurately than Carter Thompson. Oh, they always added that my boy could run faster than you, Wells, but then they always say that about black quarterbacks. You've heard that said since the 70s, haven't you?"

Wells again nodded. There was nothing he could do to prevent Thompson from finishing his list of complaints. With the passenger side door so close to the retaining wall, there was no escape from the SUV. The pistol in Thompson's hand was low enough that a passer-by—in a car or on foot—would judge the scene as nothing more than two men talking before the vehicle pulled out and went on its way.

"Daniel Wells—big war hero and the greatest quarterback in UNEV history. Far greater than that mixed-race—but in everyone's eyes, black—kid who's led the school to its first major bowl game in its history.

Thompson's voice quivered and his eyes expanded, moist with tears. He was about to go over the edge. Wells had no choice; he had to speak.

"Miles, Carter is the best we've ever had at the position. Your friends were just fucking with you, that's all."

"I said *shut... the fuck... up.* As Thompson lifted the pistol and tightened the muscles in his forearm, the driver's-side door jerked open. Two hands grabbed Thompson's coat and yanked him out of the car—but not before his finger squeezed the trigger.

The bullet slammed into the padding above passenger-side window, a scant five inches over Wells's head. By the time he crawled across the driver's seat and saw what had happened, Thompson was lying on the street on his back, sobbing and begging for the other man not to shoot him.

"Henrik?" Wells was flabbergasted. His good friend had pulled the larger Miles Thompson out of the car and disarmed him.

"Thank Andrea for your life, Daniel. She called me, concerned about your coming up here." Emotional to the point that Wells had never seen, Nordenson's voice also quivered. "How the hell did I get here in time?"

Wells saw the Glock on the street some fifteen feet away. Thompson remained on his back emotionally distraught.

"I wasn't going to kill you, Wells. I just couldn't bear to hear... My boy... My son, he's the best.... I don't know why I shot the gun... I wasn't going to..." Thompson voice trailed off into sobs.

# CHAPTER 28

Helene got off the phone with her new "beau," as her best friend Paula liked to call him. In one sense she was happy she wouldn't be sharing her bed with him tonight. First, it was late and she was tired. But she also wanted to take some time and think carefully about the relationship. She had warmed to his appearance, charm, and thoughtfulness from the time they met outside of Bistro Cacao, a couple of blocks east of the Hart Senate Office Building. She, Paula, and six other female White House staffers were sitting outside on a pleasant late fall afternoon, when a gust of wind took her bill and hurled it toward Massachusetts Ave. Helene let out a howl and rose from her chair to make chase. But she saw a handsome man bounding his way between cars until he picked up the bill, which had come to rest against a car's tire across the street. Where he came from and how he saw the paper in flight she didn't know, but he acted as though he witnessed the whole scene. She stood to shake his hand when he returned the bill to her. "You probably don't really want this, but here it is for your records." What struck her most weren't so much his good looks and his chivalrous and "death-defying" deed, but rather the fact that he looked only at her. Few men would have been able to resist staring at three of the staffers, who were all gorgeous and in their mid-twenties—and she believed Paula was also better looking than she—but he did. Helene had always been insecure about her looks. She told Paula she was the "owner of a Middle-European peasant's face," and never believed her friend when she said that Helene's "near porcelain skin and mysterious green eyes" more than made up for whatever deficiencies she believed she possessed.

A few days later, Helene was at the Folger Shakespeare Library on an errand for the first lady. Cecilia Erskine wished to see the Library Theater's production of *Antony and Cleopatra* and was looking for a way to attend without fuss and fanfare. She even volunteered to go incognito. When Helene came out of the Folger after talking to the director and several staff members about the possible visit, she walked west on East Capitol Street to hail a cab on 2nd Street.

"Well, good morning. Did one of your restaurant bills blow over here too?" She was delighted to see him again, but highly anxious over what to say to precipitate a social meeting with him. She needn't have worried. He asked if she would like to have lunch.

"I think I could do that. What day?"

He seemed shyly hesitant. "Is today too soon?"

"Well, I've got to get back to the White House, but... but yes, I can meet you today."

"Great. Wait. Do you work at the White House?" She spent the rest of the morning at her desk relishing the fact that he reacted so positively first to her saying yes to lunch and second to the fact that she worked in the White House. In addition, he didn't ask for whom she worked. She would tell him at lunch and find out where he was employed. She hoped he wasn't just in the city temporarily.

They met at 1:00 at the Old Ebbitt Grill—her choice, since he left it up to her. She wanted badly to impress him; therefore the closeness of the Grill to the White House would help accomplish that goal. She took fifteen minutes longer for lunch, at which time she learned that he worked for the Justice Department in a capacity that required considerable discretion. His elusiveness made him even more appealing. In short, several dinners followed this lunch, and staying overnight at her place became a twice weekly event for the past two weeks. He always asked if his overnight stays were acceptable, and he never insisted on lovemaking. For her, he was an ideal lover—never forceful and always allowing her to take the initial romantic steps.

But now she wondered not only where the relationship was headed but also if it was way too early to worry about such things. After an hour thinking about their time together and following her third glass of Prosecco, Helene decided just to let matters take their course without pushing anything along.

Opening the drawer on her side table, looking for the theatre program she brought home from her and Paula's outing to The Little Theatre of Alexandria, Helene saw the envelope she was supposed to deliver to the home of the recently deceased Coach Jack Ketchum in Virginia. The first lady had given her a sealed letter with instructions for delivery: "Don't mail it, Helene. Be sure you put it in Coach Jack's hands." Helene was to drive up the following afternoon, but word came of Ketchum's death, making the assignment unnecessary. She waited for Cecilia to ask for the letter back, but she hadn't mentioned it until today. The new directive came in a brief note. "BURN what I gave you to deliver." Helene understood from Paula that the first lady was especially fond of the former coach, having visited him on several occasions when she was a student at UNEV and dating then quarterback Daniel Wells—a biographical detail, shared by Paula, that was not for public consumption, although Helene had let the fact slip on two occasions. Paula also informed her that the first lady kept in touch with Coach Ketchum over the years since, sending him a special Christmas card and birthday wishes after moving into the White House.

Entering the kitchen with the envelope and pouring herself another glass of Prosecco, Helene felt the familiar sign that she had a bit too much to drink: she wanted to indulge her curiosity. Still, she made a tepid attempt at doing what she was told. She pulled from one of the cabinets a box of wooden matches and stood over the sink holding the envelope in one hand and the box of matches in the other. But why not read the contents before setting fire to them?

She opened the envelope carefully, as if by doing so, she lessened the seriousness of her actions. There was one folded sheet of White House stationary in the first lady's familiar hand.

*Dearest Coach Jack,*

*Do forgive my failing to make clear all I said to you during our last call.*

*Others were nearby when we talked, forcing me to lower my voice. I received your note asking for clarification. I hope you didn't mind giving it to Paula. As I said, I can't be sure who might read anything mailed to me here.*

*As I told you, I have great difficulty speaking directly about my stepbrother. I'm sorry I can't be more open about my past with him. No, there is no one named Lewis Kreese that I know or have known. What I said was "Lucrece." And I shouldn't have said that. In fact, I don't know why I blurted that out. It just escaped involuntarily.*

*Again, I wish I could be more forthcoming. But it's just too painful.*

*With love and much respect,*
*Cecilia.*

###

"You want to go to bed now? It's almost two."

"I'll be lucky to fall asleep tomorrow night. Sleep tonight? I don't see how."

"I shouldn't have asked Henrik in for a drink. He doesn't exactly have a poker face when it comes to these things." Wells felt the full effects of three glasses of Scotch and the traumatic events of the night. Andrea was one drink ahead of him, although she cut her vodka with cranberry juice.

"I think Henrik was more shaken up than you were, baby. I'm yet to have my own emotional breakdown. What if I hadn't called him to go up there?"

"And what if he hadn't come exactly when he did? Next time, I want you to call *me* if you're that concerned."

"Ha. You'll just say, 'I'll be fine' and 'Please don't act like a mommy.'"

"Okay, okay. I stand guilty as charged. But as I said, from now on..."

"Yet, I wonder if Miles would have really hurt you."

Wells and Nordenson shared with her Thompson's behavior after he was pulled to the ground. He sobbed and apologized, holding his hand in front of his head, as if he were in danger of being shot.

"I don't know, man. I just don't know why I got all filled with hate at you, Daniel. Everything is just so messed up in my head right now. My boy's playing his biggest game, and I went ahead and did this. He's never going to forgive me. Never, man. Never."

"He's not going to know, Miles—don't worry."

Thompson began crying again after Wells's assurance. He and Nordenson helped Thompson back to his SUV and asked for his home phone number.

"I can't talk to my wife. Not like this. I can't. Just let me drive back there and I'll be all right."

Nordenson shook his head. "We can't let you drive, Miles. We'll call your wife for you. Tell me the number." With Wells's urging, Thompson agreed, and Nordenson made the call. "She's on her way. Leave your SUV here tonight, and I'll be sure that you're not towed."

The men stayed with Thompson until his wife arrived, with Nordenson keeping him hydrated with bottled water. Jana Thompson explained through her own tears the change in her husband's behavior and her fear he was suffering from signs of early CTE. "Thank you so much for not arresting him, officer, and thank you, Daniel for agreeing not to publicize what happened. It would break Carter's heart to know what his father did tonight."

After the Thompsons left in Jana's car, Wells gave Nordenson a full account of his time with Miles and his suspicion that the distraught man might have murdered Reilly. "You think it's possible, Henrik?"

"Given his state of mind, I'd say it's possible, but I'd be reluctant to bet on it."

### ###

Chas Overby tightly gripped his smart phone, coming close to tossing it against his hotel-room wall. Lisa wouldn't pick up—and he believed he knew why. She was with someone else, having spent the night, not at her place, but in a hotel bed. To his thinking, she was likely still in it. It was 6:30 a.m. Eleven hours earlier, she had canceled their dinner date, claiming she had a hastily scheduled work-related meeting at the hotel at 8:15 p.m. "I'll call you tomorrow, Chas" was all she said before hanging up. There was something reminiscent in the awkward pace and tone of her voice. He heard it from his mother years earlier.

After much thought, Overby capitulated to his instincts and drove to her place in order to see her before she left for her meeting at the hotel, if that's what she was indeed planning. Failing to find her there, he parked at the Kimpton George Hotel on 15 E Street NW, a few blocks from the Canadian Embassy. By the time he made it inside the hotel it was 8:05. Knowing the surroundings, he made his way to the conference rooms. Only one of the rooms was in use, but it was at the tail end of a business meeting having nothing to do with Canadian and American relations. He waited until 8:30 but saw no one but hotel staff.

Overby approached the desk and asked if Lisa Busby left anyone a message. The young man didn't have to look. "She left about half an hour ago but said that if you called for her she was running a bit late and would meet you at The Visiteur at the Georgetown Marriott." The young man was puzzled. "She expected you to call here, not come, I guess."

Overby forced a smile, straining to keep his composure. "I think we got our signals crossed."

"Would you like me to call the restaurant and see if she's waiting for you, sir?"

"No, I'll call her from my cell. Thanks so much. Have a good night."

"And you as well, sir."

Overby made his way across town to the Georgetown Marriott and walked directly to The Visiteur. There was no sign of Lisa anywhere in the restaurant.

###

"Guess what I'm going to do today, my dearest love?"

"Appear nude at your press briefing?"

"That was my second choice. I'm going to submit my letter of resignation."

Maria Hernandez face exploded with joy. "Oh, my God. I can't believe it." She threw her arms around her husband and kissed him all over his face.

"What are you doing," he laughed.

"My father used to call these the 'kisses of pride' whenever I brought home all A's or won my races. I am so, so very proud of you, Álvaro."

An hour later, Hernandez stepped inside Grant Paulson's office with a cup of coffee in one hand and the draft of his resignation in the other. Paulson knew from the relieved expression on his friend's face what was in the letter. He winced as he read the text. Hernandez was resigning for "personal" and "family" reasons but would remain until the end of January to assist the new press secretary if the president so wished it. Hernandez ended by making clear he was honored to have served the administration and that his resignation had nothing to do with others at the White House.

Paulson shook his head. "You're lying about your resignation having nothing to do with others, my friend. Part of your decision is based on the treatment you've received from Kyle—isn't it?"

"In part, yes. But I don't see any need to state that to the president—or to the press."

"Would you stay on if Guidry were to go?"

"No."

"Don't bullshit me, Álvaro."

"I'm not. Really, I'm not."

"You make a bad liar. Let me think about this for a while."

"Grant, it's my decision. Besides I told my wife I'm resigning."

"Right. But don't submit anything—or say anything to anyone here—you haven't yet, have you?"

"No, you're the first I've mentioned it to other than Maria."

We'll have lunch tomorrow and talk about it."

"I'm not changing my mind."

"As a favor for me—just wait until tomorrow afternoon, okay?"

Hernandez sighed. "All right. Tomorrow afternoon."

After Hernandez left the office, Paulson tore up the draft of the resignation letter. "That fucking Guidry." Not only was he going to cause considerable harm when the press started questioning his inordinate fascination with Cecilia Erskine, but he was forcing a popular press secretary to resign before the president's reelection campaign kicked into high gear.

# Chapter 29

"Anything new on the killings or the car bombs?"

"They're following up on several possible suspects and may have a lead on the bombs. Materials may have been purchased near Hagerstown. I'll be calling—maybe driving up there later this morning. And I'm following up on..."

"On what?"

"Let me do a little more digging today and I'll let you know later."

"That sounds ominous, Henrik."

"No—just prudent. Don't worry. I'm looking out for you, my friend."

"I can never say this enough, but thank you for coming to my rescue last night."

"We should both thank Andrea for acting on her instincts. I'm still rather shaken by how close it was."

"Do you think he would have shot me if you hadn't come along?"

"I... I don't know. I really don't. But..."

"Yeah, I agree. Drive safely if you go up to Hagerstown. Are you still checking your car?"

"Yes, and I assume you and Andrea are doing the same."

Wells finished his coffee and placed a call to Carla Aronson to discuss a memorial service for her father. Her desire was to wait until the bomber was found and arrested. "I can't run the risk that he might do something during the service." Wells supported her decision and accepted with gratitude her formal invitation for him to eulogize his old coach. The rest of the day he planned to work at his office, have lunch with a friendly member of the Veterans Committee, and then call the heads of other east coast veterans organizations in order to plan a come-together in Manhattan at the end of January. He would bring Andrea, who had at the same time an important meeting with the editorial board of her magazine. Each of them had been to Manhattan on many occasions, but never together. A room at The Lowell, two Broadway shows—*Hamilton* and Andrea's birthday gift *Springsteen on Broadway*, dinners at Eleven Madison Park and Gramercy Tavern, and bundled-up walks around the southern end of Central Park were part of their January plans—and it was important to be with Andrea for these romantic moments in order to help dilute the persistent memory of the his last trip to the City with a woman he loved.

Fifteen years earlier, he and Cecilia Finch drove to Washington D.C, and took the train from Union Station to Manhattan. With more limited finances, they stayed at the Sheraton on 53rd and 7th, saw on Broadway Ibsen's *Hedda Gabler* and *Rent*, dined at Abruzzi in Midtown and Rosie O'Grady's near the Sheraton, and walked hand in hand up the east side of Central Park. Usually to Well's left when they strolled, she held the hand he later lost in Fallujah. He was deeply in love with her then, but couldn't believe a young woman as beautiful as she could be devoted to him, regardless of what she said. He loved her laugh—so feminine and controlled. He couldn't imagine her guffawing at a vulgar joke or bending over in a paroxysm of giggling. He ached for her whenever she responded emotionally to what she heard or saw—such as her reaction to the plight of Hedda Gabler and her tragic end. Cecilia's tears, which were also shed over poor Mimi in *Rent*, struck Wells particularly. It was as if Cecilia's emotional response was more than sympathy or empathy; it seemed to him as if she could not disassociate herself from Hedda's effacement of her spirit by marrying a man she didn't love. Her response to Hedda's suicide appeared to be one of resignation rather than deep sadness or shock.

These moments only made Wells love her more ardently. She told him he was perfect for her and praised his polite manner and respect for her interests and intelligence. Cecilia also encouraged his professional football ambitions and vowed to move wherever he ended up, yet saying nothing of marriage. He understood she was frightened by the prospect, surely owing to her parents' divorce when she was so young. Many were the times she politely changed the subject whenever Wells brought up her family. He only knew she had a step-father and two step-siblings, whom she spoke of in an emotionless manner. All offers to meet her family were met by a kiss and a shake of the head. Appreciating her sensitivity, though not completely understanding it, Wells ceased any mention of her family until she informed him, after he was cut from his team over the summer, that she had to go back home. Her mother had just been hospitalized for arterial surgery, and Cecilia was insistent she be at the hospital during the procedure. Wells especially needed her at that time, since his initial attempt at a professional football career failed, but he made it clear he supported her decision to be with her mother.

They talked the day of the surgery, and she informed him she would be back the day after tomorrow and to have reservations for dinner at their favorite restaurant. Wells promised to call the following evening to learn the exact time she'd be back, but when he did a man answered the family phone. Wells asked for Cecilia.

"She's not here. She left this morning."

"Oh. Did she say she was returning to her place?"

"Who is this?"

"I'm Daniel Wells. Cecilia and I are—"

"She's gone. I don't know where she went. Goodbye."

Wells assumed at the time he had spoken with Cecilia's step-father. It took several years before he realized he had in fact spoken to Hoyt Reilly.

### 

The first lady sat on the rolled-arm bench in her bedroom changing from her gray-plaid suit to a green long-sleeved sheath dress suitable for her lunch with the spouses of the House and Senate leadership—of both parties. Fortunately, she felt comfortable among these women and men and especially enjoyed the humorous stories and teasing banter of Larry Bridwell, the Majority Leader's husband and Vice President Jerald Connerly's wife Tina, whom Bridwell had "gone steady with" when they were both in high school. Cecilia believed she had few opportunities to laugh and relished each opportunity. Paula Bradford-Adams could always make her smile and no one, she felt, was as loyal. And Paula needed to be, since she was the only one who knew about the meeting the first lady recently had with someone from her past. As a girl, Cecilia was a giggler, but her smiles became fewer the older she got, when she had to endure the cruelties of her step-brother and sister. Her mother's dismissal of her complaints with "Just try to get along" left her feeling betrayed in another devastating way—and by the time she was thirteen, she kept everything to herself.

Although she said nothing specific about her family experiences to Daniel Wells, he never pushed her to speak more openly and somehow he found his way to her dormant humor and made her laugh. She felt each broad grin and chuckle so liberating–at least for the moment—and harbingers of what she hoped would come from a life with the handsome athlete. She loved him even more for his attention to her and understanding of her need to find humor even when he was going through the disappointment of being cut at the end of training camp. If she had never given in to her sense of responsibility and returned home when her mother was in the hospital, she would have married Daniel—and loved him dearly, lifting his spirits when he returned from Iraq with part of his arm gone. But she had gone home, and in the aftermath of what occurred she believed she was ruined and that he would never look at her in the same way again. She therefore avoided him, calling off the relationship and refusing to take his calls or accept his pleas to see her. She fabricated a lame reason for the break-up a high school freshman would have constructed—but without the "We can still be friends" tag line. Cecilia never knew what Daniel went through—she was too frightened to know—too frightened to see his face.

It was soon afterward that Cecilia verified her belief in her unworthiness by agreeing to sleep with an acquaintance of Daniel's, who would surely reveal to Wells his sexual encounter with her. On one date, the young man took her up to see the Gettysburg Battle Fields and bought her a scaled down civil war cannon as a souvenir of their outing. She kept the cannon as a reminder of her betrayal of Daniel and her unsuitability as a wife to him. Of her lovers in London and Paris, only the latter laid his finger on her soul in a way she never could have imagined. He bought her a small conch-shelled cameo from a boutique on the *Rue Saint-Honoré*, which depicted a beautiful lady blowing a swirled horn. Her lover insisted that the image looked remarkably like Cecilia and that her heart's longing was to blow the horn and make others hear the sound. She kept both gifts, now in the glass cabinet in her East Wing office, side by side for all these years as reminders of the contradictory feelings about herself. Upon first meeting Stephen Erskine, she was filled with self-loathing, yet still in dire need of stability and at least a semblance of a future. Erskine provided both—and accordingly she married a man she felt comfortable enough around, a man she admired for his ambition and decency. But she didn't give her heart to him and never attempted to do so. There was but one man she truly loved and another by whom she was utterly fascinated. It was only to the latter that she finally revealed what had happened to her the afternoon she was at her house after returning alone from the hospital to see her mother.

On that horrific day, Cecilia placed her suitcase on the bed of the guest room—which was formerly her room. She picked out a pair of jeans, a colorful top, and sandals, which she would wear when she met one of her high school friends at a local bookstore. The afternoon sun illuminated her room and burnished her mood. Medically, her mother was going to be fine, and her love for Daniel Wells gave her future a chance to be bright indeed. Yet being in this house—in this room, the scene of several traumatic and distasteful experiences with her step-brother and step-sister filled her with anxiety. Both Hoyt and Martha had visited the hospital the night before, and Martha mentioned they were both leaving the following morning. Even though they were gone, Cecilia wanted to change her clothes and head out to the bookstore as quickly as possible. Removing her dress and shoes, she had the colorful top in her hands when she detected his voice. She hadn't heard him enter the house or make his way up the stairs.

"My, my—oh, my. You get better looking every time I see you. Glad I hung around for another day." She could barely breathe, let alone respond to Reilly's smarmy compliment. He was a man who had just turned thirty—but his manner had never changed since he joined her family years earlier. Her muscles finally able to respond, she attempted to put on the purple top, but Reilly lurched forward and caught her arms over her head. "No, no. I want to see your tits little sis. They've gotten bigger since I was here last, haven't they?" He jerked the top out of her hands and threw it on the bed. "Here, let me take this off." He pulled down hard on the front of her bra, exposing her breasts. For some reason she never understood, she stood defiantly where she was. She wouldn't give him the satisfaction of showing fear. "Remember when you first began to bud, Cecilia—and I took your little nipples in my fingers and moved them up and down and side to side?" She was fourteen then. "We had a number of special little moments like that, didn't we, but never the big one—right?"

Cecilia's defiance collapsed from the weight of her terror. "Get out of—" Her demand was silenced by a blow to the upper part of her stomach. As she doubled over, Reilly grabbed the suitcase and hurled it from the bed. She could barely catch her breath, and the pain at the bottom of her ribs made breathing difficult. Reilly threw her on the bed, with the back of her head hitting the footboard. Reilly pulled her panties off as he stepped out of his loafers and then removed his pants. Cecilia opened her eyes to see him withdraw something from the pocket of his pants. "I'll can come back home real quick, sis—so our secrets need to be just *our* secrets—as they *always* have. You *don't want* me to come back." She pressed the palms of her hands on the bed to push up her body, but her step-brother brought his fist down on the same spot where he had earlier punched her. She moaned in pain and closed her eyes as she felt his wet finger enter her. "I'll be through in a minute, sis, don't worry. I'll even time it." After that she heard nothing until she was awakened by the phone in the room. She rolled off the bed, her abdomen and lower ribs in considerable pain, and made her way to the phone. She answered as she felt a small trickle of fluid running down her thigh. It was her friend asking why she wasn't at the bookstore.

# Chapter 30

"You're not going to believe this, my friend."

"At this point I'll believe just about anything, Henrik."

"Then hold on to your cap. I've done some further digging and can now tell you that your old friend, Dylan Nieporte..." Nordenson paused for the dramatic reveal. "...has a father and older brother..."

"Really? What exciting news."

"Let me finish."

Wells smiled. He had periodically teased his friend about his habit of dramatizing shared information. "Go ahead. Sorry."

"Nieporte has a father and brother who are explosive engineers."

Wells needed no further explanation about why this information was important. "And the eldest son and his younger brother Dylan might have worked a summer or two with old dad?"

"You got it. But even if he didn't, he would have had every opportunity to learn about explosives. My uncle in Norway was an explosive engineer and he taught me the basics before I entered *Ungdomsskole*—a secondary school to you knowing only one language."

Wells's logic didn't rebel against the possibility that Nieporte might have been responsible for the minor bombs placed under his, Gina's, Andrea's, and Henrik's cars—but what about the large explosion that killed Jack Ketchum? "Henrik, is there any way you can check to see if Nieporte knew Coach Ketchum and if there was some kind of problem between them?"

"Other than the fact that Ketchum thought of you as an adopted son?"

"Yes. Jesus. Could it really be Nieporte?"

"I'll see what I can find out."

### ###

Chas Overby sat alone on the lower steps of the Lincoln Memorial, looking east and watching the growing darkness in the distance. He paid no attention to those walking and running up the steps to see the famous statue of a sitting Lincoln, staring as it were toward the Capitol, keeping an eye on the government he, with herculean effort, managed to hold together over a hundred and fifty years earlier. But Overby's thoughts at the moment were deeply personal rather than political. He had done much in his life he hadn't been proud of but always thought it necessary to sooth or to satisfy his sense of self-worth, which deplored disloyalty and mendacity. Yet he wasn't immune to engaging in duplicity or retribution when he felt attacked or betrayed. His treatment by Hoyt Reilly and Reilly's affair with his mother led to more than his leaving the team and university. After he enrolled elsewhere, Overby paid two hundred dollars through channels to have two men jump Reilly and beat him senseless. But when Reilly broke the nose of one of the assailants, the other ran off. The pair kept the money, leaving Overby checkmated. For the next six months he sent anonymous letters to Reilly's school and athletic department—as well as the local paper— charging the coach with lewd and threatening behavior, but nothing was done.

On a previous visit to Washington, Overby spoke to Daniel Wells over several beers, expressing his desire that the UNEV community be made aware of Reilly's reputation and "despicable behaviors." Wells sympathized and agreed with much of what his friend accused Reilly of, but he couldn't promise actually to do anything. For the first time Overby judged Wells as a man with phony principles who wouldn't leave his comfort zone to help a friend. But that reaction was minor compared to the next evening, when Wells joined Overby and Lisa Busby for dinner at Robert Wiedmaier's lush Siren Restaurant. Wells came alone, and Lisa gushed about how much she had heard about him from Chas. Throughout the pre-meal cocktails, she asked Wells questions about his cause, his athletic career, and his experiences in Iraq. Unlike so many others, who didn't wish to talk about Daniels's war wound, Lisa asked questions about prosthetics and how Wells managed certain tasks with the use of just one hand. By the time the main courses arrived, Overby was barely able to restrain his jealousy, and like many men so afflicted, tended to blame Lisa's attentions on the inappropriate effusion of charm by his old high school friend.

Later, Overby found he could keep his cool if he saw Wells without Lisa's being present—and such had been the case until now. Yet as he sat on the Lincoln Memorial steps, he was dead certain she had met Wells at a hotel and slept with him. Overby gave no thought to Wells's overly positive and affectionate relationship with Andrea Chase. Wells was a red-blooded male, wasn't he? The dinner at Siren occurred weeks before Wells and Andrea became romantically involved, didn't it? There was likely unfinished business between Wells and Lisa, wasn't there? Overby rose from the steps determined to avenge his wrong. He started walking east on the north side of the Reflecting Pool. He was confident he'd come up with something by the time he reached the Washington Monument.

### 

Kyle Guidry smiled at the genius of his idea as the florist placed baby's breath in the arrangement of the dozen red roses he just purchased. He checked his watch. 6:54 p.m. He had plenty of time before he was to meet his nephew at 8:00 for dinner and a discussion of the boy's college options for the following fall. He took one of the cards and hesitated before writing the note in green pen. It had to be letter perfect and it needed to be printed. His handwriting was so distinct it would be easily identified. He pulled out a folded piece of paper and printed the three lines on the card.

My bounty is as boundless as the sea,
My love as deep; the more I give to thee,
The more I have, for both are infinite.

Because he took the verse from Shakespeare's *Romeo and Juliet*, he thought it would be most appreciated as well as appropriate. He wasn't aware, though, that the lines were Juliet's, not Romeo's. He placed the card inside the envelope and sealed it. One the outside he printed "For the First Lady."

He imagined she would find the arrangement the following morning or be given it by someone in the White House and wonder whose gift it was. Guidry guessed she would suspect him, owing to his earlier gift of Kaleidoscope roses, and whether she sought him out or not, they would see each other eventually. How she looked at him would tell him much about her reaction to these roses. If she looked kindly, even if she said nothing to him, he would be emboldened to present her with other arrangements or small gifts, which would also please her—and that was enough for him. His fantasies about Cecilia Erskine would then have a literal and sincere complement. He left the florist's, intending to walk the two blocks to the White House and set the flowers on the table in the Vermeil Room, which the first lady habitually entered every morning, being sure to look intently at the painting of Jacqueline Kennedy for what Guidry guessed was inspiration. If security questioned him on the flowers, he would say they were a surprise for one of the staffers. In any event, he doubted he'd be questioned. He had these past two months brought into the White House a cake, several balloons, and a small Christmas tree.

The city was now dark and wintry. Guidry forgot about the headlights shining in his eyes—something he reacted strongly too, especially when he drove. He blinked rapidly as he made it one of the two blocks between him and the White House. A moment later, a car pulled up next to him with the window lowered. A woman pushing a shopping cart along the sidewalk saw Guidry lean over and speak to the driver. With horns blaring behind the car, Guidry entered the passenger side. As the car pulled away, the woman noticed a bouquet of roses lying on the street. What was that all about, she wondered?

Looking to her right and left, she waited until there was a slight break in the traffic before she stepped out on the street to retrieve the flowers.

###

"It's very important to me to know we'll be together if I'm re-elected."

"Are you expecting me to leave you after you win the election, Stephen?"

"Cecilia, I know this is far from being a perfect marriage, and lately you've seemed even more distant. I admit the possibility of your leaving *has* entered my mind."

"You can set your mind at ease. I have no intention of doing so if you're re-elected. I realize the horrible effect that would have on your presidency."

"And how so many—so very many—would be devastated if you weren't first lady."

"I seriously doubt that. But let's be honest. I can't promise anything once your term or terms are up."

The president lowered his eyes. "I know. Cecilia, thank you for assuring me—and you know I want you to be happy and do what you want while we're in this house. I wish your presence wasn't required as often as it is, but other than that..."

She smiled and sighed. "We can always use the example of Harriet Lane, I suppose."

"I'm sorry—who?"

"She was bachelor James Buchanan's niece, who served his term as White House hostess. I believe she was the first to be called 'The First Lady.'"

The president laughed. "Well, you were always smarter than I, Cecilia. I guess I need to brush up on my history." Erskine took his final bite of crème brulee. This was an exceptionally good dinner, wouldn't you say?"

"I would agree." She lifted her wine glass and both of them toasted the White House chef.

Later that night, after she finished the last act of Shakespeare's

*Measure for Measure*, she considered her fate compared to that of Isabella in the play—the role she refused to play years earlier. Isabella had given her life to God and desired a nun's life, but she was caught up in a sordid plan by the powerful deputy Angelo, who would save her brother's life if she would give herself to him sexually. She escaped the loss of her virtue when another woman was substituted for her in bed. Later, the Duke returned and restored order to Vienna, and as a reward to Isabella decided to marry her. Shakespeare gave her no lines after the Duke's pronouncement; therefore, her reaction to her reward was left to the reader's imagination. In Cecilia's case, her sordid step-brother had his way with her a number of times in her young life—culminating in rape when she was twenty-one. There was no bed-trick to save her—and in a devastating state of shame she gave up the man she loved and in whom she had invested her future. Her eventual "reward" for what she endured was a marriage to an important man who was elected President of the United States, making her first lady. But she never judged her elevated status as a reward for what she suffered. She had lost too much of herself ever to be regained or adequately replaced in spite of the attention she received nationally for her sincerity, kindness, beauty, and style, elevating her favorability numbers sixteen points higher than her husband's in a recent poll.

Dressed in casual pajamas, Cecilia made her way to the East Sitting Hall outside of the Queen's Bedroom. Understanding that she was in the midst of another full reflection of her past, she took a sip of the Negroni a member of the White House staff left on the table in front of the sofa. She first had the drink in Brussels when she was there at age thirty. She wasn't sure the mixture of gin, Campari, and sweet red vermouth would blend well enough for her tastes, but she was pleasantly surprised. Her lover at the time was the one who suggested the cocktail the night before he was assaulted and hospitalized. She believed then she would never see him again—never need him again—but when he contacted her three weeks ago through a message delivered verbally by Paula Bradford-Adams, she realized the error of her assumption. Of all her men, he was the one she confided in the most, although parts of her history she never mentioned. No one knew about the rape except for Hoyt Reilly and his sister Martha—and both were now dead. Cecilia lay on the sofa and thought again her recent meeting with the man who was twice her lover.

As Paula later related to the first lady, the man called the staffer, who listened to him explain his relationship with Cecilia Finch fifteen years earlier and their subsequent meeting several years ago. "Please tell Cecilia that... that Mr. Thorn is in Washington and would love to see her."

"Mr. Thorn, the first lady is rather busy, as you can imagine. She has very little time to see old acquaintances, I'm afraid."

"I understand that, but I think she'll be very disappointed in you if you don't share my message with her."

Paula flushed with anger at the man's temerity, but he quickly apologized for his manner and choice of words. "Please forgive me for making another suggestion. If you would just mention to her that Mr. Thorn called you, you can observe what her reaction will be. If she wants to see me, you can tell me when I call you back at this number tomorrow night. If you find that she doesn't, just tell me and I won't trouble you again. Can you do that?"

Paula quickly thought it over and agreed with Thorn's logic. "All right. I'll be back here after nine tomorrow night."

"Thank you so much, Ms. Bradford-Adams. Once more, forgive my tone earlier."

The following morning, the first lady walked into Paula's office and handed her a coffee. "Good morning. Thought you could use a caffeinated pick-me-up. How was your night?"

"I received a call."

"Really?" Cecilia saw that Paula was fumbling for her words. "From a man, I assume?" Paula nodded. "Asking you out? What did Mr. Adams have to say about that? Wait, he's in San Francisco for a few days, isn't he?" Cecilia's teasing failed to draw a smile from her staffer.

"His name was Thorn."

The first lady's smile evaporated from her lovely face. "Who, Paula?"

Paula related the specifics of the call and Thorn's request to see the first lady, who listened with her eyes moving back and forth in what Paula judged as agitated excitement.

"Eat lunch with me at noon, and I'll let you know what I think." The first lady left her office and returned to the second-floor residence. When they met for lunch in the East Sitting Room, Cecilia was relaxed and composed. "When he calls, say that—"

Paula grinned. "Mr. Thorn, you mean?"

Cecilia forced a smile. "Yes, I mean Mr. Thorn—and tell him I would be happy to see him."

"Here at the White House?"

"No. As you know, on Friday evening, I'll be speaking at a dinner in Wilmington and plan to meet with some party officials coming down from Philadelphia for breakfast the next day. But I haven't yet told you that several of my high school friends are dropping by the DuPont to see me Friday night. Tell Mr. Thorn that if he doesn't mind driving or flying a hundred miles or so to see me on Friday—assuming he's in D.C.—then I'll be happy to see him then. Oh, and you'll be going with me."

"Okay. What time should Mr. Thorn expect to see you on Friday night?"

"I guess around ten or ten-thirty."

"*After* you see your other friends?"

"You can stop smirking, Paula. It may be after—I don't know."

"Security—Secret Service?"

"You'll be there as escort and chaperone."

"I serve at the pleasure of the first lady."

"That's why I love you and *trust* you the way I do, Paula."

### 

"Come on. This is where I fish with my brother and father. It's a really neat spot." The teenage couple made their way from the Lee Hwy down to Bull Run—on the eastern side of the Manassas National Battlefield Park.

"It's ten till eleven. I've have to get back home by 11:30, Nathan."

"We'll stay ten minutes and then we'll leave—I promise." Nathan believed they'd make it back to her place in Sudley Springs with plenty of time to spare."

"Nathan, what's that?"

"Where?"

"There." She pointed to a person who seemed to be asleep near the water's edge.

Nathan whispered. "Probably a homeless person. I bet there's an empty bottle of whiskey on the ground near him. No, wait. He looks better dressed than that."

"We better get back to the car."

"Don't be scared, Lori." Nathan was going to show off for his girlfriend. "Hey. Hey, Mister. Hey!" He ignored Lori's insistence that he stop calling out to the man. "He must really be out cold."

"What are you doing, Nathan?"

Nathan walked closer to the man and spotted a short piece of a broken branch. He picked it up and tossed it, hitting the man in the back. Lori headed for the car, as her boyfriend stepped closer to the man. She froze when she heard Nathan's words. "I think he's dead."

Lori ran to her boyfriend as he got to his knees and pulled away the man's arm, which was covering his head. "God!" Nathan fell backwards. He had just seen the bloody hole in the front of the man's face and the pool of blood soaked into the dirt. Having watched enough crime dramas, Nathan reached for the dead man's wallet. "I've got to see who he is." There were at least two one-hundred-dollar bills in the wallet. Nathan lifted out one of them.

"You better not steal his money."

"Don't come any nearer, Lori. Call 9-1-1."

But when Lori frantically reminded him that they would have to remain there and then go to the police station—thereby getting the both of them in big trouble with her father for breaking her promise not to drive out from town—they made a quick decision to return to their car and go straight back to Sudley Springs. "He's dead, Nathan, so there's nothing we can do to help him. Someone will find him tomorrow morning. Did you get his name?"

"No, I didn't. Here, I'm putting the wallet back and I'm not taking any of his money either." Nathan felt both the terrifying effects of coincidence—he, his father, and brother were scheduled to fish this spot sometime in the morning—and the bad luck of having a fifteen year-old girlfriend with a suspicious and intimidating father.

# Chapter 31

"Another glass?"

"Why not? I don't have to be up until 10:00 tomorrow."

Wells poured the Prosecco into Andrea's empty flute. "Interview?"

"No. I'm part of an ESPN panel discussion on the forthcoming major bowl games. I'll be the 'authority' on UNEV's chances. That I don't mind, but I'm sure they'll ask about the murders of the head coach and starting linebacker—whom I was with not long before he was killed. I'll have to discuss Carter Thompson and his skill-set, right after his father held a gun on you and might have killed you if not for Henrik's exquisite timing. Long story short, I'm not really looking forward to being on the panel."

"'Let's not borrow trouble,' as my mother used to say, always adding, 'You get enough for free anyway.'"

Andrea patted the sofa. "Come on, my love, and sit. We'll snuggle and see where that leads—although I have a pretty good idea where." She playfully pointed to her bedroom. But before Wells could reach the sofa, his cell phone rang. He didn't recognize the number.

"This is Daniel Wells."

"Daniel, it's Chas."

"Hey, Chas. What's up, my friend?"

"Just got word that I'll be flying back to Ottawa tomorrow night. Wanted to see if we could have a drink later tomorrow afternoon before I head to the airport."

"Sounds good. When and where do you want to meet?"

"I'll call you back in a bit about where. But how about 3:30?

"All right. But why are you going back so soon? I thought you were—" Overby had already hung up.

### 

Cecilia finished her Negroni as she entered her bedroom. She undressed and slipped into a blue cotton nightshirt with a green "FLOTUS" monogrammed on the front, a birthday gift from her staff. Daniel Wells told her fifteen years ago that blue and green were her colors—and that they went so well with each other. In the fall and winter, he liked wearing a solid blue shirt under a green sweater and vice-versa. On several occasions he took the first combination and she took the second. Yet when she returned from Europe after her first visit following their break-up, she wore more red and its variations, from maroon to garnet, but never pink. She had been told by her lover that red was her color—the color of a "flesh and blood goddess," not an "ethereal" one. When she saw him again six years ago, she wore exclusively red or its sibling colors. When Paula brought him to her hotel suite three weeks earlier, she was dressed in light maroon dress with yellow highlights.

Lying on her bed in the Queen's Bedroom, Cecilia played once again the events of that evening in Wilmington. Her last two visitors had finally departed—she was growing fearful they wouldn't—a little after 10:00 p.m. As soon as they left the suite, Paula stepped inside alone. "Are you sure you want to see Mr. Thorn, now that it's after 10:00? I can tell him you're very tired and have him come to the White House when you get back."

"No, that's all right, Paula. Just give me a second." Cecilia closed the bathroom door behind her and remerged a minute later with her hair freshly brushed and her lipstick reapplied. Bring him in but don't leave. I..." The first lady was uncharacteristically nervous. "I may want you to go into the... into the bedroom and close the door behind you."

"But I..." Paula was both startled and confused.

"I'll give you a nod if I want you to do that, okay? Wait--wait. Just plan on excusing yourself after I ask him to sit down. Yes, do it then." Cecilia looked away from her stunned senior staff member, seeking further words that would explain her request. She again met Paula's stare with her own. "You know how much I need you and love you, Paula. And more than that, I trust you like no other person in my life."

Paula shook free from her dazed state. "I won't say anything to anyone. If asked, I'll swear I was in the same room with the two of you the entire time. Just tell me what he is—or was—to you, so..."

"He is one of the friends I met when I traveled to Europe the fall after I graduated from UNEV. After I left London for Paris, I met him." The first lady's look informed Paula that she and Mr. Thorn were once lovers.

Paula stepped out of the room and within a few moments, she brought the man in. She quickly excused herself and entered the bedroom, softly closing the door behind her. After a moment, Cecilia heard the television come on—a little louder than expected.

Thorn came to her without a word and kissed her deeply. She didn't resist, but she wouldn't return his passion. "Why have you come here?"

"It's been several years, Cecilia. I couldn't wait any longer."

"She turned her head toward the bedroom door. "Please speak softly."

"'Speak low if you speak love.' Is that not correct, my dearest one."

Cecilia smiled at his recalling the line from Shakespeare's *Much Ado About Nothing*. "You must know that I can do nothing now. I cannot—will not—leave my husband until his presidency is over."

"So I will have to wait another five years? I read the poll numbers. Your husband is very likely to be reelected. You can't expect me to go all that time without seeing you—without holding and kissing you."

Overcome by his ardent words, Cecilia returned his kiss. "You can't know how I've missed your touch and how often I've thought of our moments together." She broke from him and sat in one of the soft chairs. "But I do neither of us any good by dwelling on what we once had."

He sat on the sofa across from her. "You speak as though you wish never to see me again."

"No, it's not that, but I can't do what I wish. I am the First Lady of the United States." She pronounced the identification with sadness. "You must see there is nothing for us now or even..."

His breathing increased—either from his rising hurt or rising anger—she wasn't sure which. "I won't believe it. I have waited for you for almost fifteen years. My affections and devotion have not changed. No one can love you more than I. No one is a better man for you than I. No one knows you better than I. And I am strengthened by the fact that you have loved no man better than you have loved me."

Cecilia stifled a gasp at the opportunity he now presented her. She knew he would never leave her alone—regardless of the danger inherent in an unrequited courtship with her—a danger to the both of them and her husband's presidency. She believed at this moment there was just one option left to her.

"No, you don't know me as well as you think. I was not the 'forest innocent' you called me when we first fell in love. I had three lovers in the States and one in London before we met at the *Musee d'Orsay*. But more than that, I was raped by my older step-brother before I ever went to Europe. Raped. By my step-brother." He lifted his head, and a flush of agony altered his features. She had never been this cruel to any one in her life, and now she was about to damage him with one more brutal fact. "And you are wrong. I *have* loved another more than I ever loved you. Before I met you. And he remains the man I have loved the most in my life."

"Who?" His voice sounded dead.

"It's of no matter who. I won't reveal his name to you. I won't." Tears ran down her face. "So that's why we can never—"

"Please have your assistant take me down." He stood and seemed composed. Cecilia was grateful he wasn't crying as she was. She went to the bedroom door and knocked. Paula opened the door looking for any indication of what had transpired since she removed herself from the room.

"Paula would you please escort Mr. Thorn out and see that he gets a cab if he needs a ride." Cecilia touched Paula on the shoulder and entered the bedroom, closing the door behind her.

###

"What's going on, Álvaro?"

The press secretary stirred his morning coffee and shook his head. "POTUS is hot, Helene. I've rarely seen him this mad. If I may be so indelicate to quote his exact words, he shouted at me "Where the mother fuck is Guidry?" I had to put my hands out to stop him from getting up in my face. After I told him I had no idea, he headed upstairs to Kyle's office. But he wasn't there or anywhere else in the West Wing. There was a scheduled meeting in the Oval Office with the solicitor general dealing with the writ of *certiorari* Kyle had been working on. But no Kyle."

Helene's initial thought was incorrect, she determined. The president had not found out about his chief counsel's dangerous infatuation with the first lady. If he was this mad about his missing a meeting, she only imagined how he would react when he learned about that. She left the White House Mess and took her coffee and pastry to the East Wing and her office on the second floor. She smiled, knowing how much Paula would enjoy the crisis over in the West Wing. Or rather that Kyle Guidry was at the center of that crisis. Perhaps she would call her friend this afternoon and inform her.

Twenty minutes later, the president's press secretary and his director of public liaison Grant Paulson entered the Oval.

A calmer president gestured for them to sit. "I take it you haven't been able to reach Kyle, Álvaro?"

"No, Mr. President. I've tried both his cell and his home number. I even tried his ex-wife, but she hasn't heard from him in over three weeks."

"Sit, sit. What about you, Grant?"

"Me, sir. No I haven't seen him since... no, I haven't."

Both the president and his press secretary glared at Paulson, given his visible nervousness. He shifted in his chair and forcibly pressed his palms on his thighs.

"Grant?"

"No, excuse me, sir. I'm... I don't know."

Hernandez stood. "Are you aware of something we're not? Has he texted or left you a message." Hernandez looked at the president then back at Paulson.

"No, no. I'm just... I'm just worried about him, that's all. He's never been late to any meeting since we came here."

The president leaned back in his chair behind the Resolute Desk. "No he hasn't. Something's happened to him. Álvaro, get some staff to call all the hospitals and police departments here and in northern Virginia and in Maryland. There might have been a car accident, but I wouldn't doubt he got involved with some married woman and her husband found out and... well, get on it. Help out too, Grant."

"Yes, Mr. President."

It was all Hernandez could do to leave the Oval Office without grinning, being well aware of Guidry's inordinate infatuation with Cecilia Erskine. Before commencing his calls, he had to go over to the East Wing and find Helene. She would find most appropriate and hilarious the president's speculation about a jealous husband being involved in Guidry's absence.

### ###

"Sure. That will be fine, Chas. I have a meeting at 2:00 and that should be over in plenty of time to get over there by 3:30. See you then, buddy."

"Where does he want to meet you?"

Wells and Andrea had just sat down for an early lunch at Busby and Poets on 5th and K Streets.

"The Rye Bar at the Rosewood. I've actually never been, so this will be a treat."

Andrea noted that she'd been at the Georgetown hotel twice and conducted an interview last summer at the Rosewood's Rooftop Bar and Lounge. "Best setting for an interview I've ever had. Too bad it's the end of December and not May. But I hear the Rye Bar is quite handsome. Get there early and take a look at the hotel's collection of contemporary and abstract art. It's impressive."

"You know me better than that. If it doesn't have a recognizable face painted on the canvas, it isn't art to me."

"Philistine."

"I'll take that as a compliment, Ms. Art Minor in College." Wells couldn't help remembering Cecilia Finch's love of the French Impressionists.

The server brought Wells's Cubano Panini and her Cauliflower Sandwich. As she watched Daniel take his first bite, she wondered if he was in any way as concerned about his safety as she was. Perhaps his experience in Iraq made a fatalist out of him or he was far better at compartmentalization than she thought. Regardless, if he hadn't agreed to spend the night at her place, she would have forced her way into his apartment and set up camp.

She hadn't told him she pestered Henrik Nordenson about the progress of the investigation—or investigations as Henrik cautioned her. He was always patient with her—and she loved him for that. She also tried contacting Miles Thompson's family ostensibly about his health but also to learn anything relating to his current psychological state. Was Daniel right in insisting that Miles should not be charged for aggravated assault in the front seat of Thompson's SUV? Henrik briefly argued with Daniel before conceding the matter to him. She did learn that Thompson was flying out to Arizona this morning to see his son play in the bowl game, but had Miles boarded the plane? And what about the other matter Daniel shared with her—Henrik's discovery that Dylan Nieporte's father and brother were in the explosives business?

"So what do you have planned for this afternoon, Andrea?"

"A little writing and several phone calls—that sort of thing." She finally took a bite of her Cauliflower Sandwich. "Mmm. Love this."

"I was a weird kid. Unlike all boys my age, I loved broccoli, but cauliflower... not so much."

"I'll convert you yet. Remember what I did about your fear of avocados."

"Right. Now I only *dislike,* rather than fear them."

He made her laugh as he always did when they dined together, which reinforced her belief she had found the man she wanted to spend the rest of her life with. She suppressed the frown at the occasional thought that their relationship wouldn't last. After all, he still seemed reluctant to make it permanent. Her thoughts returned to what was most important. She needed to make a series of calls this afternoon—and one of the first was to find out if Miles Thompson had taken the flight to Arizona.

# Chapter 32

Satisfied that his afternoon meeting went well with three other representatives of respected veterans organizations, Wells looked forward to the rest of his day and evening—a couple of drinks with Chas Overby and dinner with Andrea at Tortino, where they had their first date exactly one year ago. He smiled recalling the grief both of them received from friends, who asked if either of them knew how to cook, since they went out to eat so often. "One of the best things about living in Washington," Wells often responded.

Wells recalled being in the area near the Rosewood when he took Andrea to see the famous "Exorcist Steps," a little more than half a mile west of the hotel in Georgetown. Andrea had seen the 1973 movie only once—when she was fourteen—and refused ever to see it again. As they stood at the top of the outdoor concrete steps Father Damien Karras threw himself down at the end of the film, she began to shudder—in spite of the July heat. Wells teased her as they stood at the top of the stairs, because she refused to walk down them. "I thought you were fearless—especially with your sports background—and you won't even walk down these stairs in broad daylight?" She responded with "But I'll remember them in the dark, Daniel. It took me nine months before I'd sleep without a night-light after I saw that movie."

"Here we are, sir."

"Thanks. Keep the change." Wells earlier conceded to Andrea's wish that he take a cab to the Rosewood and ask Chas if he would drive him back to her place. She remained concerned about a car bomb being planted under his car, even though he checked both their vehicles before driving anywhere—a chore he was already tired of. Tomorrow he'd have lunch with Henrik and learn all he could about the current state of the investigations. Once more he thought of Dylan Nieporte and his likely knowledge of explosives. But what about the shooting of Hoyt Reilly and the assault on Carla Aronson in which the perpetrator was after the information her father possessed on Reilly? And then there was UNEV's starting linebacker, who was murdered after he spoke with Andrea. Nieporte couldn't be involved in all of these incidents—surely not.

As soon as he entered the hotel, Wells made up his mind to enjoy the rest of the afternoon with Chas and later with Andrea and think no more about these troubling matters until he spoke with Henrik tomorrow. Gazing at the Rosewood's handsome red-brick façade, Wells wasn't prepared for the feeling of intimacy and sophistication reflected in the hotel's interior. And he was even more taken by the stunningly handsome Rye Bar, with its brown to yellow color scheme, impressive furnishings, parquet flooring, and intoxicating back lighting. Wells imagined the bar as a whiskey-lover's altar or shrine.

"Daniel." Overby was situated in a lush brown chair, near the windows that looked out at the Chesapeake and Ohio Canal. As Well's reached the table, Overby had his hand extended. Wells shook it, but didn't feel the usual firmness Overby employed when he shook hands. Overby was already working on his first drink, or so Wells assumed.

"What are you drinking?"

"Pendleton 1910 on the rocks." Overby explained that it was a Canadian rye he had recently fallen in love with. "Here's the drink menu. I'll buy the first round—so get want you want." Given the mesmerizing surroundings, the drinks were priced accordingly. When the server arrived at the table, Wells was ready. "I'll have the Oak Aged Manhattan. Thanks." He hadn't had a Manhattan in quite a while—and this one with rye, Dolin rouge, and byrrh quinquina looked too good to pass up. "So, when are you flying back to Ottawa?" For the next forty-five minutes, fortified by another round ordered by Wells, the men's talk was dominated by sports and politics. Neither man broached the subject of their respective girlfriends.

###

"Good God." The president's head slumped behind the resolute desk in the Oval Office. His press secretary had just given him highlights of the police report from Virginia. The body of Kyle Guidry had been discovered lying not far from Bull Run. He had apparently lain on the bank for over twelve hours before being discovered by two fishermen, who took their sweet time calling the authorities. The police found Guidry's wallet had apparently not been touched. All off Guidry's credit cards, identifications, and licenses seemed to be there, as well as a substantial amount of cash. The White House received word before the press was notified.

"Álvaro, prepare a statement. My shock and deep regrets. Concern for his family. Has his ex-wife been notified?"

"I don't know, sir."

"Arrange a call. I'll want to talk to her. Oh, if you get asked, just respond that I will find a replacement as chief counsel when the time is right."

"Yes, sir."

Erskine stood and looked out the window toward the South Lawn. "Álvaro, I'm thinking of Grant's peculiar reaction this morning when Kyle failed to show for the meeting. Find Grant. I want to see him—now."

"I already looked for him, Mr. President. He left the White House late this morning and hasn't come back."

###

"Well, I could stay here another two hours, but I have to get back and start packing. You said you came by cab, right? Well, no need to call another one. I'll drop you by your place."

"Thanks, Chas. You can leave me off at Andrea's. Much closer to your hotel."

"Sure."

The men paid their tabs and headed out of the lounge. The two Manhattans left Wells feeling very much at ease but not inebriated—at least to his mind. As they walked to where Overby parked, Wells's friend stopped suddenly. "Oh, shit."

"What is it?"

"Remember I talked to you in the lounge about the Ambassador's young son?"

"Right." Overby mentioned how he had befriended the boy and how the nine year-old had asked Overby to bring him some special gifts from Washington.

"One of the things he wanted was a picture of me in front of all the presidential memorials. I have on my cell phone a photo of me in front of every one of them except Teddy Roosevelt's on Roosevelt Island. You've told me how much you like going there—and since I've never seen it and since we're not that far from it..."

Wells smiled. "I'd be happy to take your picture in front of old TR. But we better hurry since there's not much daylight left."

Following Wells's directions, Overby drove down to Whitehurst Ferry NW and then melded onto 66 South, following the road until they made it to the Theodore Roosevelt Bridge. Crossing the structure, the car headed north on the George Washington Memorial Parkway until Wells had Overby turn at the exit to the park. Overby pulled into the parking lot, and Wells informed him they would have to take the pedestrian footbridge to get to the island. As they headed for the footbridge, Overby excused himself for a moment and headed back to his rental car. When he got here, Wells noticed him opening his trunk. When he returned to the footbridge he apologized to Wells for the delay. "I bought a couple of sweaters at Bonobos before we met at the Rye Bar. I didn't want to tempt a break-in by having the bag in plain sight. You know me. Cautious to a fault."

Wells laughed. "No one knows that better than I." He recalled Overby insisting, when he was in D.C. during the summer, that they move to another table at the Blue Duck Tavern because the waiter seemed too enamored of Lisa. Caution indeed. "Let's pick up the pace, Chas. Daylight is fleeting."

The men crossed the pedestrian bridge and Wells led Chas down the short Woods Trail where the statue of TR and the memorial plaza and fountains were located. The few others who were on the trail were headed out, rather than in—so the only sound they soon heard was that of their own shoes walking on the pea gravel. "The statue is right there, Chas. When he was president, Roosevelt used to lead dignitaries and members of the government on difficult hikes through the area—which of course wasn't as manicured as it is now."

"Seems wild enough to me."

Wells was struck by the almost lifeless tone of Overby's reply. "And here we are." The men approached the memorial plaza, which was dominated by the seventeen-foot statue of TR in a frock coat with his right hand elevated, ready to make one of his bully points or to clobber a political opponent—or so Wells liked to think. To the surprise of Andrea and his friends, when Wells came here he would look at that raised right hand and feel fortunate he lost his left one in Iraq. He would say that, as a right-hander, he could do all he needed to get along fairly well, except to applaud and wrestle alligators.

"Let me have your cell phone, Chas, and I'll take four or five shots— with and without the flash. They should come out all right." Wells turned to take Overby's phone and found pointed at him what he recognized as a FNX 45 Tactical pistol, with a sound suppressor attached. Wells didn't ask what Overby was doing or why. His first words were matter-of-fact. "So you had the pistol in the trunk and put it in the inside pocket of your jacket."

Overby took a deep breath. "Move behind the wall, Daniel. Toward the trees." The centerpiece statue of Roosevelt stood before four 21-foot high granite tablets, wider that the statue itself. "Move. Now."

As he stepped behind the tablets, Wells took a quick look at the darkening surroundings. Were it summer, he could bolt for the trees and, considering the shadows and present dimness of light, perhaps conceal himself enough to leave him a fighting chance to escape being shot. But it was the end of December and the bare trunks of the trees would provide insufficient cover. Talking his way out the situation gave him his best—and only—chance of surviving. Overby's voice was harsh but quivering. His nose was also running, forcing him to wipe it with the sleeve of his jacket. Wells couldn't rely on him to explain why he was holding a pistol as though he would momentarily shoot and kill his good friend.

"Chas, I don't know why you're holding that pistol on me. Before you do anything, will you tell me what you think I've done?"

"Shut-up." Overby whispered forcefully, looking to his left and right. "Don't play stupid with me, goddamn it. Press your back against the wall and extend your arms forward and then out to your sides until I tell you to stop." Wells obeyed, realizing that Overby wished to prevent any part of his hand and arms to extend past the width of the granite tablets. Considering the type of weapon he held, equipped with its silencer, the instruction suggested that Overby's plan was carefully thought through. Wells considered that if others approached the TR statue, they wouldn't see what was happening behind the granite tablets. Wells had to get Overby to raise his voice in the hope that someone in the area would hear them and perhaps thwart Overby's apparent plan to shoot him.

As if he knew what Wells was thinking, Overby broke the silence. "No one will hear the shots, Daniel. Just two clicks. You'll drop right there, where no one will see you for some time, and I'll get out by crossing the moat. That's right. I've been out here before, checking the lay of the land." Once more, Overby wiped his runny nose with the sleeve of his jacket. "Then I'll find Lisa and tell her what I've done."

Lisa? What had she to do with Chas's behavior? Were they working as a team? Wells's mind now opened to another possibility. "Chas, just let me ask this. Did you plant the car bombs? The one at Jack Ketchum's home? Have you killed anyone else?"

Overby's head drew back and his eyes squinted more menacingly. "I told you to shut up, god damn it. You're not going to confuse me or talk your way out of this. I'm fully concentrating, you disloyal piece of shit." His arms shaking from his emotional state as well as the cold, Overby extended the pistol another few inches, both hands gripping the weapon. But he didn't realize that he had just raised his voice above a loud whisper.

"Wait, wait, Chas. I'm a dead man. I know it. Just tell me why you need to tell Lisa."

Overby took another step closer with the pistol still pointed directly at Wells's face. "To let her know that her lover is dead. Why the fuck else do you think I want to tell her what I've done?"

"No, no, no. You're wrong about that, Chas. I swear you're wrong."

"Don't fuck with me, Daniel. You've been seeing her while I was in Ottawa and you just saw her and fucked her in the hotel. Did you think I wouldn't figure it out? She stood me up to fuck you. She and I were..." His voice succumbed to his pain as he seemed now to be suppressing sobs, even though his spewing of profanities increased the volume of his voice even further, and Wells tried to match it.

"I did *not*, Chas. I've never been with her. Not in *any* way. I *swear* it."

"You lying son-of-a-bitch." Tears fell across his face. "I can't let you... I can't." Overby stepped forward another several inches, moving slightly to his right so that the suppressor's end was almost touching the portion of wrist remaining on Wells's left arm. Wells's eyes expanded as he realized his right hand might be able to swing quickly to his left and knock the pistol from Overby's grip. He took a full breath in preparation of the risky move, but at that same instant Overby stepped back almost two feet. His face contorted into an expression of utter hatred.

"You've ruined everything. I've got nothing left to lose." Wells closed his eyes. The shot was fired an instant afterward.

# CHAPTER 33

Wells slammed into the granite tablets. By the time he realized he wasn't hit, he had slid down into a sitting position, his back resting against the lower tablet. He looked to his left and saw Overby's body splayed on the ground—a pool of blood forming under his head. Shifting his eyes to the right, he saw the shoes, pants, and waist of someone standing there. Wells craned his head upward and saw the face. He prefaced his remark with an inadvertent laugh.

"How is it you always end up in the right place at the right time?" Wells was amazed that yet again Henrik had saved him from harm. There remained the possibility that Miles Thompson wouldn't have pulled the trigger inside his SUV, but there was no doubt Chas Overby had planned to kill him. Wells made a motion to get up, but Nordenson gestured for him to stay seated.

"You've had serious scare, Daniel. You had best remain still for a few minutes." Nordenson sat on the ground some six or seven feet in front of Wells, who saw what looked like either a Glock 19 or a Glock 22 in his hand, the barrel still pointed at Overby's body.

"How do I repay you for this, Henrik?"

"No need. Just something I had to do." He paused. "I promised Andrea I would."

"Andrea?"

"She called me, just like she did when you went up to meet Thompson. Quite a woman. She seems to have a sixth sense when it comes to you and when you're in serious danger. She said you were meeting Overby at the lounge in the Rosewood Hotel and that he might be driving you home."

"But what made her think I was in harm's way?"

"She received a call from Overby's girlfriend, Lisa somebody, who told her that she got home and found a note under her door from your friend here, who wrote that he was going to pay you back for fu... having sex with her—Lisa, I mean. I think I have that right." Wells groaned. "No, don't worry about Andrea, Daniel. Lisa told her it wasn't true. Besides, Andrea wouldn't believe that of you anyway."

"So Andrea asked you to find me?"

"Right. I was outside the lounge, looking in on you every few minutes. I figured he wouldn't try anything there. But when you left and headed for his car, I realized he'd take you somewhere private so he could kill you. Well, I got into my car and caught up with you as you were turning onto 66. I pulled in just as he was getting something out of the trunk. But when I made it to the footbridge, just as the two of you had crossed it, I showed my credentials and insisted that everyone get away from the park and trails because shots might be fired. I had to make sure everyone was out before I confronted Overby. There were more people milling around at the end of this trail than I expected, so I was delayed. I carefully made my way to the plaza and saw no one there. I guessed you were both behind the statue's backdrop, and as I got closer I began to hear your voices. It's been my experience and training to assume that in situations like this, the perpetrator wishes to explain to the victim his reasons for doing what he's about to do. Withdrawing my weapon, I slowly slid around the granite wall, not wanting to startle Overby into firing, and I saw that he was ready to shoot. Then I fired—not a second too soon, I guess."

"Jesus." Wells put his hands up to his face and tried to rub the tension out from around his eyes. "What time is it, Henrik?"

Nordenson pulled a pocket watch from his coat. "5:04 to be exact."

The sun had just set, and Wells could hear the wind scattering the fallen leaves in the area. Wells laughed. "Well, as my mother used to say, all good and bad things come in threes. You have one more life-saving rescue in you, Henrik."

Wells watched Nordenson lean to his right and retrieve Overby's FNX 45. "I'm afraid there won't be a third time, Daniel." Nordenson pointed Overby's pistol at Wells's chest. "Don't try to get up, my friend. Before we say goodbye, I have a bit of a tale to share with you. He offered a sad smile. "As I just said, the perpetrator wishes to explain his reasons for doing what he's about to do."

Wells wanted to laugh off the implications of Nordenson's words—as if Henrik were joking—but his mind registered only the fact that he was about to be murdered.

"You'll of course wish to know why I'm doing this—and our friendship compels me to inform you. Please know how much I regret your having to be part of all this. I also feel for this poor soul lying here. You see, I fully understand his feelings and his need to put all his hurt behind him by killing you. Ironic, isn't it? Or perhaps it's just coincidental?"

"Henrik, have you too misunderstood something I'm supposed to have done?"

"No. There are no false impressions in play, Daniel. And what's most tragic is that you haven't done anything since I've known you. It was all done before. And sadder still is that it was done *to* you, not *by* you."

Damn it, Henrik. I don't understand." Wells couldn't see any way he could go for the pistol and disarm Nordenson.

"Don't interrupt me. Please—just listen, my friend. Some time ago, I took a holiday from my work for the National Bomb Squad in Oslo. I had been there for two years, due in part to the influence of my father, who ranked highly in the Emergency Response Unit. I had a very close call that summer and looked forward to my visits to Copenhagen, Amsterdam, Paris, and London. While in Paris I met a young woman, with whom I fell instantly in love. She was an American, also on holiday. I cancelled my plans for London and spent the rest of my holiday with her. I invited her back to Oslo, but she was unable to accompany me then. When we parted, we vowed to correspond regularly and phone each other from time to time. This we did, and during the next several years I flew to the States and spent time with her in Boston and New York. But then I received a dry letter informing me she was to be married, but that she didn't love her intended husband, although it was necessary that she marry him. I assumed she was with child, but would come to discover that she never had children, and so I assumed she had terminated her pregnancy. Later I would learn that she was never pregnant."

The wind increased its intensity and Wells shook from the cold; yet his hopes were warmed by the possibility that Nordenson's story would open the door for him to share his own similar romantic disappointment, thereby preventing Henrik from his still incomprehensible decision to shoot him with Overby's pistol.

"Did you ever see here again, Henrik?"

"Twice more. Six years ago in Brussels and once recently." Nordenson looked up at the sky, although Overby's weapon was still pointed at Wells's chest. "I would have waited. Five or six years more if necessary, and I have long believed we would be together after that, but..."

As dark as it was getting, Wells could see the emotion on Nordenson's face. "But what, Henrik?"

"She insisted we could never be together. So I planned to leave and return to Norway, but I couldn't yet because she told me a dreadful story about what had happened to her, and I couldn't let that go without avenging her assailant. And I learned more from a woman who works with her—a woman I have been seeing—who was very free in speaking about a man who was enamored of her and was about to cause her serious problems. I felt badly killing him because I understood what he felt. I know you understand too."

"Henrik, I'm at a loss. How would I understand as well?" The wind blew Nordenson's light hair across his eyes as he dropped his head. If he closed his eyes, Wells might be able to lurch forward and grab at the pistol—but he would only have use of one hand in the attempt.

"I know it doesn't make sense to others who are not like us, Daniel—and the late Mr. Guidry."

Guidry? Wells had heard the name before but he couldn't

remember who the man was.

"We both know that falling in love with her was easy. How many other men have felt the same way and attempted to win her?"

Wells's mind still couldn't fully process what he had so far heard. "Andrea?"

Nordenson brushed the hair from his face and smiled. "Oh, you don't believe I have given my heart to Andrea, do you? I love her in a much different way. Like a sister—or a close friend. I feel for her. Believe me, I do. And in case you're concerned, I would never harm her—not in any way. I will truly miss her when I return to Oslo—as I will miss you."

Another gust of cold wind brought clarity to Wells. "Dear God, you're in love with Cecilia."

"More in love than even you can comprehend. You see, you have apparently moved on from her—even though..." Nordenson's face turned dark. "She told me when I saw her last that another was her one true love—not I. Only days ago, I learned you were that man. I then knew I couldn't let you live. When Cecilia hears you were killed by your friend Overby here, she may come to me yet. I cannot—will not—give up hope that we will be together. Especially when she knows what I have done for her."

Now Wells recognized the name Guidry as the lawyer who worked for the president and who would therefore have occasion to see and communicate with the first lady.

"Henrik, what else have you done for her?"

Nordenson ignored the question. "I feel ashamed that I put you and Andrea through the car bombing business. And I wish I could apologize for forcing your assistant Gina to spend a night in the hospital."

"You planted the bomb in my old car—and under Andrea's?"

"Yes, and I lied about finding one under my car, although I did soon afterwards set one off severely damaging my Passat in order to make it look as though I was a victim as well. I could buy the impounded Black Canyon I borrowed and followed you in when you drove to Virginia the other day, but I'll probably make do with something more economical."

There was no irony or sadistic humor in Nordenson's comment about his car and borrowed truck. He mentioned it as though he and Wells were talking over beers.

"And that business about Dylan Nieporte having experience with explosives."

"A happy coincidence—yes, it was true."

"But why the charade?" Wells knew that every question he asked and Nordenson answered helped increase the chances he could survive the moment—even if the odds were slim.

"So that you would trust me with your safety, which is why I dropped several red herrings along the way—the 'Boom!' note on Andrea's car, for instance. That Miles Thompson might have killed you had I not been there served the purpose as well. And of course Overby here."

Wells was too concerned about his own life to be affected by the dead body lying a few feet away. "But had either one of them killed me, you would have been guiltless of murder and your desire to have me dead would still be satisfied."

"No. There you are wrong, Daniel. I wished to serve my lady—my goddess Freya, as I called Cecilia. All matters of vengeance and satisfaction would have to be done by me—in the old chivalric way. Unfortunately, I had to behave in a less than salutary mannner in order to make possible my being with her after her husband's tenure as president was over."

Wells's thoughts returned to the minor car bombs Nordenson had set. He didn't wish to kill anyone, even though Gina suffered minor injuries. But someone hadn't been so lucky. "Henrik, did you set the explosive that killed my old coach?"

"I'm sorry, Daniel, but I did. I hoped to destroy the papers he possessed that might have information on me. He had spoken with Cecilia, and she might have identified me. That information might have been in his head—and so I felt I had no choice."

Wells felt a return of his grief, now compounded by his anger—but he maintained his composure. There was more to learn. "And that was you who confronted his daughter in Chapel Hill, wasn't it?"

"Yes, I wanted copies of her father's notes you happened to mention to me. I treated her as kindly as I could under the circumstances—and yes, it was I who broke into your place in search of the notes. But I soon realized you must have looked at them and, based on your continued behavior to me, that there was nothing there I needed to worry about."

"So you killed three people then? Jack Ketchum, Guidry, and Chas."

"I wish I could say that it was just three, but that would ignore, for one, Paula Bradford-Adams."

Wells no longer felt the chilled evening air; his tension and heightened anticipation warmed him to the point of physical discomfort. After asking permission from Nordenson, he partially unzipped his jacket. "I assume she was the woman you were seeing— the one working in the first lady's office."

"No, her name was Helene Eckermire—a woman I've been dating for a few weeks and enjoyed being with, actually. She was one of those who trust quickly those who flatter and pay attention to her and was willing to share Guidry's behavior as it related to Cecilia. I never told her my real name, or where I've really been working for the past eight and a half months."

Now Wells fully understood why Nordenson left Norway and came to the Metro force in D.C. He had to be as near as possible to the woman he adored. As Wells knew, Nordenson's reputation in the profession was sterling. Another friend on the force noted how fortunate it was to get him, even if he might return to Norway the following spring. "Wait. You said you killed the other woman— Paula?"

"Again, a cruel and regrettable necessity. She was a go-between when I recently met Cecilia at her hotel in Wilmington. She of course saw me and may have learned my name from Cecilia. I informed her that my name was Thorn—you see Cecilia teasingly called me 'Mr. Thor' after I told her she was the goddess Freya come back to life. I was confident she would then know "Mr. Thorn" was I. In my heart, I believe Cecilia never mentioned me to anyone else—but since Paula had learned of my connection to the first lady and knew my face, I was forced to end her life—sad to say."

"Where did you...?"

"Off a road in Virginia near Falmouth. I'm not sure anyone has yet found her. I deeply, deeply regret that Cecilia will grieve for her. It was my vow that I would never hurt her but only protect her... and avenge her wrongs."

"You avenged her wrongs?"

"About ten days ago, we talked to three players on the UNEV football team about careers in law enforcement. I asked one of them whether he knew who you were—he did, I am happy to say, and he also knew that the president, the first lady, and several members of the administration were alumni of his school. He went on to speak of Cecilia's attractiveness and how a line back—forgive me, I'm still not fully versed in American football—a line-backer on the team often made lewd comments about his apparent fantasy of having sex with her. I made it a point to learn who this player was and recently overheard him myself speak in such a disgusting manner to other teammates. I planned initially to wear a ski mask and beat him severely, but I discovered he was going to be interviewed by our darling Andrea. I was there the night they met, and I could see Andrea was upset by the interview. Given that and what he had said about Cecilia I avenged both her and Andrea's honor by killing the useless pig."

But Wells knew there was one more puzzle piece left to be placed. "You killed Hoyt Reilly too, didn't you?"

"It was my responsibility and considerable honor to do so."

Wells was struck by the possibility that what he had feared all these years had occurred. "He beat her when she was young, didn't he?"

"He might have."

Wells was overcome with agitation at the answer. "What do you mean, he *might* have?"

"You didn't know—of course. I would otherwise wish to keep it from you, but now I see no reason why you shouldn't know." Nordenson shook his head in pity. "He had sexually abused her on several occasions when she was twelve and older—with the assistance of his sister—Cecilia's step-sister, whom I killed as well. But when Cecilia was twenty-one and just out of college, Reilly raped her."

Wells closed his eyes and felt the unique pain a complete understanding of a painful memory can bring. He felt his chest pressing backwards, making his next breaths difficult. What he couldn't comprehend or accept for fifteen years was now made perfectly clear. Cecilia had been raped and her debasement forced her to end their relationship.

Nordenson withdrew a pocket watch from his coat. "See this? I took it from Reilly when I shot him on the track. Cecilia told me he pulled out a pocket watch when he raped her. I assumed this was the same one. I've kept it as something tangible to remind me to avenge what he did to my Freya."

Well's thoughts were not on his precarious predicament but rather on Cecilia at age twenty-one and younger dealing with what no girl or woman should have to endure. His heart told him that he would have married and loved her regardless of her brutal experience.

Both he and Nordenson were silent as each grieved in his own way for the woman he had lost. But soon they both remembered how different their fates were or could be. Nordenson believed he had still a chance to be with the woman he loved. Wells knew he was unlikely ever again to see the woman he was now devoted to, in spite of the pain he felt over the one he once adored.

"I do so wish we could remain friends forever, Daniel. I do so wish it."

"Henrik, I love Andrea now. *My* time with Cecilia is long past. I could never come between you."

"But you forget that her time with you is *not* past, my friend. She has told me so. Only by your death can she and I have *our* time." Nordenson stood and stretched his arms their full lengths, both hands holding Overby's weapon. "I will shoot you twice in the heart and then replace the pistol near Overby's body. Who wouldn't believe that I arrived just too late to save my close friend, but was still able to take down the perpetrator? I'm so very sorry, Daniel. You have been a dear,

dear friend to me."

Once more Wells awaited his imminent death. This time, though, he kept his eyes open. Perhaps he could capture Nordenson's own and force pity to travel through the windows of Henrik's soul.

The sound of the shot was loud, reverberating it seemed through the entire plaza and the trees behind it. Nordenson screamed as the bullet tore into the top of his left hand, forcing him to drop Overby's weapon. He fell on his knees and reached for the pistol with his right hand, but the second shot caught him high on the right side of his back. After his face hit the ground, he didn't move until he was in the ambulance, half way to George Washington University Hospital.

# CHAPTER 34

She was able to get through the afternoon's reception for several female leaders of national Healthcare Programs, which took place in the Yellow Oval Room, on the second floor of the residence. It was all Cecilia could do not to look out toward the South Lawn and wish she could be left alone on the grounds to cry. But she had held up well, although Helene Eckermire could not and had to leave the White House in the wake of the news about Paula's death and the devastating revelation about the man she had been seeing for the past few weeks. As soon as Paula's body was found and identified, the White House received notification following that given to the next of kin. The first lady and Helene were informed a mere twenty minutes before the reception began in the Yellow Oval Room. After the reception concluded, Álvaro Hernandez shared with her other details regarding the events during and leading up to the shooting on Roosevelt Island.

Now Cecilia sat alone in the Queen's Sitting Room—right off her bedroom. She had been there for over an hour crying. At first she gave no thought to why she was crying; she simply had to release the pent-up emotion that began building with the news about Paula. Cecilia had always found the décor and the heavy cotton *Toile de Jouy* fabric in the room too busy and, oddly, too depressing to spend her private time there rather than in the East Sitting Hall. But today the surroundings seemed so very appropriate for the state of her soul. She had been responsible for Paula's murder because she wanted to see her old lover one more time. Why hadn't she considered in time the possibility that his passion for her might lead to his committing acts of violence against those who did and did not deserve it. When she learned of her step-brother's and step-sister's deaths, she wanted to believe he had killed them both, and she was flushed with righteous vanity that her Norwegian Galahad might have satisfied her honor. But learning of Kyle Guidry's murder deeply pained her. Yes, she well knew he was enamored of her, and she might have made the situation less politically dangerous had she spoken frankly with him and made clear that she didn't appreciate his interest in her as a woman. Why didn't she, she wondered? Was it another example of her vanity dominating her better sense? Could she actually have enjoyed the fact that her husband's chief counsel was smitten the way he was? Or was it more likely she wished to avoid confrontation at all costs or at least to avoid hurting yet another man?

Álvaro told her another man was killed by her former lover—a man who worked in the Canadian Embassy in Ottawa but that there seemed to be no connection to her. Yet she couldn't help believing that there was. Once more, sheer vanity on her part? Or was it a manifestation of the all-encompassing guilt that tortured her since she was twelve and was first abused by Hoyt Reilly? Daniel Wells might have been killed by this man—and the thought made her reach for the second of the two drinks she ordered before she entered the Queen's sitting room. Twice, her Daniel had escaped being shot. Her Daniel. She hadn't thought of him in that way for over fifteen years. She had hurt him deeply—the regret over which she felt acutely ever since. But she believed at the time that she couldn't spend her life with him—not after her spirit had been crushed by her stepbrother's brutal act. She hadn't seen her Daniel, except on television and occasionally in the newspaper and online, during all that time. She accepted she could never face him. How he must have hated her. But was he told what had happened to her right before her lover Henrik Nordenson was shot? How had she never learned that her "Thor" had worked for D.C. Metro for over eight months, as Álvaro told her this afternoon? But her biggest sin, she believed, was that she used her feelings for Daniel to dissuade Henrik from maintaining the impossible hope she would divorce the president in order to be with him. She might indeed separate from Stephen when his term or terms were up, but she could never have agreed to be with Henrik. The intensity of his devotion—so satisfying and necessary earlier—was at this point in her life too frightening to accept or even contemplate. Yet it was true. Daniel Wells was the love her life—and always would be.

### 

"Grant Paulson called me to say he'll be at Jack's memorial service tomorrow. He also said the test results on his wife revealed a benign, not a malignant, tumor. Said he'd been a wreck all day fearing the worst. He had to apologize to the president for being out of it yesterday.

"Great news. I'm so happy for them."

"Also great is the fact that you'll be going with me to the memorial service. How did you get out of your commitment?"

"These pro athletes are a lot more understanding than the public believes, my love—even when you have to cancel an interview." Andrea began crying. Wells put us arm around her as they approached the entrance of Tortino. "I'm sorry, Daniel; I just couldn't help imagining having to go to *your* memorial service. It was so close—it still frightens me."

"If they didn't get me in Fallujah, they weren't going to get me on Roosevelt Island. I just wish... never mind."

"What?"

"Nothing. I was going to say that I wish you were with our unit in Iraq—but that doesn't make any sense."

"Perhaps not—but it was a sweet thought. At least I think it was."

They went down the stairs to the basement entrance of the unpretentious though quite charming and welcoming restaurant. It was so perfect for their first date, they both thought, because each believed the description fitted the way they saw each other. More neighborhood-like than upscale, but with food that always delighted.

Andrea noted on their first date that a section of the interior reminded her of her favorite monastery near Florence she had visited as a girl, whereas Daniel thought the bar and tables close to it were just like the basement of his great uncle Dominick's Long Island home, where good meals and conversation titillated even the young Wells. He loved the fact that Andrea had a sentimental streak running through her heart to match his own.

As Andrea perused the menu, Wells couldn't take his eyes off her lovely face. Would their relationship have to change in any way now that he owed her so much? How many times had he commiserated with her about barely missing a medal in the short pistol competition at the World's in Munich when she was in her early twenties? She had won a host of championships in national 25 mm. pistol competitions when she was a teenager and young woman in college. As Wells knew, her failure to medal at the World's cost her both her confidence and a spot on the 2012 Olympic Team. Besides, her career as a sports journalist had begun, and she felt honored to be assigned the women's shooting events in London, which led to a full article in her magazine. When Wells asked on one of their first dates if she kept up with her shooting, she laughed and told him she hadn't been out to the range since she gave up competing in the sport. And still she had hit her target area with both of her shots on Roosevelt Island. She shot to save Wells and to incapacitate—not kill—Henrik Nordenson, and she had been successful.

When Andrea looked up from the menu to order her Blood Orange Cosmo, she knew she couldn't keep one fact from Daniel any longer. In the immediate aftermath of the shooting the previous evening, she admitted she came to Roosevelt Island because of something Henrik said on the phone, when she called him fearing that Chas Overby would harm Wells. She told Daniel at the time, "Henrik's voice sounded very peculiar—and just as he was hanging up, he said under his breath, 'That's not Overby's job...' and then cut himself off. So I panicked and drove out to the Island, calling the police as I drove. I knew I wouldn't get there before Henrik or Chas did, but I had to try and warn you, so I grabbed my Beretta and headed in as fast as I could run. The police pulled up while I was on the pedestrian bridge. I saw no one at the Teddy Roosevelt statue and stopped when I reached the plaza. But then I heard Henrik's voice—and then yours, so I crept up as quietly yet as quickly as I could. I didn't want to shout out for fear it would provoke any violence against you. When I reached the statue I quickly came around and as close to Henrik as I could so I wouldn't miss the shot I knew I'd have to take." Most of what she told Wells was spot-on accurate, but one part was an outright fabrication.

Wells ordered a Gray Goose martini and the *Prosciutto di Parma* as an appetizer. Andrea wanted to wait until the drinks arrived before she confessed. In the interim, she elaborated on her interview with the police after the shooting and with the detectives earlier today. "One of the detectives told me Henrik was operated on without incident and would be arraigned right afterward. I don't know what makes me sadder—the fact that someone I truly liked and trusted committed these horrible crimes or that I had to be the one who had to shoot him."

Wells smiled. "You wouldn't take that back, would you?"

"Of course not—it's just that..."

"Let's move on to something really important—like football."

Andrea teased Wells about the amount he put on the big game. "UNEV is a thirteen point underdog. Are you tempted?"

"Not tempted at all. I've already made the bet. UNEV and the points."

They discussed the fact that Miles Thompson was now in Arizona to see his son play. "I've learned that he's agreed to a medical workup and counseling. At first I wasn't sure you were right not to press charges, but I know now you made the right call."

The server brought the drinks and Andrea raised her glass. "Here's to you, my love."

"Here's to *you*, my knight-ess in shining armor. Thanks for saving my life. I'd say that I hope someday to return the favor, but I really hope not to have that opportunity."

"Hear, hear." She grinned but soon her features altered. "Daniel, I have to tell you something."

His fist tightened. "Oh, God. Don't say that you're having second thoughts about you and me."

"No, no. I love you and I want you to be around every day so I can continue to do so. It's just that I wasn't honest in everything I told you about why I came out to Roosevelt Island."

"Can I take a sip of this before you go on?" He lifted the martini to his mouth; his hand was shaking the contents. Andrea took her drink and wondered why her hand wasn't trembling as well.

"It wasn't that I suspected Henrik. He really didn't say anything under his breath about Chas. I trusted him completely. Not two minutes after I hung up, I got a call... from the White House."

"The White House?" Wells was finally able to take a sip of his martini.

"From the first lady. She said she had read about our relationship and that she was afraid for your safety. She told me a little about Henrik's love for her and what he might do." Andrea paused, bracing for the look on Wells's face that might tell her if or how much Daniel was still enamored of Cecilia Erskine. At Thanksgiving, in perhaps an unguarded moment mixed with one too many glasses of sparkling wine, he told Andrea about his "dating" relationship with Cecilia Finch back then. Before that, he merely admitted he had known her at UNEV. For a full month now, Andrea looked for any evidence that Wells was still in love with her—or at least with the memory of her. "Should I go on, Daniel?" She was surprised by the look on Wells's face. He seemed almost to smile as he took a much longer sip of his vodka martini.

"You don't have to, my darling. While he held his gun on me, Henrik confessed his love for Cecilia and what she told him about me and how I was the one she loved most—not Henrik."

Andrea reacted as if her greatest fear had been realized. "And..."

"And what?"

"You felt what when he told you that?"

"Scared to death he was going to shoot me." Wells reached across the table and took Andrea's hand. "Andrea, my darling, I loved her very much fifteen years ago. I love you more than that right now."

Andrea's normally steady hand shook in his as she closed her eyes and took a deep open-mouthed breath. The server returned with the

*Prosciutto di Parma* and asked if they were ready to order their entrees.

"Go ahead, Daniel."

"All right. The Caesar salad and the New York Strip, medium rare. Thank you."

Andrea grinned—her face and mind now completely relaxed. "I'll have the Seafood Linguine. No salad for me. I'll eat some of his." The server departed and Andrea squeezed Daniel's hand. "So we're having exactly what we ordered on our first date."

"Well not quite. Thought you'd like an additional appetizer along with the prosciutto." He reached in his jacket pocket and retrieved a small white box. Now with both hands shaking, Andrea opened it and was barely able to see the ring through her forming tears.

The End

# ABOUT THE AUTHOR

During his career as Professor of English at the University of Georgia, John Vance was the author of six books and numerous articles devoted to literary biography and criticism. He also began indulging his love of theater as actor, director, and playwright, with thirty-five of his plays staged. Now he has turned exclusively to fiction, and is the author of thirteen books, including the historical novel *The King's Favorite*, the humorous memoir *Setting Sail for Golden Harbor*, and the BookBub featured *In Mind of the Vampire*. He lives in Athens, Georgia with his wife Susan.

Thank you so much for reading one of our **Political-Thriller** novels.
If you enjoyed our book, please check out our recommended title for your
next great read!

*Death by Mournful Numbers* by John Vance

"*an ingeniously plotted, deftly paced political-thriller*"
—Iain Reid, winner of the Taylor Prize Emerging Writer Award
and author of *THE TRUTH ABOUT LUCK*

View other Black Rose Writing titles at www.blackrosewriting.com/books

and use promo code **PRINT** to receive a **20% discount** when purchasing.